# D FORCE

## A John Decker Novel

# ANTHONY M.STRONG

**WEST STREET**

# ALSO BY ANTHONY M. STRONG

## THE JOHN DECKER SUPERNATURAL THRILLER SERIES

Soul Catcher (prequel) • What Vengeance Comes • Cold Sanctuary
Crimson Deep • Grendel's Labyrinth • Whitechapel Rising
Black Tide • Ghost Canyon • Cryptic Quest • Last Resort
Dark Force • A Ghost of Christmas Past • Deadly Crossing
Final Destiny

## THE CUSP FILES

Deadly Truth

## THE REMNANTS SERIES

The Remnants of Yesterday • The Silence of Tomorrow

## STANDALONE BOOKS

The Haunting of Willow House • Crow Song

## AS A.M. STRONG WITH SONYA SARGENT

### Patterson Blake FBI Mystery Series

# DARK
# FORCE

West Street Publishing

Cover art and interior design by Bad Dog Media, LLC.

ISBN: 978-1-942207-32-0

*To Sonya*

# DARK
# FORCE

# PROLOGUE

THE BARTHOLOMEW MEADOWS WORKHOUSE sat like a crouching predator against the black night sky, hunkered down and ready to strike. It was a large stone structure with two imposing four-story wings that spread one on each side of a central building that had once been Mavendale's manor house.

It was almost midnight. The waxing moon hung low in the sky, partially obscured by scudding clouds. The ground was wet because it had rained for most of the day and well into the evening. Even though it was technically summer, a chill wind cut across the landscape, causing Eddie Lamb, one of a trio of night porters, to pull his coat tight around his rake-thin frame as a shiver ran through him.

He approached the building from the east, passing through the open iron gates set into an archway made of blocks pillaged from the old monastery that sat in ruins twenty miles away, thanks to the actions of Thomas

1

Cromwell and the man he served, King Henry VIII, over three-hundred years before. This entrance, nicknamed the Archway of Despair by the villagers, had earned its reputation through the many horrors inflicted upon the residents of Bartholomew Meadows, many of whom arrived via that very gate on their way to a life of hard labor and cruelty at the hands of the uncaring and often sadistic workhouse staff.

Eddie was one of the lucky ones. Although he was paid little more than the men and women who toiled within the dreaded institution with little hope of release, he could walk away every morning after his shift ended and return to the small cottage he shared with his wife and three children on the outskirts of the village.

When he was halfway up the driveway, Eddie paused and looked up at the building as he often did when arriving for work. As always, the urge to turn and walk back to the village came upon him. He hated this place and loathed all that it stood for. It was institutionalized barbarism at its worst. Fearful of encouraging idlers, the government made sure that this place, along with almost two-thousand other such establishments just like it all across the country, instilled terror in the hearts of the population. No one wanted to find themselves in a workhouse if there was any other option available to them.

But Eddie didn't turn back toward the village. As always, he continued on toward the building, because without this job he and his family might find themselves on the receiving end of the Poor Laws that condemned so many, which was, in his opinion, a fate worse than death. He would be separated from his wife. His children, young as they were, might end up sold to a factory as free labor or even end up down the mines.

Eddie reached the front of the building, but instead of mounting the steps and entering through the imposing double doors of the old manor house that lead to the staff quarters and suites of rooms kept by James Grayson, the workhouse master—a man of immeasurable viciousness and brutality who loved the whip so much it had earned him the nickname Old Flogger—he turned to circle the building and make his way to a more mundane entrance at the back of the south wing. This was where lowly workers like himself entered.

Even this was better than the entrance in the north wing, which housed the receiving area for the paupers condemned to a life inside the workhouse. Once they entered through those doors, inmates would be searched, stripped of their clothes, and checked for infectious diseases before being unceremoniously bathed. Those who passed this humiliating ordeal were sent to their respective wards, which were nothing more than large dormitories that afforded no privacy. Here they were assigned a cot before being put to work. Those who did not pass muster were sent to the infirmary, which was often as good as a death sentence.

Eddie shuddered and moved off, but then he noticed something unusual. He turned back to the manor house and realized what had made him so uneasy. The fancy carved wooden doors stood open, the space beyond dark and foreboding.

They were never left open, even during the day.

The breath caught in Eddie's throat.

He took a faltering step toward the doors, called out.

"Hello? Is anyone in there?"

Silence answered him.

Eddie mounted the four wide stone steps leading to the entrance. He poked his head inside and looked around.

Beyond the doors, he found a wide lobby with checkerboard tiles and a high ceiling. A staircase swept upward to the second floor where the master's chambers and bedrooms for other important staff, including the matron and chaplain, were located.

Eddie had only visited this area of the workhouse a few times. He spent his nights in the south wing where the men's and women's dormitories were located because, even though his official title was a porter, his actual job was more akin to a prison guard. But he knew enough to realize there was a problem here. The gas lamps that should have lit the lobby were dark. The only illumination came from the upper landing, where a single lamp burned.

Eddie moved across the threshold, looking left and right. There should be other staff here, those who lived at the institution. Even if they had been asleep, whatever that occurred would surely have roused them. But he saw no one. At least, until his eyes alighted on a crumpled form sprawled on the far side of the lobby. It was Robert Trent, the physician who oversaw the invasive and demeaning medical examinations of the female inmates. He had a special proclivity for the younger, more attractive women whom he paid special attention to. With those, he would spend an hour or more in his private room in the north wing. The rumors of what occurred there were probably true, given what Eddie had overheard during the man's conversations with other staff members.

He wouldn't be paying attention to anyone anymore.

Upon his approach, Eddie saw the man's head had been staved in with a heavy object. A halo of crimson blood was spreading around his scalp, a sign that the crime had only just occurred.

Had one of the good doctor's special inmates found him

to exact revenge? If so, how had they escaped the female wards, which were as secure as any prison in the country?

Eddie turned back to the stairs, and in doing so caught a flash of movement near the doors through which he had entered. Beyond them, out on the driveway, he saw a pale form clad in the workhouse's signature inmate uniform. It was a woman he recognized as Annie Clement; a long-term resident consigned to Bartholomew Meadows by her erstwhile husband after their divorce many years before, on the grounds that their separation had rendered her penniless. Now she was making her way toward the gates at a clip, making the most of her newfound freedom. Behind her was another female inmate that Eddie didn't recognize. In her hand, she clutched a small ax. Was this the weapon that had dispatched the workhouse physician? It was impossible to tell from this distance, but Eddie suspected it was.

From somewhere above, on the second floor, a swiftly silenced scream interrupted Eddie as he watched yet more freed residents come into view. Both male and female. He tore his eyes away and started for the stairs, mounting them two at a time.

When he reached the top, he saw that the door to the workhouse master's private quarters, which he occupied with his wife Bethany, stood ajar.

Eddie approached with caution. He pushed the door and let it swing inward. The sight that greeted him dissuaded Eddie from venturing any further.

Bethany Grayson stood motionless in the suite's small front parlor, holding a heavy meat cleaver that must have come from the kitchen.

Upon Eddie's arrival, her eyes snapped up from the figure lying at her feet on the floor in a pool of blood larger than the one Eddie had witnessed below.

"What the . . ." Eddie recognized Old Flogger not from his face, which was now nothing but mushy red pulp, but from his Savile Row suit custom fitted for him by tailors in London, and the gold fob watch that adorned his breast pocket.

"He needed to pay for his sins," Bethany said in a rasping voice that sounded little like her own.

"You killed him," Eddie stammered, taking a quick step backward. "Sweet Jesus. You murdered the master."

"He will be just the first of many," Bethany replied in that same unholy voice, a twisted grin snaking across her face. Then she lifted the knife to her own throat and opened it in a quick and hard sideways motion.

Eddie didn't wait around to see what would happen next. He was fleeing back down the stairs in a blind panic, even before Bethany's lifeless body hit the ground.

# ONE

JOHN DECKER LOOKED up at the townhouse on Hays Mews with a mixture of revulsion and awe. Entombed in the cellar, inside a bricked-up room that would not be discovered for more than a hundred years, was a man who called himself Abraham Turner. Except he wasn't a man in the true sense of the word. He was, for want of a better expression, a vampire who stole the life force of those he killed to extend his own existence. And the generations that came after didn't refer to him by that name. They had a more sinister title for the monster who terrorized Victorian London's East End back in the eighteen-eighties. Jack the Ripper.

The street itself looked much the same at the beginning of the twentieth century as it did in the second decade of the twenty-first. No cars were parked at the curb, and the streetlamps still used gas, but in many other ways, it was just like he remembered it.

But Decker hadn't come here to reminisce or destroy the

7

abomination in the cellar while it still slumbered through the years, even though the thought had crossed his mind. Such an action would alter the future in ways Decker could not predict. He had come here because it was the last place he could think of to look for Mina.

His last glimpse of her came as they flew over Singer Cay in the Lockheed Electra. Their plan to escape the Bermuda Triangle and return home hadn't gone as expected. The lightning storm, supercharged by the Triangle's unique properties, should have returned them all to the day of Decker's wedding. Instead, it had brought him to London in the year 1911. Where Colum, Rory, and Hunt had ended up, he didn't know, except that it wasn't here. He hoped they had made it back. Mina was a different matter. She had been next to him on the plane. They had been holding hands when the lightning hit. Afterward, as they fell through the void that Decker hoped would take them home, he saw the rest of his team tumbling ahead of him. But Mina was still holding his hand, at least until she was ripped away. Then he woke up in this strange time and place.

Their previous trip back through time, as they explored the ruined Grand Fairmont Hotel, had left them separated but in the same era. Decker hoped that the same thing had happened now, which was why, after realizing where and when he was, he spent all night and most of the morning on London's cold and rainy streets searching for her. He visited the university she was attending, or rather would attend many years distant, but she wasn't there. He went to the hotel he and Colum had stayed in on their last trip to London, but she wasn't there either. In the end, he was left with one location—the Ripper's old townhouse.

If she had arrived here at the same moment in time as him, Mina would have made her way to one of these places to wait. Of that, he was sure. Which meant he must face the reality that she was either in another era or too far away to reach any of the locations he expected her to go. Decker was alone, with no way to get back to his life or the woman he loved.

This thought troubled him the most.

He could only imagine what Nancy must be going through if the others had made it back and he wasn't with them. Thinking about it was almost too much to bear.

There was a pub at the end of the street. The same bar had been there in the twenty-first century when Decker last visited this location. It even bore the same name. The King's Head. He lingered a moment longer, hoping against hope that Mina would appear, then walked toward it at a brisk pace. He needed to regroup. Think about his next move. He was also starving. With any luck, the pub served food. But as he entered, Decker realized that he had another problem. Money. He didn't have any.

Frustrated, he turned to leave.

"Hey, you," A voice called from behind him. "Not so fast."

Decker glanced back over his shoulder. It was still early, and there were few customers in the place. The voice belonged to a burly man with a thick beard and shaved head. He stood behind the bar with an empty beer mug in one hand and a dishcloth in the other.

"Don't worry, I'm leaving," Decker said. He was in a bad enough situation already. He didn't need extra trouble.

"You got anywhere to go?" The man asked.

"Not really," Decker admitted, taken aback by the strange question.

"Bet you're hungry too, I'll wager."

"Little bit."

"Come on in then. Take a load off." The landlord pointed to a table in the back of the room.

Decker hesitated, then did as he was told. In his years as a cop, he had learned to read people and wasn't sensing aggression. Quite the opposite, in fact. He went to the table and took a seat. A couple of the other patrons glanced his way, then lost interest and continued with their own conversations.

After a minute, the landlord ambled over with a plate in one hand and a pint of beer in the other. He placed them both in front of Decker. "There you go. It ain't much, but it'll keep you going for a few hours, at least."

"Thank you." Decker looked down at the plate, upon which sat a sandwich made from thick-cut bread, ham, and a chunky brown condiment he couldn't identify. The beer was dark and foamy.

"Ham and pickle," the landlord said. "On the house."

"Much appreciated." Decker looked up and smiled at the man.

"That accent. American is it?"

Decker nodded. "Louisiana."

The landlord shook his head. "You're a long way from home, mate."

"If only you knew," Decker answered.

"None of my business and you can tell me to bugger off if you like, but how does a fellow from so far away end up on the streets of London?"

For a moment, Decker wasn't sure what the man was asking. But when he looked down at himself, at the damp and ill-fitting army-issue khaki pants and shirt he'd been given on Singer Cay, coupled with his general disheveled appearance, he understood. The landlord thought he was homeless. And in a way, he was.

The man was still waiting for an answer.

Decker shrugged. "It's a long story."

"I'm sure it is. I'm Edward, by the way. Just like the king."

Decker looked at him blankly.

"King Edward VII. God rest his soul." The landlord studied Decker for a moment, then. "Well, don't just sit there, mate. Tuck in. When you're done with that, I'll bring you some of the wife's spotted dick."

Decker hoped spotted dick wasn't as bad as it sounded, but the ham sandwich looked good despite the strange condiment, so he followed Edward's advice and ate. He wasn't sure what his next move would be, but the landlord's generosity had bought him some time to figure it out, and at least he wouldn't be hungry while he did.

# TWO

DECKER FINISHED the sandwich in a minute flat, then turned his attention to the beer. Now that his stomach was full, he could think clearly about what to do next. The situation was unlike any he had encountered before. Even on Singer Cay, he wasn't alone. He also had Rory, who was knowledgeable in matters Decker couldn't even begin to understand. Without Rory, they would never have captured the Smilodon and made it off the World War II version of the island. That something had gone wrong, at least for Decker, in the final moments of their trip back to the twenty-first century was obvious. How to fix the situation was less so.

But there was one glimmer of hope even if he couldn't find Mina. The Order of Saint George. They were the precursor to CUSP, formed at the end of the nineteenth century by Queen Victoria to combat the forces of the unknown. They were also responsible for walling Jack the Ripper up in his Hays Mews prison. Since this was the year 1911, a good thirty years before the formation of CUSP, they would still be out there somewhere.

The question was, where?

As a secret organization that fulfilled its mandate in the shadows, it would not be easy to find. He couldn't just ask where their headquarters were located or look them up in the phone book. Not that there were any phone books at this point in history.

But he had one piece of information that might be useful. The names of the two men who dealt with Abraham Turner. Frederick Abberline and Thomas Finch. The latter of the two was instrumental in forming the Order of Saint George. Queen Victoria herself had handpicked him out of the Grenadier Guards for that very purpose. Decker knew this because of his previous interaction with Stephanie Gleason. She was Finch's great-great-granddaughter and the latest member of Finch's family to be entrusted with safeguarding Abraham Turner's watch and the relic within.

But locating Finch would be hard. Decker had no information on him beyond that which Gleason had provided. He didn't know what happened to the man after the Ripper encounter. It was 1911. Twenty years had passed. Thomas Finch could be anywhere. Or he could be dead.

But the man who was with him on the night they walled Jack the Ripper into that Mayfair cellar would be easier to find. Decker knew about him, not from Stephanie Gleason, but from the history books. Police Inspector Frederick Abberline had led the Ripper investigation even before Finch and the Order had become involved. Officially, the case was never solved. Abberline took the secret of Jack the Ripper's true identity to his grave, much to the consternation of conspiracy theorists and Ripperologists ever since.

Decker's knowledge did not extend to the inspector's career after Jack the Ripper, but he was a well-known figure even in his own time and could very well still be alive. If

Decker could find anyone connected to the order, it would be him. The only question was how to go about it.

"You ready for that spotted dick?"

The question pulled Decker from his thoughts.

The pub's landlord, Edward, had come back over and was standing next to the table.

"The sandwich is more than enough," Decker said, unsure he wanted to tackle a dish with such an unsavory name. "I don't wish to take advantage of your generosity."

"Nonsense." Edward clapped his hands together. "What kind of host would I be to let a man back out onto the streets with less than a full belly?"

"In that case, how can I refuse?"

The landlord shuffled away toward the door next to the bar and soon returned with a bowl and spoon.

Decker was relieved to find that spotted dick was nothing but a steamed pudding containing raisins and dried fruit. It came with a thick yellow sauce that Edward identified as custard.

He placed the bowl in front of Decker and then pulled the chair from under the table and sat down. He leaned forward. "If you don't mind me asking, do you have anywhere to stay tonight?"

Decker shook his head. "I don't."

"That's what I thought." Edward rubbed his chin. "Listen, I know a man over at the Whitechapel casual ward. He was a regular when I ran the Horn of Plenty some years ago. Jack Finlay. Go over there and tell him I sent you. He'll make sure you have a bed for the night."

"That's very kind of you. If you don't mind me asking, what exactly is a casual ward?"

"You really aren't from around here, are you?" The landlord laughed. "It's the workhouse. But don't worry. They won't keep you in. The casual ward only lets you stay for one night."

"That's reassuring." Decker wasn't an expert on British workhouses, but he knew enough about them to be wary. "I wonder if you could direct me to another location within Whitechapel."

"Where would that be?"

"The police station."

Edward studied Decker for a moment through narrowed eyes. "Now why in the name of everything that is holy would you want to go there?"

"I have my reasons," said Decker, hoping the landlord would not press him on the matter.

"You realize vagrancy is a crime in London, right?"

"I'm not exactly a vagrant," Decker protested.

"You have nowhere to live. You came in here soaking wet and looking half-starved. I'll wager you don't have a penny to your name. How would you describe yourself?"

"A traveler," Decker replied.

"As you please. Call yourself whatever you want, but my advice would be to stay away from the police. They won't be as open-minded."

"I appreciate the warning. But I really need a police station. It's very important." Decker had asked about the police station in Whitechapel for one simple reason. It was the obvious place to look for Abberline.

The landlord shrugged. "Your funeral I suppose. You'll want to head over to Leman Street. H Division."

"Thank you for the information."

"Don't mention it." Edward leaned back in his chair and folded his arms. "Whatever your business there might be, I'd advise you to tread carefully. The less attention you draw to yourself in your current situation, the better."

"I'll heed the warning," Decker said.

"Make sure that you do." Edward pushed his chair back and stood as if to leave, then paused. He reached into his pocket and withdrew two coins, which he placed on the table. "Here are a couple of shillings. That should get the ticket to Whitechapel on the Underground. Take the train to Aldgate East. The police station will be a short walk away on Leman Street."

Decker took the coins and pocketed them. "I appreciate this."

"Don't mention it."

As the landlord turned to leave, Decker asked him one last question. "Just out of curiosity, why did you help me?"

"What else is a man to do?" The landlord replied. "Let a fellow human being starve?"

Decker thanked the landlord again and watched him walk away. His problems were far from over, but at least he had a plan now, and a place to look for the Order of St. George.

# THREE

AFTER DECKER LEFT the King's Head, he made his way to the tube station, following directions given to him on his way out by Edward the landlord. A short while later, he exited another tube station on Whitechapel High Street near the intersection of Leman Street. After that, it didn't take long to find what he was looking for.

Leman Street Station, home to Division H of the Metropolitan Police, was a dirty and drab five-story brick building with a pub on one side and cooperative wholesale society on the other, which Decker surmised was the early twentieth century English equivalent of a modern wholesale club.

Decker mounted the front steps and entered the building to find himself inside a small lobby with cream-colored walls and a checkerboard tiled floor. He made his way directly to the reception desk on the other side of the lobby.

A bored-looking sergeant looked up at Decker's approach. He was in his late thirties or early forties and wearing a black frock coat with shiny silver buttons. The shoulder number 23H was attached to his collar.

"Can I help you, sir?" He asked in a thick Cockney accent.

"I hope so," Decker said. "I'm looking for a detective inspector that might work here."

"You are, eh?" The sergeant leaned back in his chair and studied Decker for a long moment. "And who might that be?"

"Frederick Abberline," Decker replied.

"You're a little too late," the sergeant said. "*Chief Inspector* Abberline has been retired for near on twenty years."

"Is he still in the city?" Decker asked. "It's very important that I find him."

"Don't know where he is these days. Only met the man once when I was new to the force. Heard he got a job working casinos in Monte Carlo for the Pinkerton detectives, but I doubt he's still doing that."

"Would anyone else here know where he is?" Decker asked. With no easy way to track down Thomas Finch, Abberline was his only hope of finding the Order of St. George.

"Couldn't rightly say," the desk sergeant replied. "Not that it matters. I can't imagine Abberline would want to talk to the likes of you."

"Not sure I follow," Decker said.

"A dirty vagrant."

"I'm not homeless." Decker sensed the conversation was veering into dangerous territory. He didn't like the way the desk sergeant observed him, or the man's tone of voice.

"Right. What's your address then?"

"I don't live in London," I'm just visiting."

"Let me guess. From America."

"That's right."

"In that case, you'll be staying somewhere hereabouts. Where are you lodging while you're in our fine city?"

"It's complicated," Decker said.

"Is it now." The desk sergeant scratched his chin, then pointed to a wooden bench against the wall on the other side of the lobby. "Listen, why don't you go take a seat over there, and I'll ask around, see if anyone can help you."

Decker considered this for a moment, then nodded and went to the bench, where he settled. The desk sergeant's sudden helpfulness felt out of character. It was unlikely he was fetching someone who knew Abberline and could give Decker the retired chief inspector's address. It was more probable that Decker had done exactly what the landlord of the King's Head warned him not to do and stepped into a situation. Which was why he waited until the desk sergeant ambled off into the back of the police station, then rose from the bench, intending to make his escape, but he never got the chance.

Decker hadn't even made it halfway to the door when the desk sergeant was back, accompanied by a pair of uniformed policemen.

"Where do you think you're going?" The sergeant asked as the two policemen hurried into the lobby.

"Figured I'd taken up enough of your time," Decker replied. "Thought I'd be on my way."

"Not so fast." The sergeant stood in the doorway and watched the two constables approach Decker. "How do I know you won't go back out on the streets and commit some felony?"

"And why would I do that?" Decker asked.

"Why do criminals do anything?"

"I'm not a criminal," Decker protested as the constables grabbed his arms.

"See, that's where we disagree. You don't have nowhere to go tonight, which makes you homeless. In case you didn't know, vagrancy is a crime in this country."

"So, because I don't have a hotel room, you're going to lock me up?"

"You catch on fast." The sergeant motioned for the pair of constables to remove Decker from the lobby. "Take him down to the cells. Maybe a night or two behind bars will give you a chance to think about the path you're on."

"And then what?" Decker couldn't imagine they were just going to cut him loose the next morning.

"And then a judge gets to decide what happens to you. More than likely, you'll be heading for the workhouse where you can be beneficial to society."

Decker resisted the urge to fight back against the constables. The last thing he needed was a charge of resisting arrest. But he wasn't going down without a fight. "This is a violation of my rights. I haven't done anything wrong."

"Tell that to the judge." The sergeant laughed. "Gotta hand it to you. It ain't every day a vagrant rounds himself up."

"I told you before, I'm not a vagrant. I came here looking for Frederick Abberline."

"And I *told you*, he ain't here and wouldn't see you even if he was." The sergeant stepped out of the way as the constables led Decker deeper into the police station. As they entered a narrow and gloomy corridor, the desk sergeant called after him. "You want to tell me your name and save me the hassle of coming down to the cells and asking later?"

"Not really," Decker said, not bothering to keep the annoyance from his voice. But then he changed his mind.

What harm could it do? It wasn't like anyone in this era knew who he was or how he had gotten here, and it might dissuade the sergeant from asking more uncomfortable questions later. He glanced back over his shoulder. "John Decker. My name is John Decker."

# FOUR

THE CELL WAS small and cramped, located in the bowels of the police station beneath street level. There was a small window secured by iron bars near the ceiling that looked out on the pavement above and a steel door with a peephole and a narrow flap at the bottom through which a tray of food could be inserted. A concrete ledge with a thin mattress on top provided space to sleep. A foul-smelling bucket in the corner had attracted a horde of flies that circled relentlessly.

Decker sat on the concrete ledge with his arms folded and eyes closed. He had been here for several hours already. It must be evening now, because the sun was setting. The patch of weak light cast by the window had crept across the floor and was now climbing the opposite wall, growing dimmer as it went. There was no artificial illumination. Soon the cell would be plunged into darkness.

Earlier, as the constables escorted him down to the cells, Decker had protested his arrest to no avail. Afterward, when the metal door slammed shut and locked, he banged on it and demanded to be set free. But it soon became clear that either no one was listening, or they simply didn't care, so he gave up.

Now he sat and waited, counting off the hours, figuring that eventually someone would have to pay him some attention. His patience was rewarded when he heard the bolts on the other side of the steel door draw back.

Decker squinted against the brighter light outside the cell as the door swung open. Soon, his eyes adjusted, and he saw a figure silhouetted in the doorway. A slender man in a peacoat. Further back in the corridor were a pair of constables, no doubt ready to intercept Decker if he tried to escape. They were not the same men who escorted him to the cell earlier.

The stranger in the doorway took a step inside the cell.

"Good evening," he said in a clipped accent. "I do hope the accommodations are to your liking."

"The maid did a horrible job cleaning the room," Decker said. He glanced up toward the small window. "The view isn't great either."

"I'll relay your concerns to management," the stranger said. A bemused smile touched his lips.

"You do that." Decker climbed from the ledge, stood, and stretched to work the kinks from his sore muscles. "While you're at it, you might want to mention that the door sticks. It wouldn't open no matter how much I tried."

"You're a funny man."

"I do my best."

The stranger nodded. "When you came in here earlier, you identified yourself as one John Decker."

"That's right."

"And you're American."

"Right again."

"Yet you look like a tramp and only had a single shilling upon your person. A paltry amount for a foreign traveler."

"I had two shillings before I took the underground from Mayfair," Decker said. "Does that help?"

"Not really." The stranger cleared his throat. "Again, just to be clear, your name is John Decker."

Decker confirmed that it was.

"You have no way of proving your identity, I assume?"

"Do I need to?" Decker pushed his hands into his pockets. "Seems to me that my unwarranted incarceration has little to do with my identity and more to do with the fact that you think I'm a vagrant."

"Vagrancy *is* a crime."

"That's what people keep telling me." Decker looked the man straight in the eye. "What difference is it to you what my name is?"

"I like to know who I'm dealing with, that's all."

"Well, now you know."

"Indeed I do."

"You thinking of letting me out anytime soon?" Decker asked, fearing that he already knew the answer.

"I believe we'll keep you tucked up a little while longer," the stranger replied. "Think of it as free bed and board, courtesy of his Majesty."

"For how long?" Decker had struck out looking for Abberline, and didn't know what to do next, but he knew one thing. He didn't wish to be locked up.

"We'll see." The man turned to leave.

"Wait," Decker shouted after him. "I told you my name. How about you tell me yours?"

The man glanced back over his shoulder. "Fair enough. My name is Detective Inspector Harry Sim of the Met."

Met was short for Metropolitan Police. This much Decker

knew. Founded in 1829, they were one of the oldest constabularies in the world and the model for most other forces around the globe. None of that helped right now.

"Is it usual for someone of your rank to show an interest in a vagrant?" he asked quickly.

"Good night, Mister Decker," the detective inspector replied, ignoring the question. He stepped out of the cell and motioned for the closest constable to lock the door. "Sleep tight."

# FIVE

DETECTIVE INSPECTOR HARRY SIM returned to his desk on the second floor of the Leman Street station and settled back in his chair. Outside his door in the common area, he could hear the chatter of uniformed officers—blue uniformed bobbies who would soon be out walking their night beats on the rough and tumble streets of the Whitechapel district.

He closed his eyes for a moment, replayed the conversation with the American down in the cells. The man didn't look anything special. A down and out wearing khaki fatigues that hung loose on him. Was he a soldier down on his luck? If so, he didn't serve in the British Army. And why would an American soldier be over here on the streets of London in uniform? A soldier with nowhere to lay his head.

Sim opened his eyes and reached for a poster lying on his desk. The paper was yellowed; the wording printed upon it had faded to a coppery brown. Its edges were curled and brittle. The poster dated back at least twenty years. One of many distributed around the city decades earlier, the poster had hung on the wall in the common room for as long as he could remember until he removed it an hour before.

**Notice**
*Wanted by the London Metropolitan Police*
*John Decker*
*An American*
*About forty years of age*
*If seen, please contact*
*Frederick Abberline*
*Of H Division*

Sim had barely given it a second glance in all the time he had worked at H Division, even though oversight of the case it related to had been assigned to him as a young man by Chief Inspector Frederick Abberline in the weeks before his retirement back in 1892. Why the high-ranking Abberline had kept this particular case close to him during his tenure with the Met, Sim didn't know. He had retained no other cases upon his promotion to Chief Inspector.

Sim also didn't know why Abberline had passed the mantle to him personally, summoning him and relaying the details, sparse as they were, in person. He impressed upon the young Sim how important this particular case was. If Sim were to do nothing else of note at the Met, he must be vigilant regarding this strange case.

And it was indeed strange, comprising nothing but a sheet of paper with a name and description upon it. No details beyond that. A person wanted for unknown reasons. In the early days, when he still believed they would find the man in short order, Sim had wondered if Abberline knew more than he was letting on. Certainly, the Chief Inspector had acted as if he did, refusing to answer Sim's questions except to say that powers higher than he had an interest in locating John Decker.

In the years since, Sim had come to believe that he would never find his quarry, who would by now be in his sixties. Which was why he was so surprised when the desk sergeant informed him they were holding an individual who matched the description and name on the poster. Except this person was too young by at least a couple of decades. When Sim visited the cells and confirmed this, he didn't know what to make of it. The name and nationality matched. But his appearance . . . It was closer to the age the man should have been when the poster was printed all those years before. This could not be who he was looking for, could it?

Maybe.

Abberline had left him with one last order before retiring and heading off to Monte Carlo. Regardless of when this man shows up, you must follow my instructions to the letter, even if you don't believe you have the right person. No matter how inexplicable you find the situation, even if it appears impossible, you are to do your sworn duty.

Sim had taken an oath that day in Chief Inspector Abberline's office. He had given his word as a policeman. Which meant that he would do as Abberline wanted, and follow his orders, regardless of the fact that he didn't understand them. Which meant sending word across town to another man who had been in that meeting between Abberline and Sim almost twenty years previously. A man who still asked about the case to this day, making sure the detective inspector did not forget the name John Decker.

Sim tore a sheet of paper from a notepad on his desk and wrote upon it. That done, he rose from his desk, the sheet of paper in hand, and left his office to find a suitable messenger.

# SIX

DECKER LAY on the hard ledge that passed for a bed in his cell and tried in vain to sleep. Darkness swirled around him like a shroud. It had been hours since the sun went down and now the only thing visible in the cramped space was a crack of light around the door.

Earlier, after his visit from the detective inspector, someone had pushed a tray of food through a narrow oblong flap at the bottom of the cell door. It was barely edible. A lump of hard stale bread with no butter and a thin broth that bore a faint taste of chicken but contained no meat or vegetables. A tin mug of water accompanied the inedible meal. Decker drank the water to quench his raging thirst, but ignored everything else, pushing it back the other way through the flap.

Sometime afterward, when darkness had already come, there was a commotion in the corridor outside Decker's cell. Slurred shouting and cursing in a thick London accent followed by what sounded like a brief scuffle before a cell door banged closed. Another unfortunate being given unwanted bed and board for the night, no doubt. For an hour or more the cursing continued, along with a barrage of salty threats and ringing thumps as the prisoner beat his fists against the door much like Decker had done earlier. Eventually, also like Decker, the man tired of his useless tirade and quieted down.

After that, Decker was left in a cocoon of silence broken only by an occasional wail or groan from one of the other cells. He stared up into the void of nothingness that surrounded him, and his mind wandered. Many years in the future and a continent away Nancy was surely thinking he was lost forever and probably dead. This weighed heavy upon him, tearing at his heart. When and if he ever got out of here, he would find a way to send her a message across the decades. He didn't know how to achieve this feat . . . yet. But he would figure it out. Even if it was his lot to remain trapped in the past for the rest of his life, he wanted Nancy to know he was alive and loved her.

Decker shifted on the thin mattress and tried to find a comfortable spot. A losing proposition in the dark and dirty cell. Tomorrow or the next day he might be hauled up in front of a judge, at least if the desk sergeant was telling the truth, and Decker could see no reason for the man to lie. While he relished getting out of the cell, Decker couldn't help but wonder if worse awaited him. He knew little of English workhouses save what he had read at school in classic novels like Oliver Twist. Even from this, he knew they were appalling places where disease was rife. The idea of ending up in such an establishment left a pit in his stomach. But there was nothing he could do to prevent such an outcome, which sounded all but certain. Unless he could convince the judge that he was not homeless. A tough thing to do when you were from another century and had only a single shilling to your name.

Decker rolled back over and observed the crack of light around the door, because it gave his eyes something to focus on.

From somewhere deeper in the cells, another inmate coughed, the sound rasping and full of phlegm. Someone else grumbled for the man to quit his hacking. Yet another inmate shouted at this individual, which started everyone off, slinging insults back and forth in thick accents until a bobby showed up and hollered for them all to settle down or else.

Decker sighed. It was going to be a long night.

# SEVEN

EUNICE GLADSTONE SAT near the window of the solicitor's office where she worked on George Street, and looked out across Tower Hill Road to one of London's most famous landmarks. The Tower of London had been there much longer than the building Eunice now occupied, but both had served the same function over the years. To protect the kingdom from threat . . . Because poring over legal contracts and resolving disputes was not the main function of this particular establishment.

The balding, portly, white-haired solicitor who occupied the inner office had been with the firm of Crosley and Dutton for as long as anyone could remember. In fact, he was one of the founding partners, his own last name being Dutton. But his true employer, the one who had approached him with an offer he couldn't refuse decades before during the reign of Queen Victoria, and a year after the eponymous Crosley was hit and killed by one of the then new cable trams on Highgate Hill, was not in the legal business. Instead, the solicitor was expected to keep shop without plying for clients, and subtly dissuade any foot traffic that did wander into the office with high prices and a surly attitude. He was, in short, nothing more than a smokescreen. For the trouble of effectively giving up his profession, he earned more than he ever could practicing law and got to spend his days snoozing and taking long lunches.

This was why it surprised Eunice when an unannounced visitor showed up less than thirty minutes after she had opened the offices for the day. He wore a cheap corduroy jacket and pants under an unbuttoned double-breasted Ulster coat. A bowler sat atop his head, which he slipped off upon entering.

"Good morning," he said in a voice that carried a faint trace of a cockney accent. He wiped his coat shoulders to remove the dampness that clung there from the morning drizzle outside. "Fine weather for ducks."

"That it is," replied Eunice with a demure smile before slipping into her usual first line of defense. "I'm afraid Mr. Dutton is busy right now preparing court documents and cannot be disturbed. If you would like to leave your name, along with a brief account of the reason for your visit today, I'll inform him that you stopped by."

"I'm not here to see the solicitor," the man said, stepping closer to the desk. "I have a message for Mr. Phillips."

"I see." Eunice hid a flicker of surprise behind a well-practiced neutral expression. Few people asked to see Mr. Phillips, who was not in fact a real person, but rather one of several pre-arranged code names designed to allow clandestine communications between her true employer and various establishments, including law enforcement, the military, and Whitehall politicians. In this case, the name told her that the Metropolitan Police were reaching out even before the man in the wet Ulster introduced himself.

"My name is Inspector Clover." He held out a neatly folded slip of paper. "I bring an urgent message from Detective Inspector Sim."

Eunice observed the policeman for a moment, then reached out to take the message.

Clover hesitated, apparently unsure if he should release it. "I was told to deliver this message personally."

"And you have," Eunice replied.

"I'm not sure I should leave it with a . . ." Clover paused a moment before continuing. "With a secretary."

"You mean with a woman," Eunice retorted.

"It has been impressed upon me that my message is of a most sensitive and urgent nature." Clover looked uncomfortable, perhaps regretting his words. "I merely wish to guarantee it arrives in the correct hands."

"Did Detective Inspector Sim give you specific information regarding which hands those might be?"

"No, ma'am, he did not."

"Then I suggest you finish your task and give me that message so that I may complete mine."

Clover hesitated a trifle longer before releasing his grip on the folded sheet of paper.

Eunice took the sheet and studied it for a moment before glancing back up at the messenger. "Is there something else?"

"No, ma'am, there isn't."

"Then I suggest you be on your way."

"What should I tell Detective Inspector Sim?"

"That we will take the appropriate action." Eunice did not elaborate further, partly because she didn't know what action that might be, and also because she never imparted more information than was necessary.

For a few seconds, Clover didn't move, as if he expected her to be more forthcoming, but then he nodded and excused himself before pulling the coat tight around his frame and stepping back out into the chilly London morning.

Alone again, Eunice stood and locked the office door, turning the sign hanging in the window from open to closed. That done, she headed toward the back of the room, removed a key from around her neck, and unlocked another door that led to a dimly lit corridor with an ornate birdcage elevator at the end.

After glancing briefly over her shoulder to double-check she was alone and had not been observed, even though she knew that to be the case, Eunice stepped into the corridor. Behind her, from one of the inner offices, came a rumbling snore. The aging solicitor, Dutton, was asleep in his chair as usual, with the London Times spread across his desk, no doubt.

She pulled the door closed and locked it behind her, then started down the corridor toward the elevator, carrying the message from Detective Inspector Harry Sim. A message that comprised just four short words.

*I have John Decker.*

She didn't know why her employer was looking for him, or who John Decker was, but the man she was going to see would. Of that, she was sure. And if this John Decker had attracted their attention, then it would not end well for him, because it never did for the people who fell afoul of her organization.

# EIGHT

JOHN DECKER AWOKE to rough hands pulling him up from the thin mattress by his lapels. He must have fallen asleep at some point during the night, even though he didn't expect to. Now he opened his eyes to find a pair of blue uniformed policemen dragging him to his feet.

"Come on, sleepin' beauty," one of the pair said with a snigger. "Yer wanted upstairs."

"What's going on?" He asked. It was morning now. Sunlight was filtering in through the transom window near the ceiling. He didn't know what time it was, but it felt early.

"You'll find out soon enough," the other policeman said.

"Are you taking me to see a judge?" Decker remembered the desk sergeant's words from the day before. Would he be an unwilling resident of a workhouse by day's end?

"Chatty one ain't you." The policeman to his right gave Decker a hard shove toward the door.

He stumbled forward out of the cell. The two police officers followed and led him along a narrow corridor with water dripping down the walls. They passed other cell doors.

A few stood open, but most were occupied. As they walked by, the occupants called out and grumbled. One of the cops withdrew a thick truncheon from his belt—the British version of a nightstick—and banged on the doors to quiet them down.

Soon they reached a set of stone steps that rose steeply toward ground level. Decker was hustled upward and escorted through the police station to a small and featureless room with no windows that contained nothing but a wooden table and three hard chairs. Two on one side and one on the other. Decker was pushed down into the single chair and his wrists were secured with a pair of metal handcuffs which were themselves swiftly shackled to an iron ring set into the tabletop.

Their task completed, the pair of bobbies retreated and left Decker momentarily alone. A quick glance down told him that the table was bolted to the floorboards. No chance of an escape even if he had wanted to. Not that he had any intention of trying to flee. Even if he made it out of the interrogation room, there were a lot more officers between it and the station's front doors. And even if he could've made it, where would he go with his wrists bound by handcuffs? Better to wait and see what would happen next.

He didn't need to wait long.

The door opened and two men strode in, one of whom Decker recognized as Detective Inspector Sim. They settled on the two remaining chairs and observed him wordlessly for a moment before Sim cleared his throat.

"I trust that my officers were not too heavy-handed in bringing you up here," Sim said to Decker, his tone softer than their previous interaction.

"They were nothing but professional," Decker replied, sensing a change in the dynamic between them. He looked from Sim to the other man, who was in his late forties or early fifties and sported salt and pepper hair and a thin mustache. "Who's this? Another one of your detectives?"

"All in good time," Sim replied casually. He leaned back in his chair and folded his arms. "Please, state your name."

"You already know my name. I told you already."

"Tell me again, for the benefit of my guest."

"John Decker."

"Thank you." Sim kept his gaze firmly fixed on Decker.

Now the other man spoke. "You're a long way from home, Mr. Decker."

"I'm from Louisiana in the United States."

"I'm aware of that." The man studied Decker's face for a few seconds before speaking again. "Could you be more specific . . . How about a town?"

"Wolf Haven."

"Is there a Mrs. Decker waiting for you back there?"

"Not there. But I have a fiancée." A twinge of yearning tugged at Decker's heart. His interrupted wedding on Singer Cay felt like another life. "Her name is Nancy."

"Very interesting." The man rubbed his chin. "I just have one more question, and it may appear odd, but I ask that you answer, anyway."

"Ask away." Decker had found the whole interview strange. This wasn't a courthouse, and he clearly was not speaking to a judge. The man had offered him no name, and Decker didn't think he would get an answer if he asked for one. There was an air of secrecy swirling around the stranger sitting next to Detective Inspector Sim. It reminded him of another man that was now, hopefully, back on the island many years in the future and safe. Adam Hunt.

"What was your father's occupation?" The stranger asked, fulfilling his promise that the question would be strange.

Decker didn't answer for a moment, wondering if it was a trick question. When it became obvious that he was not, he drew in a long breath before speaking. "He was the town sheriff."

"Thank you," the stranger said, a look of satisfaction passing across his face.

"Well?" Sim glanced sideways, taking his eyes off Decker for the first time. "Is he the one?"

"I believe he is." The stranger rubbed his hands together. "You can make the paperwork regarding his arrest disappear?"

"As if he was never here," Sim replied.

"And your men?"

"They'll keep their mouths shut if they know what's good for them."

The man nodded. "I'm pleased to hear that. Because if they don't—"

"You can trust the men of division H just like you always have," Sim replied, cutting off the stranger. "No one in this station will utter a word of this. There's no need for implied threats."

"Very good," the stranger said. Then he stood and left the room, letting the door swing closed behind him.

# NINE

NO SOONER HAD the enigmatic stranger left the room than the two policemen who had escorted Decker there earlier stepped back inside.

Sim leaned forward, placing his elbows on the desk. "I don't know who you are, or how you came to be here, and I know better than to ask, but I sincerely hope that your situation improves. I really do."

"It could improve right now if you took these handcuffs off me," Decker said, tugging at his shackles.

"I think not." Sims smiled. "I wouldn't want you escaping on the short trip to your new lodgings. Not after we spent so long looking for you."

"Care to expand on that last statement?" Decker asked. He had arrived in London less than forty-eight hours ago and had spent at least half of that time locked up in the basement of Leman Street Police Station.

"I would not." Sims motioned toward the two officers, who stepped forward and released Decker from the shackle attached to the table. They did not unlock his handcuffs.

"In that case, how about you tell me where I'm going?"

"You'll find out in due course." Sims stood and turned to the pair of officers. "You have your orders. Take him away."

Decker started to protest, but there was no time. He was hustled from the room, down the corridor, and through what looked like a file storage room with boxes piled on wooden shelves. From there he was unceremoniously manhandled through a back door that led into a small courtyard where a black motorcar with sweeping fenders and ridiculously thin tires on large spoke wheels idled. To Decker, it looked like an antique, but to the citizens of 1911 London, it must have looked ultra-modern. A twentieth-century replacement for the horse-drawn carriages that dominated the streets up until that time.

A driver dressed in black with a peaked cap sat behind the steering wheel. He didn't react as Decker was led to the vehicle and deposited in the back. But no sooner had the door slammed than they were moving. The driver steered them out of the courtyard and through a set of open wooden gates onto the road beyond. They drove through narrow back streets past cramped, squalid housing and rundown businesses including a cobbler, bakery, and a stable yard with a farrier—a blacksmith who made and attached horseshoes—standing outside wearing a leather apron.

But soon the slum housing and dirty streets gave way to larger, more ornate buildings. The River Thames came into view. Decker saw the unmistakable outline of Tower Bridge spanning the river, and beyond this, the building that gave that landmark its name. The Tower of London.

For a moment, he thought that was their final destination, but then the car veered left into a side alley and navigated past buildings that crowded in close enough to feel claustrophobic. Finally, just when Decker wondered where they were headed, the car pulled into what must have been a stable at one point. It was now a garage concealed behind the buildings fronting the river.

No sooner had the car stopped than two men stepped up and pulled the car's back door open. They waited for him to step out and then led him toward a metal door that looked like a service entrance to some business or other. As they made their way inside, Decker noticed a sign affixed to the door.

*Crosley and Dutton*
*Solicitors*
*Private—No Entry*
Clients: Please use door *at front of building*

This was weird. Decker had expected to end up at either another jailhouse or a courtroom. Maybe even the workhouse. The last place he expected to be taken was a lawyer's office. The men accompanying him felt wrong, too. Unlike his previous escorts, they were not police officers. They also didn't look like they were in the legal business. The way they held themselves, the swagger in their walk, and muscular build, suggested something else entirely. They looked more like soldiers even though they wore everyday clothes—work pants made of duck cloth, leather suspenders, and cotton shirts—instead of uniforms. But why would a pair of soldiers be leading Decker into the offices of a solicitor who probably spent his days drawing up legal contracts for banks and moneylenders?

They were in a corridor much like the one at the police station, except this one was brighter and more recently painted. From a door at the other end that probably led to the front offices where the solicitor entertained clients, a woman appeared. She hurried toward them with a warm smile.

"Mr. Decker, I've been informed of your arrival," the woman said. "My name is Eunice Gladstone. I'll be accompanying you from this point on."

"Accompanying me where?" Decker asked as the two burly men flanking him turned and retreated. They disappeared through a small archway Decker hadn't noticed to the left of the outer door.

"Please, no questions," Eunice said. "All will be explained in due course."

"Could you please take these handcuffs off?" Decker asked, holding up his chafed wrists to show her the shackles.

"I'd love to," his escort replied as she led him back along the corridor toward the door from which she had appeared. "But I don't have the keys. That is not my job."

"What is your job?" Decker was curious.

"Didn't I just say there would be no questions?" Eunice glanced back over her shoulder toward Decker.

"You did." Decker glanced over his own shoulder toward the door through which he had entered the building.

Eunice Gladstone must have read his mind. "If you're thinking of making a run for it, I would urge you against that course of action. You won't get very far. The two men who brought you in here are still close at hand and will happily chase you down. Frankly, I think they're bored and would relish the exercise."

"It was just a thought," Decker said. "A man has to weigh his options. Especially when that man doesn't know where he's about to end up."

"Quite." Eunice nodded. "To put your mind at rest, your new accommodations will be much nicer than the place where you slept last night."

"I'm pleased to hear that. I would still like to know where I am and who is providing those accommodations."

"My goodness, you are a persistent fellow, aren't you?" There was a hint of amusement in Eunice's voice.

"When necessary." Decker followed Eunice through the door at the end of the corridor and found himself in another short passageway with doors on both sides. One door stood open to reveal what looked like a rear office that had not been used in many years. A desk and leather banker's chair occupied half the space. Bookcases containing legal volumes and case law lined two of the walls. A heavy layer of dust coated everything. From behind another door, this one closed, came a sound that startled Decker. A low snore.

"That would be Mr. Dutton," Eunice said. "He was a fine solicitor once until the opportunity to do more worthwhile endeavors came his way."

"Like sleeping?" Decker asked.

"He does a lot of that," Eunice admitted. "And all of it in the name of patriotism."

Decker found this last comment odd. Actually, the whole situation was odd. When he asked his unflappable escort what she meant, Eunice just shook her head.

"Now, now, Mr. Decker. You won't get any more information out of me. I'm too good at my job."

"Worth a try," Decker said as they made their way past the offices to another door which brought them into a front lobby area.

Without another word, Eunice led Decker through the small lobby toward yet another door. Behind this was a barely lit passageway that ended at a gold-colored metal birdcage elevator. They stepped inside and Eunice pulled the cage door closed. She pressed a button, and Decker found himself descending below ground and into the unknown for the second time in as many days.

# TEN

THE WORLD beneath the solicitor's office was a wonder to behold. Decker stepped out of the elevator into a wide arched tunnel. Green tiles ran halfway up the walls to an ornate dado rail freeze in a floral acanthus leaf pattern. Above this, curving up around the arch, were clean white porcelain tiles.

They followed the tunnel for what Decker estimated to be around a hundred feet until it opened out into a wider area that Decker realized with a jolt was a ticket hall with kiosk-style windows set into the far wall. The intricate tile work continued. There were no gas lights here. Electrified chandeliers hung from the ceiling, and smaller light fixtures curved out above each ticket window. This had all the hallmarks of a London underground station. Except there were no passengers. Instead, a pair of men in similar garb to those who had escorted him into the building sat at the far end of the ticket hall near a reinforced metal door. At their hips, Decker observed, they wore pistols.

"Don't be put off by the security," Eunice said, noticing

the look of alarm on Decker's face as they walked across the hall. "It's an unpleasant necessity that ensures our safety."

"Am I about to find myself in some kind of covert prison?" Decker asked. "Because this sure as hell isn't a regular tube station."

"I assure you this is no prison," Eunice replied. "And you are correct. This is not a regular tube station. It is, in fact, all that remains of the Tower of London station opened in 1882, only to close two years later when the Metropolitan Railway and District Railway were merged to form the Inner Circle. This station was no longer needed. At least, not by the rail company."

"So who does it belong to now?" Decker asked as they reached the guarded door.

"All in good time," Eunice answered, then engaged in a brief hushed conversation with one of the guards who eyed Decker with suspicious curiosity.

The guard used an antique-looking telephone device mounted on the shelf next to the door to converse with someone on the other side. A moment later, the sound of a lock disengaging could be heard. The two guards stepped aside as the metal door swung slowly inward.

Eunice motioned to Decker. "After you."

Decker hesitated, unsure if he should step across the threshold into the unknown. But what choice did he have? Besides, he had a suspicion of where he was, and if that hunch proved correct, his situation might improve greatly.

"We don't have all day." Eunice gave him a gentle prod in the back.

"Okay. I'm going." Decker stepped forward beyond the door. He found himself in a dimly lit chamber roughly ten by ten feet in size. It contained nothing but a small desk behind which another guard stood to attention. This man's weapon was less subtle. He carried what Decker recognized to be a Winchester Model 1910 self-loading rifle and also a pistol on his belt. This place, regardless of if Decker's hunch was correct, was well defended.

"What time is it?" The guard asked.

Decker thought this to be a strange question for such circumstances until Eunice answered the guard.

"Time for tea," she said.

"It's always time for tea," the guard responded.

"With milk and two sugars."

Decker suppressed a grin. This was a uniquely British code exchange meant to verify the identity of anyone who showed up here.

"And your guest?" the guard asked, looking at Decker.

"He only drinks tea in the afternoon."

This was, no doubt, more code play. Eunice's response probably told the guard what Decker's business was in whatever lay beyond this chamber.

The guard used a phone similar to the one near the outer door, dialed a single digit—the number three—and exchanged another round of code phrases with whoever was beyond the inner door. This done, he replaced the receiver and nodded to Eunice. "You may proceed."

"Thank you, Tom."

The sound of another set of locks being drawn back reached Decker's ears before the inner door opened. Again, he was herded through but soon stopped in awe. The large oblong underground chamber beyond the door was even more elaborate than the tiled tunnel from which they had entered the underground complex. Iron columns with intricate scrollwork capitals and fluted shafts supported the ceiling at intervals. The walls here were tiled, too. An inset mosaic panel formed the words Tower of London. The space reminded Decker of something, but he couldn't quite put his finger on it until he heard the throaty rumble of a train passing on the other side of the wall to his right.

"This is an old platform," he said, surprised.

"Yes." Eunice nodded. "We blocked off the track side of the platform. The trains run beyond that wall without the passengers ever guessing this is here. In fact, as far as anyone is concerned, the station was demolished back in the late 1880s. Nothing remains of it topside."

"Which is why we had to enter through a solicitor's office?"

"Precisely. The office backed up to one of the station's original lift entrances. We merely added onto the building and incorporated it to give us private access."

"And the sleeping lawyer?" Decker asked, remembering the snores coming from the office above.

"One of the original partners. We bought the business for many times market value and retained him for appearance's sake at a grossly inflated salary much higher than what he could have made in his previous occupation."

"Why bother?" Decker asked.

"Because we don't want anyone getting curious about a solicitor's office with no solicitor," a new voice said from behind Decker. It belonged to the man who sat in on the interview at the police station earlier that morning. He was standing in a doorway on the station's back wall. "Welcome to our underground lair, Mr. Decker."

"Thank you," Decker said. It was time to test his theory regarding where he was. "The Order of St. George has done a good job concealing themselves."

"Yes, we have," the man said, confirming his suspicions.

"And to whom am I speaking?" Asked Decker. This man

was clearly not Frederick Abberline because he was too young.

"Of course. Where are my manners?" The man replied as Eunice turned and wordlessly headed back toward the door they had entered through, leaving Decker alone with the stranger. "My name is Thomas Finch, formerly of Her Majesty's Grenadier Guards."

# ELEVEN

"COME ALONG, my friend, let us find a more comfortable location within which to converse," Finch said, turning on his heel and heading back toward the door through which he had come. "We have much to talk about."

"Wait." Decker held up his shackled wrists. "Any chance of losing these?"

"Of course." Finch turned back and produced a small key, which he used to unlock the handcuffs securing Decker's wrists. "They were a precaution, nothing more. I apologize for your treatment."

"You could have told me who you were back at Leman Street," Decker grumbled, rubbing his sore wrists. "You didn't need to bring me over here like a common prisoner."

"On the contrary," Finch replied. "We had to ensure you were indeed who you claimed to be. These are dangerous times."

"Aren't they always?"

"Quite." Finch headed back toward the door again. "And now, please save your questions a while longer, and I promise to tell you everything you wish to know. But let us do so in more genteel surroundings."

"Suits me." Decker was all for some creature comfort after his night in the cells. Even though he was brimming with curiosity, he bit his tongue until they had passed through another large chamber behind the old station platform, this one occupied by several men and women hunched over wooden desks in pools of light cast by lamps. A few of these gave the pair curious stares as they passed by but then quickly put their heads down again and continued their work. Moments later, they arrived in a lavish office the size of a small apartment.

It was furnished with plush rugs and silk hangings. An oak executive desk occupied the middle of the room, behind which was a large leather chair. Two more leather chairs occupied the space in front of the desk.

To Decker's left was a purple chaise lounge with ornately turned legs. A carved mahogany writing desk stood against the far wall. It looked old and valuable, even to Decker's untrained eye. Opposite this was a bar cabinet made of similar dark wood. Next to this was a sideboard, atop of which was a teapot and four porcelain cups.

"Please, take a seat," Finch said, closing the door and heading straight for the sideboard.

Decker settled into one of the two plush leather seats in front of the desk and marveled at the room's opulence, which included a large hanging chandelier above the desk that illuminated the space in soft yellow light. "Nice digs you have here."

"Thank you. Can I interest you in a drink?" Finch nodded toward the liquor cabinet. "I would offer you a nip of whiskey, but it's a little too early even for me, so how about a cup of tea instead? Freshly made. Oolong."

"Sure." Decker wasn't sure what Oolong was, but he was parched.

"Excellent. I had the tea leaves imported directly from China."

"Sounds expensive," Decker replied.

"Not nearly as expensive as my other weakness." Finch poured the tea.

"Whiskey, I presume."

"Very astute. Queen Victoria, God rest her soul, introduced me to the joys of whiskey drinking. I enjoy Irish. Victoria preferred scotch, which is, in my opinion, a second-rate product. The Irish did invent the drink, after all. Even the name is derived from an Anglicized version of the Gaelic. Translates as water of life."

"I'm more of a bourbon man myself."

Finch gave Decker a long and mildly disapproving stare, then placed the teacup in front of him before settling down in the seat across the desk. "Maybe later I'll open my latest bottle direct from the Emerald Isle and change your mind. Fifteen-year single malt."

"In the meantime, maybe you will answer my questions?"

"Like?"

"Well, for a start, how did you find me, and why were you even looking?"

"That question is easy to answer. We've had feelers out for many years. Two decades, to be precise. Chief Inspector Abberline, prior to his retirement, was instrumental in involving the Metropolitan Police, which made things considerably easier. When he departed, the mantel was passed to Detective Inspector Sim, whom you have met."

"Not a very charming man," Decker said. "At least from my perspective."

"He's a little rough around the edges but mostly agreeable."

"I'll take your word for that." Decker picked up the cup and sipped his drink. The hot tea, with no sugar or milk added, was better than he expected. It was sweet with a mild fruity taste and an aroma of honey. "You still haven't said why you were looking for me or how you even knew about me."

"Because of me," a female voice said from behind Decker. "I told him to look for you."

Decker swiveled in his chair to see a familiar figure standing in the doorway. Relief flowed over him like a wave. "Mina!"

# TWELVE

"I HOPE you saved some of that tea for me," Mina said, stepping into the room and closing the door behind her.

Decker hadn't even heard her enter. He turned and was momentarily taken aback by her appearance. She wore a navy-blue silk day dress with a high neck, lace collar and dainty white embroidered polka dots along the skirt. She looked like Mina, but also not like her at all. The spunky, modern young woman that Decker had grown to think of as an adopted daughter over the last few years was replaced by a serious, dour woman who looked every bit a Victorian lady.

Then a smile played across her lips, and Decker shook off the strange feeling that he was looking at a living photograph from a time long in the past. He jumped up and met her in a tight embrace.

For a moment he felt her stiffen, but then Mina returned the embrace, just briefly, before pulling away.

Sensing her discomfort, he returned to his chair as she followed behind with a catlike grace he had never seen from her before. "I don't understand. How are you here with Thomas Finch?"

"That is a long story, which I should be happy to tell you in due course." Mina settled into the chair next to him. "In the meantime, I'm just happy to have found you after all these years. It's been so long I had practically given up."

"How long?" Decker asked, alarm bells going off inside his head.

"More than two decades. I arrived here in 1887. Mid October, I believe."

"What are you talking about . . . that can't be . . ." Decker struggled to find the right words. He could hardly believe his ears. The young woman occupying the chair next to him looked no older than when he had last seen her only a few short days before—at least for him. Her skin was pale and flawless, her hair luxurious. She radiated the exuberance of youth. Yet her eyes . . . Those told a different story. In them, he saw a much older soul, and realization dawned. "Abraham Turner."

Mina nodded. "He had apparently amassed quite a few stolen years of life before his essence transferred to me when you killed him."

Finch had remained silent during this exchange, but now he spoke up. "We estimate that she's aging at the rate of about one year per decade, maybe slower than that. It's been rather hard to determine, even with our resources given the unique situation."

"Only a year every decade?" Decker absorbed this news and came to a startling conclusion. He looked at Finch because he couldn't bear to see Mina's face when he spoke again. "That means that if her natural lifespan would have been eighty years, then she—"

Mina interrupted him. "It means that since I was only

twenty years of age when I encountered Abraham Turner and absorbed his life force, I have at least half a millennium ahead of me. Probably much more."

"She is, for all intents and purposes, as close to immortal as a human will ever come," Finch said.

"Oh, Mina, I am so sorry," Decker said. "If I had known the consequences of killing Abraham Turner the way I—"

"If you had not killed him, I would have died right there and then," Mina replied, interrupting for a second time. "Your actions might have extended my life by an immeasurable term, but they also saved it. I for one, would choose the latter over the former any day even if I don't relish the thought of being the world's first six-hundred-year-old woman."

"Even so . . ." Decker felt that neither option was agreeable.

"The actions that brought us to this situation are not worth discussing since they cannot be changed." Mina reached across gap between the chairs and laid her hand on Decker's. "You did what was necessary. There was no way to anticipate such an outcome. Even had you been able to, you could not have asked for my thoughts on the matter, because I was close to death. It was, as the French say, a fait accompli."

"Doesn't make me feel any better," Decker said. He studied Mina, suddenly aware of the subtle changes that twenty-odd years in the Victorian era had wrought upon her. Her accent was softer. The hard edges worn away. She didn't speak like the Mina he had known, either. Not only did she sound older and wiser, but her vocabulary had expanded, and her sentence construction was more refined. He wondered if this was an accident of her surroundings or deliberate.

She answered this question with a wide grin as she slipped briefly back into the old Mina and said, "Hey, Mister Monster Hunter, quit feeling sorry for yourself."

"Not feeling sorry for myself," Decker said, returning the grin. He was relieved to see that some glimmer of the real Mina was still there, even if she hid it well. "But there is one way to fix what happened to you."

"You mean head on over to Hays Mews and send that bastard to hell right now before he has a chance to wreak havoc on the future?" Mina said.

"Yes." Decker thought back to the previous morning when he stood outside of Abraham Turner's old residence and briefly considered that very action, even though he knew it could change the future in unanticipated ways. Still, having discovered how his actions had affected Mina, it was worth further discussion.

"Believe me, we have contemplated that very course of action," Finch said. "But if I understand it right, we would be making a grave mistake."

"This timeline, the one where we get thrown back to Singer Cay in the middle of the Second World War, and then end up here in London like this, was always meant to be."

"Mina . . ." Decker warned in a low voice, glancing toward Finch.

"It's okay," Mina countered. "He knows about many future events and has sworn to keep them secret and not interfere with the dominoes that must fall to make them happen."

"I can't say I'm looking forward to the future," Finch said. "I guess I'm lucky that, unlike Mina, I won't be around for the majority of it. I for one, am still positively mortal."

Decker nodded, accepting that Mina must have had her reasons for revealing such knowledge to Finch. It was a conversation that could wait until later when they were alone. Besides, it was already done. "Why would you think that our current situation was preordained?"

"I can answer that," Finch said. "Without Mina, we never would have been able to catch the Ripper and contain him. She's the one that started it all, admittedly with a little help from myself."

"What do you mean?" Decker asked, a prickle running up his spine.

"If she had not ended up back here when she did," Finch continued. "There would be no Order of St. George."

"You mean . . ." Decker let that statement sink in.

"He means that I founded the Order alongside Thomas at the behest of Queen Victoria herself," Mina said. "So you see, if I never came back in time, none of this would exist and Abraham Turner would still be plying his grisly trade."

# THIRTEEN

DECKER'S HEAD was still spinning thirty minutes later when Mina showed him to a large and lavishly appointed room lined with bookcases deep within the subterranean complex that had at one time been one of the first London Underground stations in existence and was now headquarters to the Order of St. George.

She followed him into the chamber and made sure he was settled before taking her leave. There was much Decker wanted to know, but Mina said she had urgent matters to take care of even as she assured him she would return later.

At the door, she stopped and turned back. "I can't tell you how happy I am to see you again, Decker," she said.

"Me too," Decker replied. "Although I had hoped you and the others all made it home and were not trapped in the past like me."

"Colum, Rory, and Adam Hunt probably did make it back. Or at least, I don't think they are here in London." Mina flashed a sad smile. "I have a feeling that I'm responsible for your current predicament."

"How so?" Decker asked, sensing that there was much she had not told him.

"Later." The smile vanished from Mina's face. As she turned to leave, Decker thought he saw a flash of sadness in her eyes.

Alone now, he surveyed his surroundings. The bookshelves stretched from floor to ceiling on all sides of the room. They were stuffed with leather-bound volumes of all shapes and sizes, many of which looked old even given the era he currently resided in. A gorgeous, tessellated floor beneath his feet incorporated encaustic tiles into a stunning red and white mosaic pattern. Above him was an intricate, coffered ceiling made of at least two contrasting woods. A pair of velvet couches stood in the center of the room, one on each side of the low table. Beyond this was another, higher table surrounded by chairs upon which several fat books were stacked haphazardly.

He went to one of the bookcases and browsed its contents. The books were all on the same topic. The occult. Another bookcase contained volumes dealing with ancient myths and legends. Yet another was dedicated to astrology and fortune-telling. Many of the books would not be out of place in a museum. Some were so old that they had obviously been rebound more than once.

This was, Decker realized, a research library dedicated to the paranormal. But was it also, he wondered, another jail cell much fancier than the one he had occupied back at Leman Street? There was one way to find out. He went to the door and turned the handle. He was relieved when the door swung open. Until he saw the man sitting on a wooden chair outside. He wore the same uniform as the guards they passed when Eunice was bringing him here.

Decker's heart fell. Had Mina changed so much that she did not trust him?

"Can I get you something?" The man said, looking up.

"Cup of coffee would be nice," Decker said, partly because he wanted to see if the man would leave his post and also because he was parched.

"I'll see what I can do," the man replied but didn't move.

"Thank you." Decker's eyes fell briefly to the man's waist and the holstered gun that was strapped there. "I'll take it black if you don't mind."

The man nodded and stared at Decker with folded arms. After a moment, he spoke again. "You should go back inside and close the door. I'll have someone bring your beverage at the first opportunity."

So there it was. The surroundings might be plush, and the door might not be locked, but Decker was as much a prisoner now as he had been under the care of Detective Inspector Sim. His disappointment was palpable. The Mina he knew would never have kept him restrained in such a way. Had her many years stranded in turn-of-the-century London really changed her that much? He found it hard to believe, yet the evidence of his own eyes was hard to refute.

Then again, he must keep in mind that for him, it had been little more than a week since they were all gathered on Singer Cay for his wedding. From Mina's perspective, almost a quarter century had passed. She could not possibly be the same young woman he had first met while investigating the Qalupalik in Shackleton, Alaska, and had subsequently inserted herself into the middle of his battle against Abraham Turner in London the previous year. She could not be the same person who showed up to his wedding, still trying to deal with the aftereffects of what happened to her when they defeated Turner. Even though he hated to admit it, the Mina that Decker knew was probably gone forever.

"Sir? If you wouldn't mind stepping back into the room." The guard jolted Decker from his thoughts.

"Of course." Decker retreated and closed the door. He went to one of the couches and sat down. It was comfortable, and he was exhausted after spending his first night in London on a park bench and his second on a hard concrete ledge in a basement cell. He soon found himself dozing off.

# FOURTEEN

WHILE DECKER WAITED for Mina's return in the luxurious underground library that used to be part of the Tower of London tube station, another man named Reginald Poulton waited impatiently Twenty-four miles northeast of London outside of the Black Dog pub in the small hamlet of Mavendale.

He paced back and forth, giving his watch an occasional glance. His friend was late, which was not unusual. Even though he was only twenty-two, Alastair Chamberlain was a man of means with a large trust fund, which afforded him a lifestyle that meant he could come and go as he pleased and indulge any whim. As such, punctuality was not his strong point.

Reginald sighed and pushed his hands into his pockets to keep them warm. It was already getting dark. The temperature had dropped a good five degrees, and it wasn't exactly warm in the first place. He thought of the roaring fire in the pub hearth. He was about to head back inside to banish the chill from his bones and have another pint when the toot of a car horn drew his attention.

He turned in time to see a tourer with a fat grill and brass headlamps—a bottle-green Lancaster Thirty-Eight motorcar— swoop up to the curb next to the pub. Alastair was behind the wheel. In the back were three young women, two of whom Reginald recognized as Daisy Elizabeth Cartwright— Alastair's latest conquest—who went by Ellie because she didn't like her first name, and Lady Felicity Braithwaite-Moore. They were both monied. The former because her father owned paper mills in the Midlands, and the latter because she was the daughter of Lord Robert Braithwaite-Moore, who inherited several properties in the village, including the pub in front of which they were now parked. The third young lady, a pretty girl with hazel eyes and long dark hair, was unknown to him. Not that it mattered. He had been seeing Felicity on the quiet for the past two months and even though it wasn't serious, he was rather fond of her. A little flirting couldn't hurt though, he thought to himself as he pulled the door open and slid into the Lancaster's front passenger seat.

"Your bally late," he complained, then turned to the stranger. "And who is this beautiful creature?"

"Beatrice Warburton," the young woman replied. "I'm Ellie's cousin from London."

"That's why we're tardy," Alastair said. "Had to swing by the country house her parents just acquired a couple of miles outside of town and pick her up."

"At least you're here now," Reginald said, still miffed that he'd been kept waiting. "Any longer and I was going to give up on you and get soused instead."

"We'll still get merry, don't you worry," Alastair said with a grin. "I put a couple bottles of bubbly in the boot."

"Or we could just go back into the pub," Reginald said, casting the Black Dog one last wistful glance.

"What, and miss out on an adventure?" Alastair eased the car away from the curb. "You're not getting cold feet, are you?"

"Well . . ." Reginald wished he hadn't said he would ride along on this jaunt. The previous evening, they had been drinking and playing cards at the country house Ellie shared with her parents, who were currently in London on business. The talk had turned to the old manor outside of town, and someone had decided they should go explore it since a member of Alastair's family had served on the board when the building was a workhouse.

Felicity leaned forward and stuck her head between the seats. "Come along now, Reginald. You agreed to do this. Don't tell me you're afraid."

"I'm not afraid," Reginald replied, indignant. "I just don't see why we have to go tromping around some moldy old, abandoned manor house when we could do more interesting things."

"We'll get to the interesting things later." Felicity's eyes sparkled with mischief. "When we're alone. In the meantime, you need to prove to me what a man you are."

"Isn't that what I'll be doing later when we're alone?" Reginald chuckled at his own wit.

"Don't be so crass." Felicity slapped his shoulder from the back seat. "Besides, it's so much more than a moldy old manor house. Don't you know the stories?"

"Of course I do." Reginald watched the businesses on the village high street pass them by until they left Mavendale behind and ended up on a narrow, winding lane with trees overhanging both sides. "After the family who owned it lost their money back in the mid-eighteen-hundreds, the place was sold and turned into the Bartholomew Meadows Workhouse. One dark and wet night, the inmates rebelled and slaughtered every last staff member. According to legend, it was the master's own wife who released them. She killed her husband with a meat cleaver, then slit her own throat."

"That's disgusting," Ellie said with a shudder.

"It is rather, isn't it?" Felicity was in her element. "After the massacre, the workhouse was closed down and it's been abandoned ever since. You know, they say it's haunted to this day."

"There's no such thing as ghosts." Reginald snorted. "And as for that old manor house, it's just a pile of old bricks and rotting wood. If you really want to go up there, it's fine by me. Maybe I'll even prove to you that ghosts don't exist."

"Ah, but they do." Felicity's eyes twinkled. "Maybe we'll see one tonight."

"I rather doubt it," Alastair snorted. "But if we do, the drinks are on me in the Black Dog afterward."

"Be careful, old chap," Reginald said as his friend slowed the car to turn onto a narrow track marked only by a weathered sign on a leaning wooden post that read Bartholomew Meadows. "I shall hold you to that."

"I would expect nothing less." Alastair gripped the steering wheel tightly as they bumped over deep ruts left by hay carts that belonged to the farms on either side of the trail. "Beer only. Nothing to—"

"There it is," Felicity squealed, interrupting Alastair.

Reginald leaned forward and peered through the windshield. Up ahead, in the darkness, he saw a stone archway silhouetted against the night sky. For a moment, he harbored some hope that the gates would be closed and locked. Instead, they stood wide open on hinges that probably hadn't moved in decades. And beyond the arch stood Bartholomew Meadows itself.

Looking out at the bleak and empty old building ahead of them, Reginald suppressed a shudder. Even from beyond the gates that had once closed it off from the outside world, he could feel the atmosphere of this place. It oozed from every brick and beam, bleak and diabolic. And at that moment, Reginald thought of the fire burning in the hearth back at the pub and wished more than anything in his life that he was back there right now.

# FIFTEEN

DECKER FELL INTO A FRACTURED SLEEP, and his dreams were filled with the vampiric Abraham Turner, who stalked him through dark and foggy London alleys, intent upon opening his neck with that vicious knife and stealing the years of his life.

With some relief he was awoken from this nightmare by the sound of the door opening. At first he thought it was the guard bringing his coffee, or maybe Mina returning to explain herself. But it was neither. He stirred to find Finch standing in the doorway.

"Come along," he said. "Let's go find you a hearty meal and a real bed to sleep in."

"Where's Mina?" Decker asked, pushing himself up from the couch.

"She's busy. Got called away. You'll be reunited again soon enough."

"Where are we going?" Decker asked.

"Home," came the reply. "Unless you would prefer to spend all night on that couch with a guard outside the door."

"I would not," Decker said. He wasn't sure where home was, but at that moment he didn't care as long as there was a hot meal and a soft bed waiting for him.

Finch dismissed the guard and led Decker through the complex to the same birdcage elevator he had entered by earlier that day. They rode up to ground level and exited through the front of the solicitor's office. The lights were off, and a closed sign hung in the window. Eunice and the snoozing lawyer had already left.

When he stepped outside, it surprised Decker to find that it was dark already. He must have spent longer in the old underground station snoozing while he waited for Mina to return than he had realized.

Finch stopped at the curb and raised a hand. Moments later, the same motorcar that had collected Decker from the police station earlier breezed up. The driver, Decker noted, was different. This time, it was a woman with short-cropped hair. She exited the vehicle and opened the back door for them to climb in then took her position behind the wheel. Moments later, they were whizzing through London's dank and foggy streets, heading out of the city and toward the suburbs.

Thirty minutes later, they pulled up on the driveway of a large home sitting amid manicured grounds replete with rosebushes, shrubs, and a large oak tree that spread shade over the front lawn. Other homes on the street were equally grand.

"Nice place you have here," Decker said, as they exited the car.

"Thank you." Finch led Decker toward the front door, which opened upon their approach.

A middle-aged woman wearing slacks and a sweater stood in the doorway.

"This must be our overnight guest," she said, before turning her attention to Decker. She flashed a welcoming smile. "My husband told me you would be joining us."

"I appreciate his generosity," Decker replied as he stepped inside the house.

"As you should. He's never brought his work home before."

"Is that what I am . . . work?" Decker asked, raising an eyebrow.

"I'm sorry, I misspoke. I meant to say he has brought no one from the office to our home before."

"I like to keep my home and work life separate," Finch said to Decker. "This is my wife, Lily."

"It's a pleasure to meet you," said Decker, turning to the woman. He held out a hand in greeting. "John Decker."

"You're American," Lily said, accepting the gesture.

"Yes." Decker nodded. "From Louisiana originally."

"How fascinating. Tell me, what do you do in the city with my husband?" Lily asked as they make their way down a hallway with stairs on one side and closed doorways on the other.

"Now, Lily. Don't give our guest the third degree. You know I can't discuss my work. That goes for John, too."

"Oh well." Lily shrugged as they entered a large living room with a roaring fire flanked by two sofas. "A lady can try, can't she?"

"Absolutely." Finch laughed. "That doesn't mean a lady will get anywhere."

"My husband and his secrets. I swear, he plays things close to his chest for a lowly civil servant."

Decker looked at Finch and raised an eyebrow.

"I don't mean to be secretive, my dear," Finch said to his wife. "It's just that my job isn't very exciting, and I would rather not talk about it outside of the office. Besides, it would surely bore you. I spend my days shuffling papers and sitting in dull meetings where we talk about governmental policy and the suchlike."

"You're probably right." Lily looked at Decker and indicated one of the sofas. "Please, Mr. Decker, take a seat."

Decker waited for Lily to settle on the other sofa, then sat down.

Finch moved toward a liquor cabinet near the window and selected a dark bottle with a yellowed and peeling label. "Would you like an aperitif before dinner, Mr. Decker? Cognac Gautier. A fine vintage from an excellent maker."

"I would be honored," Decker said, even though he had never tried the drink and wasn't even sure what it was.

"My husband is something of a connoisseur," Lily said.

"I have an appreciation for fine wine and spirits." Finch poured a measure of alcohol into a pair of tulip cognac glasses. "It's a small indulgence."

"Which does not come cheaply," Lily said with a smile. "He spends far too much on such things."

"No more than you spend on gowns at Paquin of Mayfair, my dear." Finch picked up the glasses and approached the sofa.

"And on that note, I shall take my leave." Lily stood and headed toward the door. "I have to check on dinner. We have a new cook, and she hasn't quite learned the kitchen yet."

Decker watched her leave, then accepted the glass of cognac from his host. He looked at the amber-colored liquid and swirled it around, noting the tantalizing aroma that rose up. He might like this drink after all.

Finch sat down on the opposite sofa. "You'll have to excuse my wife's curiosity. I try not to share the details of my work with her."

"I assume she isn't aware of your true occupation," Decker said. Finch had made it sound like he was a paper pushing civil servant in some boring government office.

"She is not, and I would like to keep it that way."

"I understand." Decker nodded. "Might I ask . . . why the secrecy?"

"Because the Order of St. George is not public knowledge."

"So you don't trust her," Decker said, and instantly wondered if he had spoken out turn.

Finch didn't appear to notice, or if he did, he did not take offense. "On the contrary, it's nothing to do with a lack of trust. It is for her own protection, and also that of my daughter, neither of whom need be exposed to the realities of my job."

"You have a daughter?"

"Her name is Daisy." Finch rose and went to the mantelpiece, where he took down a silver-framed photograph. He held it out to Decker. "She's away at boarding school."

Decker took the frame and studied it. Inside was a photograph of an attractive young woman with blonde hair cascading down over her shoulders. Decker guessed she was around sixteen or seventeen years of age. She carried more of Finch's features than those of his wife. Decker handed the photograph back. "She's very beautiful."

"Thank you." Finch returned the silver frame to the mantel. "Intelligent, too. Very headstrong."

At that moment, the door opened again, and Lily entered. "Gentlemen, dinner will be ready in fifteen minutes."

"In that case, we had better finish our drinks or there won't be time for a top-up," Finch said with a grin.

Lily turned her attention to Decker. "After we dine, I will

show you to your sleeping quarters. I've already instructed the housekeeper to air out the room and put fresh sheets on the bed."

Decker expressed his thanks.

Lily gave a demure nod and retreated, closing the door as she did so.

Alone again with Finch, Decker decided to satisfy his curiosity. He sipped his drink and waited for Finch to settle on the couch. "If you don't mind, I have a few questions."

"I'll do my best to answer if I am able," Finch replied. "What would you like to know?"

"About Mina, mostly," Decker replied. "And how she has survived here for the past two decades? It must be tough."

"I'm sure it was, at first." Finch polished off the rest of his drink and sighed. "But she's just as headstrong as my daughter. Possibly more so. She is also very opinionated and values her privacy. Which is why I'm going to decline to answer your questions and let her do so if she should so desire."

"I can respect that," Decker said, pushing back a twinge of frustration.

"Good." Finch jumped to his feet, glass in hand. "And now I think it's time for that top-up."

# SIXTEEN

BARTHOLOMEW MEADOWS WAS a dilapidated derelict building with broken windows and crumbling brickwork. The expansive grounds, a holdover from when the building was a manor house, would at one time have been maintained by the poor souls forced to endure hard labor at this place. Now they were overgrown and choked with weeds. The terraces and front courtyard were cracked and buckled thanks to years of winter frost and lack of maintenance.

Reginald Poulton looked up at the building and suppressed a shudder. He glanced back toward the motorcar parked on the driveway nearby and considered suggesting they climb back in and abandon this foolhardy escapade. The whole thing was ridiculous.

Ellie had come up with the idea the night before when they were sitting around drinking and complaining about the lack of entertainment in the village, especially now the nights were getting longer, and the first breaths of winter were upon them.

"Let's do some ghost hunting of our own," she had said with some exuberance after Alastair finished reading a particularly creepy tale from M.R. James' latest collection, More Ghost Stories of an Antiquary, which had been released earlier that year.

"And how do you propose we do that?" Alastair asked, giving her a quizzical look. "Do you know of any haunted houses hereabouts?"

"I know of plenty," Ellie replied. "But there's one place that must be brimming with unquiet spirits."

Which was how they had ended up driving out to the Bartholomew Meadows Workhouse as if it was the most normal thing in the world to go exploring a rundown and probably dangerous ruin at night.

Reginald sighed and tore his eyes away from the Lancaster motorcar. There was no point in protesting this expedition yet again. Especially since the others were moving toward the house now. Alastair was already mounting the stone steps in front of the central building that had once been the manor house. Ahead of him a pair of double doors lay half open, the blackness ahead of them a yawning an unfathomable chasm.

It appeared to Reginald that these doors had been left open on purpose. As if the building were luring them inside. A crazy thought occurred to him that this place, made as it was of bricks and stones and rotten wood, was actually a living, breathing entity. The building knew they were here, and it wanted them to step across its threshold. Then, once they were inside, the doors would slam shut and they would be trapped forever.

Reginald threw off the strange notion. He'd always possessed an overactive imagination and in a place like this it worked overtime.

"Tell me more about what happened here," Ellie said, her voice laced with excitement. She was actually enjoying this.

"Yes, do tell us," Beatrice implored of Felicity, who appeared to be the resident expert on the subject.

"I've already told you what happened here." Felicity was at the open front doors now, standing beside Alastair and peering inside the building. "The inmates broke out of their wards and murdered the staff. That's why the place was closed down."

"But that isn't the end of the story, is it?" Alastair said. "I heard that the villagers believed an evil spirit had been unleashed up here on that fateful night. They were so afraid that a few years after the workhouse was abandoned, they hired a spiritualist to cleanse the place."

"That's right." Felicity turned to face the group. "I forgot that part of the story. The spiritualist spent three long nights here battling the entity, which was supposed to have been the angry spirit of a man whose wife died at the hands of the workhouse staff."

"Sounds like a lot of balderdash to me," Reginald said, even though his heart skipped a beat.

"I'm only telling you what I heard." Felicity pulled a face.

"Supposing there's any grain of truth to this, what did the spiritualist do with this wayward ghoul?"

"Maybe he asked nicely for it to leave, and it went away like a good little ghost. What do you think?" Alastair nudged Felicity, who threw him a withering look.

"Actually, after a long battle with the enraged spirit, he defeated it using a centuries-old incantation passed down through the generations of his family that could trap a disembodied entity in a piece of pure crystal."

"He imprisoned the ghost in a chunk of old stone?"

Alastair shook his head. "I don't suppose you know where this magical crystal would be?"

"I do," Felicity said. "He didn't have a piece of crystal on hand, so he did the next best thing. He used the chandelier hanging in the lobby of the old manor house and forced the Spirit into that."

"This story is getting more far-fetched by the minute." Alastair reached a hand forward and pushed on one of the doors to open it wider. "Are you seriously trying to tell me that there's a ghost living in the chandelier inside this house?"

"No." Felicity sounded annoyed. "As I said, I'm just relaying the story I heard."

"I for one, think it's all absolutely fascinating," Ellie said, pushing past Alastair and Felicity. She stepped across the threshold and stopped. "My goodness, it's dark in here. How are we ever going to see anything?"

"With these," Alastair said, holding up a pair of oil lamps he had taken from the back of the car.

"You thought of everything," Beatrice said, stepping forward and snatching one of the lanterns from Alastair. Then she looked around the assembled group before following Felicity into the building. "Well, what are we waiting for?"

"Nothing, I suppose." Ellie tugged at Reginald's arm and dragged him toward the entrance. "Come along. Your girlfriend is already inside."

"She's not my—" Reginald started to protest.

"Don't be so silly." Ellie laughed. "The two of you think you're keeping your dalliance a secret, but it's obvious to anyone with half a brain."

"It is?" Reginald forgot the apprehension that had coiled in his stomach ever since he realized they were really going to explore the old workhouse. If his romance with Felicity was so obvious, he had a bigger problem. Her father. He would never approve of their relationship, and Reginald knew very well how protective he was of his daughter and what the man was capable of. With that disturbing thought fresh in his mind, Reginald followed Ellie past the workhouse doors and into the darkness beyond.

# SEVENTEEN

THE BEDROOM PROVIDED for Decker in Finch's home was just about as comfortable as anywhere he had ever slept, especially after spending a night on a street bench, another in the cells, and almost a week before that in a World War Two army barracks on Singer Cay.

After a hearty meal, Lily had commented that he looked tired and escorted him upstairs to their spare bedroom at the front of the house. She had also provided towels so that he could freshen up, which he did with much relief. There was no shower, so he took a bath. He knew little about turn-of-the-century homes, but he was aware from his own grandmother that only the well-to-do would have had an indoor bathroom in the first decades of the twentieth century, at least in the United States. He assumed England would be the same. If Finch had owned a lesser abode, he would probably have been forced to bathe in a tin tub in the kitchen filled with water boiled on the stove.

When he returned to the bedroom, Decker discovered that Finch had laid out clean clothes on the bed, no doubt from his own wardrobe. There was also a pair of folded pajamas. Both men were roughly the same build, so Decker figured they would fit just fine. The army fatigues he had worn since before his arrival in London were gone. Decker didn't care if he never saw them again.

Right now, though, all he could think about was getting a good night's sleep. It was still early, a little after nine o'clock, according to the mechanical alarm clock on the nightstand, but Decker didn't care. He slipped on the PJs, pulled the covers back, and climbed into bed.

His thoughts turned to Mina and their conversation from earlier in the day. Could she really be a founding member of the Order of St. George? If so, that meant she was also indirectly responsible for the formation of CUSP. It was a strange and unsettling thought. She had, apparently, set in motion the events that trapped Abraham Turner in the house on Hays Mews many years before, which in turn led to her own misfortune at his vile hands over a century in the future.

It made Decker's head hurt to think about it.

Then something else occurred to him. How much did Adam Hunt know of Mina's destiny? When Decker first met the spunky young woman in Shackleton, Alaska, Hunt was on a long-term assignment there. Was he really just guarding some old laboratories in a disused Navy building, or was he there to put in motion the events that would seal Mina's fate and send her to the past?

It wasn't much of a leap to think that CUSP knew more about the Order of St. George than they were willing to admit, at least to operatives like Decker or Colum. They might very well have known of Mina's involvement in the Order all along, and the strange circumstances that led her there. Decker wondered if Adam Hunt had been playing him. Was his boss a puppeteer pulling Decker's strings to make sure that everything happened as he thought it should? If so, then Hunt was just as responsible for Mina's ordeal in London and its consequences as he was. Maybe even more so.

Decker didn't like that thought.

But there was no way to find out what Adam Hunt did or did not know from over a hundred years in the past. But if he ever got back to the twenty-first century, Decker and his boss were going to have a long and possibly unpleasant chat.

Decker closed his eyes and forced the unsettling suspicions from his mind. He had more immediate problems. Like dealing with Mina in the here and now and finding a way home. None of which he could tackle if he was exhausted. He closed his eyes and waited for sleep to come. It didn't take long.

# EIGHTEEN

REGINALD POULTON SNIFFED the air inside the old and crumbling central building that once housed the offices and staff quarters of the Bartholomew Meadows Workhouse and wrinkled his nose.

"I say, it's rather unpleasant in here," he said. "Don't you think?"

"The place has sat empty for years. What were you expecting?" Ellie asked.

"Something a little less decrepit." Reginald moved further into the building, taking small steps, testing the ground beneath him as he went lest a rotten floorboard give way. "I can't imagine that even the ghosts want to hang out here."

"It is rather bleak," Beatrice said, raising her lamp high and letting the light play across the gloomy lobby area. She walked toward the central staircase that dominated the room and took a couple of ginger steps up. "I bet the workhouse master's quarters are up here. Maybe we can find the place where his wife murdered him."

"Oh. Good idea." Felicity's face lit up. "We should have a séance."

"I'd rather not talk to the restless spirits of the people who were murdered here." Reginald decided he had ventured far enough into the lobby and folded his arms.

"Don't be such a chicken." Felicity nudged him, then leaned close so that her mouth was near to his ear and whispered so that the others would not overhear her. "All this excitement is making me rather amorous. You wouldn't want to ruin that, would you?"

Reginald most certainly would not. If they got this over with and went back to the village early enough, he hoped there would be time for Felicity to come back to his cottage on the outskirts of town for an hour before the curfew imposed by her father. She was never allowed out past eleven, even though she was a grown woman in her early twenties. His Lordship was protective of his daughter's honor and intended her to remain pure until she was married off to a suitor he deemed acceptable. In other words, a member of the aristocracy, which Reginald was not. The chances of him and Felicity marrying were slim even though she was stubborn and resistant to her father's plans. Reginald fully expected to lose her affections one day, but until then, he planned to enjoy every moment of his time with her. He was still pondering this when an exclamation from Alastair broke his train of thought.

"I say, look up there."

Reginald followed Alastair's gaze to see a large cut crystal chandelier hanging down from the second-floor ceiling.

Ellie had seen it, too. "Do you think that's the chandelier used by the spiritualist to trap the evil spirit?"

"I think it's nothing but a dusty old light fixture," Reginald said.

"I bet that it is," Felicity said.

"It's amazing no one came here and removed it, what with all those crystals. They must be worth money." Beatrice was halfway up the stairs now. They creaked under her weight, and she paused as if expecting them to come crashing down at any moment. When they didn't, she continued on up. The oil lamp swung in her hand, causing the shadows to dance and leap as she reached the second-floor landing. "It feels pretty solid up here."

"I'm coming up," Ellie said, heading for the stairs and mounting them. "I want to see where the workhouse master was murdered."

"Why?" Reginald couldn't fathom this morbid interest in such an old crime. Who cared if the master's wife had gone insane and released the inmates before killing her husband? It wasn't like there would be any sign of the murder left. They would surely have cleaned it up decades ago.

"Don't be such a stick in the mud." Alastair was on his way up now, too. He reached the second floor, taking the second oil lamp with him and leaving Reginald and Felicity alone below.

"Hey, it's dark down here." Reginald glared upward toward his friend.

"Come and join us then." Alastair made his way down the landing and disappeared into one of the rooms beyond.

"Come on, let's go up." Felicity took Reginald's hand.

"I don't want to."

"You really are a stick in the mud."

"I am not." Reginald didn't want to admit it, but the old, abandoned workhouse was giving him the creeps. Just thinking of all those people that died here made his skin crawl.

"Look what I found." Alastair's voice drifted from above.

He reappeared on the landing holding a heavy iron poker. "I bet one of the inmates used this to bludgeon the workhouse physician."

"I doubt it," Felicity said from below. "The doctor was found down here in the lobby, not upstairs."

"Still would have made a wonderful weapon." Alastair swished it through the air, barely missing Ellie who jumped back with a squeal.

"Hey, watch what you're doing."

"Sorry. Let me make it up to you." Alastair grinned and stepped toward her. He wrapped an arm around her waist, pulled her close, and planted a kiss on her lips.

"Stop it." Ellie slapped at him. "Don't do that here."

"Why not?" Alastair released her.

"Because it's uncouth."

"It is not." Alastair swung the poker again, then he moved to the railing and leaned over toward the chandelier. "I have an idea. Let's see if there really is a spirit trapped in those crystals."

"How you propose we do that, silly?" Ellie asked, before the realization of what Alastair had in mind dawned on her. She looked at the poker, which he was already drawing back and preparing to throw. "Wait. No. Don't do—"

But it was too late. Alastair released his grip on the poker. It sailed away from the landing toward the dusty chandelier hanging in the stairwell.

A moment later, the iron rod smacked into the light fixture with a sharp crack, followed by a tinkle of broken glass. The chandelier swung wildly. Pieces of shattered cut crystal rained down, followed by the poker, which landed with a thud mere feet away from Reginald.

"Hey, watch it," he exclaimed, leaping back and almost

knocking Felicity off her feet. "What in blazes do you think you're playing at?"

"See. I knew it." There was a note of triumph in Alastair's voice. He leaned over the railing to study the smashed light fixture. "No evil spirits trapped in that chandelier."

"You bally fool." Reginald was fuming. This was too much. "Get down here and drive us back to the village right now. I'm done with this."

"Well, I'm not. We came here looking for ghosts, and I intend to find one." Alastair turned toward Ellie, intending to grab her again and plant another triumphant kiss on her lips. Then he stopped when he saw the look on her face. Her eyes were wide, her mouth curled up into a sneer.

"Are you feeling alright?"

She took a step toward him.

The color drained from Alastair's face. He took an instinctive step away from her. "Ellie, what the devil?"

"Devil indeed," Ellie said in a voice that no longer sounded like her own. Then, before anyone realized what was about to happen, she hurled herself toward him with a shriek and sent the man she had shared a bed with only the night before crashing through the rotten second-floor railing and tumbling backward into empty air.

# NINETEEN

MINA STOOD on the street and looked up at the house Thomas Finch shared with his wife, Lily. A light burned in one of the upstairs front windows, which she knew to be the guest bedroom. John Decker was up there right now, probably preparing for bed. She wanted so badly to knock on the door and ask to see him. There was much she had to explain, not least of which was the reason they were both here. But she could not bring herself to do it.

Mina had spent years searching for Decker ever since her arrival in Victorian London more than two decades before. They had been holding hands when the Lockheed Electra passed through the electrical storm over Singer Cay because she was nervous. When the lightning struck and threw them into the time vortex created by the Bermuda Triangle, she had seen Decker tumbling through the void next to her even after they had been ripped apart. Which was why she firmly believed he had ended up further in the past, just as she did.

But as the years went by and there was no sign of him, she convinced herself that Decker had made it home instead. It was with a small measure of excitement, mixed with a heavy dose of disappointment, that she received the news that he had been found the previous day. Decker had, apparently, walked into the Leman Street police station asking for Detective Inspector Abberline.

She smiled. That was so like Decker. He had probably mounted a frantic search for her, believing that she must have arrived around the same time that he did. When he came up empty, Decker did the exact thing she predicted he would do. Went in search of the only other people he knew could help him in this time. Abberline and Finch. The inspector was easier to locate. Hence Decker's trip to Whitechapel.

It was mostly luck that the desk sergeant had recognized him from the old poster that still hung there. A poster Mina herself had arranged to be printed and distributed by Abberline a quarter-century before.

When she saw Decker sitting in Finch's office, she was beside herself with joy. In the long years since they departed singer Cay, she had come to believe she would have to wait over a century to see him again. Yet there he was looking exactly like she remembered him. He was even wearing the same clothing, which made sense because for him only a matter of hours had passed since the events on the small Bahamian island.

At first, she had been excited to spend time with him. Hers had been a lonely existence stuck so far in the past, punctuated only by brief spells of happiness that never lasted. Decker was a link to her previous life. Someone she could talk to about all that had befallen her because he was there for most of it.

But then, after she left him in the research library, Mina was struck by a sudden and uncharacteristic panic. She had noticed the way he looked at her in Finch's office, as if he was trying to figure out who she now was. She had changed during her time in London. How could she not? She was living in an era that was not her own while cursed with an unnaturally long lifespan that meant she would outlive every person she ever got close to. The burden of her predicament weighed heavy. She feared Decker would not understand the person she had become. Worse, she was afraid that he would not like her anymore. And that was too much to bear. Which was why, instead of returning to the library later that day as promised, she had fled CUSP's underground headquarters on a flimsy excuse and spent the afternoon wandering Covent Garden—one of her favorite places in the city—in an effort to delay the inevitable.

Returning much later, she found Finch and Decker driving off in the motorcar purchased by the Order a year before. It didn't take a genius to figure out where they were going.

"Mina?" Finch was walking down the driveway toward her. "Is everything alright?"

"Yes. No. I mean . . ." Mina stepped from the shadows of a tall oak tree overhanging the road and met Finch halfway.

"He's still awake if you want to speak with him."

"I don't. Not right at this moment." Mina felt a lump form in her throat. "I need some time to work this out."

"Why?" Finch raised an eyebrow. "You've been looking for John Decker for all these years. Now that he's here, you intend to avoid him?"

"Maybe."

"And the point of that would be?"

"I don't know. It's difficult to explain."

"Try me." Finch took a step forward and pulled her close in a hug. He cradled the back of her head with the palm of his hand. When he spoke again, his voice was low. "Of all the people you have known since you arrived here, I might understand you the best."

"I know." Mina rested her head on Finch's shoulder. She allowed herself a moment of weakness before drawing back. "I'm afraid."

"Of what?" Finch retreated a few steps and stood with his hands in his pockets.

"It doesn't matter." Mina squeezed her eyes shut against the tears that threatened to flow. Decker's arrival had left her emotionally battered. She desperately wanted to reconnect with him, was terrified of how he would react to this woman who was practically middle-aged, yet still wearing a young and youthful body that didn't age. On the outside, she looked the same. Yet on the inside . . .

"I wish I could be of help," Finch said.

"Go back inside to your wife, Thomas."

"Come in with me. Talk to him."

"Tomorrow. I promise." And with that, Mina turned and walked back to the street. She didn't breathe easy until the swirling London fog had wrapped around her like a blanket, and she was alone again.

# TWENTY

ALASTAIR LET OUT A TERRIFIED, high-pitched scream that was quickly silenced as his body impacted the tile floor of the lobby with a sickening thud.

At first, Reginald thought his friend might have survived with nothing but a few broken bones. It wasn't a long drop after all. But it soon became clear by the way Alastair lay unmoving, with his neck cocked at an unnatural angle, that he was dead.

"Oh my God. He's . . ." Felicity's hands flew to her mouth. Her eyes moved from Alastair to Ellie, who was still on the landing above, standing in the broken gap between the railings.

Behind her, Beatrice stood frozen in mute horror.

A wide grin spread across Ellie's face. She lifted her arms out to her sides, took a small hop, and launched herself into the air as if she were leaping from a diving board.

For a moment she hung in open space at the apex of her dive, but then she pivoted gracefully in the air, and cut a swift path downward.

Felicity screamed.

Beatrice scrambled backward on the landing above, turning her head so that she wouldn't see the inevitable.

Ellie connected with the ground headfirst. There was a horrifying crack before she toppled limply to one side in a crumpled heap.

Reginald could hardly believe his eyes. He took a step toward the two lifeless bodies sprawled on the tile floor in front of him. Bile rose in his throat, and he fought the urge to vomit.

"We have to find the car keys. Get back to the village and bring help," he said in a croaky voice even as his throat constricted.

Beatrice had found the will to move now. She was rushing back down the stairs with a look of abject terror across her face.

"The keys are in Alastair's pocket." Felicity's eyes were wide with fear. "How are we going to—"

It took a moment for Reginald to register that Felicity had abruptly cut herself off mid-sentence. He turned to her, wondering if she might have fainted with shock.

But Felicity was very much awake. She strode past Reginald to the spot where the shattered remnants of the chandelier lay smashed across the floor. She bent and picked up the poker then turned back to him, ignoring the pair of corpses lying nearby.

"What in blazes are you doing?" Reginald asked, baffled by her strange and inexplicable behavior.

Further away, at the foot of the stairs, Beatrice had come to a halt. "What's happening?" she asked in a small voice as Felicity turned back to Reginald.

A tremor of apprehension shivered up his spine. He

backed away as she advanced upon him with the poker gripped in one hand.

"For heaven's sake, Felicity. Put that down," Reginald implored. But even as the words tumbled from his mouth, he knew they were falling on deaf ears. Because Felicity now bore the same maniacal look upon her face as Ellie had moments earlier. There and then, Reginald realized something. Ghosts were real and spirits could be trapped in crystal. Because he could see the entity lurking behind his girlfriend's eyes as she closed in on him with the heavy poker. When Alastair broke the chandelier, he really had released something diabolical.

He backed up further, raising his arms in defense as Felicity brought the poker up and leaped toward him with a snarl.

Beatrice screamed, the sound shrill and hollow.

Reginald turned to run, overcome with blind panic. The doors of the old manor house stood open mere feet away. But before he was even halfway to them, a blinding pain erupted at the back of his skull.

He stumbled and almost fell.

The pain blossomed again as Felicity swung the poker into the side of his head with all her might.

This time, his legs collapsed from under him. He fell to his knees. Warm, slick blood flowed down his neck even as Felicity stepped in front of him and raised the poker for one final blow.

Reginald toppled sideways. His body felt numb. Darkness pushed at the edge of his vision. He looked up at Felicity, standing over him with a triumphant look on her face. He wanted to cry out, tell her to stop as she gripped the poker in both hands and plunged it deep into her own chest. But no sound came out, and it was too late now, anyway. She was falling toward him; the light fading from her eyes even as he felt his own life force ebbing.

Soon, the darkness that danced at the edge of his vision closed in like a shroud. The last thing Reginald Poulton saw before death came for him was Beatrice, the young woman he had met mere hours before, fleeing across the lobby and out the front doors in terror.

# TWENTY-ONE

BY SEVEN THE NEXT MORNING, Decker and Finch were on their way back to the converted tube station in the black Ford motor car. They entered through the same rear entrance that Eunice had led him through the day before. They rode the elevator down under the city's streets.

As they approached Finch's office, Mina appeared carrying an overnight bag. She looked startled to see them. "Thomas. I wasn't expecting you to be in so early," she said. "I left a note on your secretary's desk."

"You did, huh?" Now it was Finch's turn to look surprised. His gaze dropped to the travel bag in her hand. "Going somewhere?"

"There's been an incident outside of the city."

"What kind of incident?" Finch sounded suspicious. Decker sensed he was missing some unspoken tension between the two.

"The same kind as always. Supernatural. It's a level two. Nothing to worry about."

Decker waited for someone to explain a level two incident

to him. When no one did, he pushed his hands into his pockets and stood in idle silence.

Finch was more vocal. "We have plenty of operatives that can handle something like that. It's hardly out of the ordinary. Does it really warrant your personal attention?"

"I don't like sitting behind a desk while others do the dirty work," Mina replied. "You know that."

"But a level two?" Finch thought for a moment, then he nodded. "I think I know what's going on here."

"What's going on is me doing my job." Mina's expression had turned stony. "Now, if you wouldn't mind stepping aside, I'll be on my way."

Finch didn't budge. "We have a more pressing issue to address before you go running off on some ghost hunt."

Mina's eyes flicked to Decker, then back to Finch. "It can wait until my return."

"Actually, I don't think it can." Finch glanced toward Decker. "The two of you need to talk."

"I agree," said Decker. For someone who had been searching for him for so long, Mina's attitude was strange. She had disappeared the previous day and promised to come back, but had not done so. Now she was trying to skip town without talking to him. It felt like she was avoiding him. He looked at Mina. "If you're mad at me because of what happened with Abraham Turner—"

"I'm not mad at you." Mina spoke quickly. She dropped her eyes, unwilling to meet his gaze. "I really am happy to see you, I mean it. And as for Abraham Turner . . . Like I said yesterday, I don't hold you responsible. In fact, you saved my life."

"Then what's the problem?"

"It's hard to explain." Mina shuffled her feet. "Look, I

know it looks like I'm running away rather than face you, but it isn't like that. Really."

"That's not how it looks from where I'm standing." Decker took a step toward her.

"Please. I just need some time to get things straight in my head. The best way I can do that is by working a case. Keeping busy. When I come back, we'll talk. I promise."

Decker felt his frustration rising. He didn't believe her. For whatever reason, Mina was trying to avoid him. Then a thought occurred to him. "Okay. Fine. How about I come with you? That way, whenever you're ready to talk, I'll be there."

"What? No . . . I mean . . ." The words tumbled from Mina's mouth. She looked flustered. "That isn't possible."

"Why not?" Decker noted that Finch was letting this conversation play out with a bemused expression on his face.

"For one, you aren't a member of the Order of St. George."

"That isn't strictly true, given my job back in the twenty-first century," Decker said. "And given my role in the events that brought you here, some might say that I'm directly responsible for founding the Order."

"That isn't . . . You can't . . ."

"He has a valid point," Finch said. "And anyway, all we need to do is declare him a member, and it shall be so."

"There are rules to be observed." Mina's exasperation was clear.

"Which we ourselves created."

"Any other objections?" Decker asked.

"Yes. You aren't familiar with how things work."

"I'm a fast learner," Decker said. "You should know that."

"Really? You've only been here a couple of days and the first thing you did was get yourself arrested."

"Because you put my name on a bunch of wanted posters

and distributed them throughout the city," Decker said. "Hardly my fault."

"Mina, this is ridiculous." Finch folded his arms. "Unless you have a valid reason why Mr. Decker cannot accompany, I think he should go. If nothing else, it will help to acquaint him with this time period and with the work that we do."

"Thomas . . ." Mina gave Finch a pleading look. "We talked about this last night."

"Which is exactly why Mr. Decker needs to go with you."

"Last night?" Decker looked between Finch and Mina.

"We had a visitor late last night, but she would not come into the house," Finch said. He focused on Mina. "Everything you've told me about the future, and Mr. Decker, leads me to believe that it would be a mistake for you to burn your bridges. You might be trapped in the past right now, but given the rate you are aging, you will need Mr. Decker's organization when you finally reach your own time again. Don't make the mistake of alienating the rest of your friends the way you did with me."

"Thomas, that isn't how it—"

"A conversation for another time," Finch said quickly. He stepped past Mina toward his office. At the door, he turned back to the pair. "What is this urgent matter that you must attend to, anyway?"

"There have been some deaths under suspicious circumstances in an old workhouse outside of London. It might be a case of possession."

"Demonic?" Finch furrowed his brow.

"That remains to be seen." Mina turned to Decker. "If you're going to come with me, you will need more than one of Thomas's old suits."

"It's all I have right now," Decker said. "Unless we bring

those old army fatigues from Singer Cay, assuming they're not already in the trash."

"I think we can do better than that." Mina started down the corridor. "I'll send someone over to Frederick Gorringe's to purchase you some new outfits before we depart. They have a surprisingly well-stocked men's section. I don't suppose you know your measurements?"

"No." Decker shook his head. "I usually just try stuff on, and if it fits, I buy it."

"Oh, dear. I forgot how frustrating twenty-first-century men could be." Mina motioned for Decker to follow her. "I guess we had better take your measurements, too."

# TWENTY-TWO

THEY DEPARTED London two hours later from Victoria Station by train. Decker found the experience of riding a steam locomotive exhilarating. It was like living a scene from an old movie. He wished Nancy were there to enjoy it with him, then felt a pang of longing.

Mina had barely spoken since their earlier conversation in the old tube station except to say that the journey from the capital to their destination of Mavendale would take around ninety minutes. She now sat across from him in the train carriage with her face buried in a book.

After a while, Decker coughed to get her attention. "Are you intending to ignore me forever?"

Mina lowered her book just enough to look at him over the top of it. "I'm not ignoring you."

"Then what are you doing?"

Mina set the book aside. She glanced around at the other train passengers, who were looking at the countryside rolling by outside, reading newspapers, or chatting among themselves. "I don't think this is the place to talk."

"Fair enough. When do you want to talk?"

"Later," Mina said without stipulating exactly when. "I promise."

"I shall hold you to that." Decker settled back in his seat. He glanced out the window. They were passing through a small village but didn't stop. Instead, the train merely blew a whistle and kept going. The rhythmic clack of its wheels on the tracks was strangely soothing. He turned his attention back to Mina, who had picked up her book and was now reading again. There was so much he wanted to know, but she was not ready to answer his questions. He would have to accept that and hope she opened up to him sooner rather than later. In the meantime, there was nothing to do but wait for the train to reach their destination.

An hour later, the train pulled into a small station with a wooden sign on the platform that read Mavendale. Apart from Decker and Mina, only a few other passengers disembarked. Most stayed aboard. The locomotive still had a long journey and several more stops before its final destination of Sheffield to the north.

As the train pulled out of the station in a cloud of belching steam and continued on, Decker and Mina made their way out of the station, where they were met by a horse-drawn hansom cab that took them into the village proper. It would not be long, Decker thought, before this style of transportation gave way to mechanized taxicabs. He had already noticed a few of them in London as they journeyed across the city in Finch's private automobile, although it appeared that automobiles had yet to reach the smaller towns and villages.

After a short and bumpy ride, they arrived at their accommodation, a public house called the Black Dog that offered rooms for rent on the second floor. It reminded

Decker of another pub he had stayed at during his visit to Clareconnell in Ireland when they went up against Grendel and his mother.

The landlord, a jovial man of large stature who would have made a good department store Santa Claus if he were looking for a change of career, escorted them to a pair of rooms at the back of the building.

"It'll be ten shillings a night for each room," he said, sniffing and wiping his nose on the back of his hand. "Payment upfront. How many nights will you be with us?"

"Five nights should suffice for now," Mina said, opening a small purse and withdrawing a five pound note, which she gave to the landlord, who quickly pocketed it. She took another two more one pound notes out and offered them to him. "I trust we can count on you to be discreet about our presence in the village."

"I can keep my mouth shut well enough," the landlord said. He snatched the bribe from her hand and pushed it into his pocket along with the original payment. "Unless you're doing something illegal. You're not planning on breaking the law now, are you?"

"It hadn't occurred to us," Mina said.

"I'll make sure we stay on the straight and narrow," Decker added. "Don't you worry."

The landlord studied Decker for a moment as if deciding whether to comment on his accent, but then he shrugged and handed over a pair of keys. "We don't serve breakfast. Lunch and dinner are available for purchase in the lounge bar downstairs. Pub grub only. Nothing fancy. If you come down to the lounge bar after seven, the first drink is on me."

"That's very gracious of you," Mina said with a smile.

"All part of the service." The landlord sniffed again. "As

my old granny used to say, you catch more flies with honey than vinegar."

"That is so true." Mina pushed her key into her bedroom door and unlocked it.

"Lavatory is at the end of the passageway. There's a bathroom too if you want to freshen up. We have no other guests right now, so you get it all to yourselves."

"Thank you." Decker unlocked his own door.

"I'll leave you to it, then." The landlord rubbed his hands on his trousers, then turned and shuffled back toward the stairs.

When he was gone, Mina looked at Decker. "Let's take fifteen minutes to get settled, and then I want to get started."

"Could you fill me in on the whole story before we do that?" Decker wasn't used to Mina being so assertive. He had to remind himself that she wasn't a young woman, barely out of her teens anymore. Even though she hadn't aged externally, her decades stranded in the past meant she was technically in her mid-forties now. In fact, she was now older than him, a thought that Decker found disturbing. "I'd like to know what we're dealing with before we run into any trouble."

"Same old Decker." The smile returned to Mina's face. "I can do better than that. First thing I want to do is pay a visit to the only person who survived whatever happened here. Would a first-hand account suffice?"

"Sure." Decker shrugged. He paused a moment before speaking again. "This is all very weird."

"Really?" Mina replied. "Your whole job is dealing with the supernatural."

"No. I don't mean this ghost hunting trip to the country. I mean traveling back in time, to turn-of-the-century England no less, and finding you like this."

"Tell me about it," Mina said. "It's freaking weird. I've been thinking the same thing for a quarter of a century. I mean, look at me. I'm a girl from nowhere, Alaska, who ended up a continent away and over a century in the past. On top of that, it appears that I don't age, thanks to Jack the Ripper, who turned out to be a vampire. And I helped create a secret society that fights paranormal entities. A group that will one day become the organization you tried so hard to shelter me from."

"Guess your high school guidance counselor didn't see that one coming, huh?"

"Not even close." Mina smiled, but it was mirthless. She stepped into her room before turning back to Decker. "See you in fifteen minutes, Mister Monster Hunter."

# TWENTY-THREE

BEATRICE WARBURTON SAT PERCHED on the edge of an overstuffed leather wingback chair in the drawing room of the country house her parents had purchased as a summer retreat to escape the bustle of London. Situated a couple of miles outside of the village on a small hill, the property had stunning views of the valley within which Mavendale sat, and the larger countryside beyond.

She was in her early twenties and possessed a Rubenesque figure that no doubt earned her a lot of attention from the eligible bachelors back in the city. Her hazel eyes, which would on any other day be one of her most striking features, were red-rimmed and teary.

Mina and Decker had arrived an hour before and wasted no time in interviewing the young woman, despite the objections of her parents that she was fragile and should not be disturbed. The local constabulary, they said, had already interviewed her at length the previous night when she had arrived home in a state of hysterics.

Mina convinced them that it was in their best interest to

comply with her request. She was cool and calculated, a world away from the impulsive and cocky girl that he first met in Shackleton. The years that had passed for her since she was last with Decker had changed her in more ways than he realized. Yet here and there he still saw flashes of the old Mina, for which he was grateful.

Now, after hearing what Beatrice had to say, he was stumped. She had gone up to the abandoned Bartholomew Meadows Workhouse the previous evening with four friends, one of whom was her cousin, after an evening of drinking and ghost stories the previous day led to the idea that they should seek a paranormal adventure of their own. The workhouse was in near ruins, having been abandoned decades before after an incident in which the inmates had escaped and slaughtered most of the staff. It didn't take long for the villagers to decide it was haunted. According to legend, they even sent a spiritualist there to take care of a wraith.

"Let me see if I've got this right," Decker said after Beatrice finished her account of the events leading up to the deaths of her four companions. "It was only after your friend Alastair damaged the chandelier that you noticed anything was amiss."

"He wasn't really a friend. I hadn't even met him before a couple of nights ago," Beatrice said tearfully. "I'm new to the village. My parents acquired this property through a business deal and thought it would make a pleasant country home since we already had family in the area. I asked Ellie to introduce me to her social circle. I've spent most of my life in London and have found Mavendale very dull and boring. At least until last night."

"What makes you think your companions were

possessed?" Mina asked. "You surely realize how far-fetched your tale sounds?"

"You think I had something to do with their deaths, don't you?" Beatrice fought back a sob. "The local constable thought so too. He all but accused me of killing them, which is ridiculous. It was only my father's influence that stopped the man arresting me."

"We never said that you harmed anyone, and we certainly aren't going to arrest you," Mina replied in a soothing voice. "That isn't why we are here. But we do need to know what really happened."

"I told you already. Alastair smashed the chandelier with a poker. Local legend says that a spiritualist trapped a vengeful spirit within its crystals many years ago. At least, that's what my cousin Ellie said."

"Did you actually see this spirit?" Decker asked.

"No. Not as such." Beatrice wiped a tear from her cheek. "But I saw the look on my cousin's face when she pushed Alastair over the railing. Her voice was different, too. It wasn't her. I'm sure of that. Besides, she would never have killed herself the way she did. She was so happy only moments before. I'm sure it was the spirit that killed her. It made her jump. After that, the entity moved on to Felicity. Oh, God. I can still see her with that poker, it was . . ." Beatrice ran out of words. She struggled to contain her emotions.

"It's alright," Mina said. "You don't need to keep repeating what happened."

Beatrice nodded. "Look, I have no proof of what I know to be true. But I'm telling you this. We unleashed something last night, and whether you believe me or not, it's out there right now. You don't think it will come for me next, do you?"

Decker exchanged a glance with Mina. "I think if it wanted to harm you, it would have done so last night."

"You really think so?"

"I do." Decker nodded.

"Will you be staying in the village for the foreseeable future?" Mina asked.

"I think so. Yes." Beatrice rubbed her eyes with the back of her hands. "The constable asked us not to leave until the matter is settled. My father is a very powerful man, and I can't guarantee that he will abide by the request, but I can assure you that I myself fully intend to."

"Good." Mina stood and waited for Decker to do the same before she spoke again. "If we have any more questions, may we come back?"

Beatrice nodded.

"In that case, we won't take up any more of your time." Mina touched Decker on the hand and motioned for him to follow her outside. After they exited the building, she turned to him. "What do you think?"

"I think we just talked to a very scared and fragile young woman."

"Do you believe her story?"

"You obviously do, or we wouldn't be here." Again, Decker was struck by the change in Mina. She had handled talking to Beatrice with a professionalism which impressed him. If they ever got home, he decided, Mina would make an excellent CUSP operative. This thought dismayed him. Ever since they first met in Alaska, Decker had tried to keep Mina away from the world he lived in. It had not worked, and now it turned out that she was, in many ways, the architect of that world. All he ever wanted was for her to lead a normal life, and now he realized, that would never be. He pushed the thoughts away and decided to focus on the job at hand. "What next, boss?"

Mina grinned. "I'm not your boss."

"In this time period, given your status with the Order of St. George, I think that's exactly what you are," Decker replied.

"On that we shall disagree," Mina said. "But to answer your question, I think it's time we go take a peek at that workhouse."

# TWENTY-FOUR

THE BARTHOLOMEW MEADOWS WORKHOUSE WAS, John Decker thought, exactly as he would expect a Victorian poorhouse to look. It was a Dickensian monstrosity with two dilapidated wings thrusting out from what had once been the local manor house.

"I hate these places," Mina said as they approached the building, passing under an arch with gates that had probably stood open for a decade or more. "They are a barbaric solution to a poorly understood social dilemma."

"I can't argue with that," Decker said, looking up at the destination looming ahead of them as a dark and ominous shape with the winter sun at its back. He glanced toward her, troubled by a sudden thought. "When you arrived here back in the 1880s, you never—"

"I didn't end up in a workhouse," Mina said. "But I have encountered those who have. Life inside a building such as this was a wretched existence that should never have been allowed in any civilized society."

"Apparently, the residents of this particular establishment

felt the same way considering they broke out and slaughtered the staff."

"Can you blame them, locked away like criminals simply because they were homeless and had nowhere else to go?" Mina's voice was full of disdain. "The people who run these places are cruel taskmasters who exploit the suffering of others for their own ends."

"There are still workhouses in operation?" Decker asked, surprised. "I thought they were a purely Victorian institution."

"Unfortunately, no." Mina shook her head. "They continue to this day. If I were not required to keep a low profile because of my situation as an interloper in this time period, I would do all in my power to ensure their closure."

"Just how much power would that be?" asked Decker. Mina had still not opened up to him, but given her position as a leader of the Order of St. George alongside Thomas Finch, he suspected she had impressive connections accumulated over decades of living in the past.

"Nice try," Mina said as they reached the building and started up the steps toward the old manor house where four people had met a grisly end only hours before.

Decker shrugged. "It was worth a try."

Mina came to a halt in front of the double doors leading into the building. She turned to him. "Look, I know you're concerned for me and want to know how I have survived these past decades stranded so far from home. And I will talk to you, I give you my word. But it needs to be at the time of my own choosing. Just give me some space, okay?"

Decker nodded. "Want to take a peek inside?"

"That is why we came here." Mina stepped forward and was about to enter the building when a voice called out from their rear.

"Hey. You two. What the devil are you doing? This area is out of bounds."

Decker turned and was surprised to see a police constable in a smart blue uniform striding toward them up the driveway. "I'm sorry. We didn't realize. There were no signs posted."

"Why would there be?" The policeman reached the steps and hurried up toward them. "The place has been abandoned for years. Doesn't mean you have the right to snoop around. Names. Now."

"I'm John Decker, and my companion is Mina Parkinson."

"Thank you." The constable produced a notepad and wrote down their names. "What are you anyway, reporters?"

"We aren't with the press," Mina said, turning back and meeting the officer at the top of the steps. "We're private detectives from London."

"Private what now?"

"Detectives," said Decker, reinforcing Mina's impromptu cover story. "Like the Pinkerton's, only we work independently. The Metropolitan police use us from time to time to aid their investigations."

"The Met, huh?" The local copper didn't look convinced. "Now, why would *they* need to use hired help such as yourselves?"

"Have you seen the crime in London?" Decker asked, hoping they weren't digging a hole for themselves.

"Fair enough. Still doesn't explain what you're doing here."

"The same as you, I would imagine," Mina said. "Investigating the demise of four young people in mysterious circumstances. The victims all had ties to London, not to mention their status in aristocratic circles. There is some discussion that their deaths might be connected to an ongoing case in the Whitechapel District."

"Or they could just have been a bunch of wealthy and entitled toffs who drank too much and got into a deadly squabble."

"You really believe that?" Mina didn't bother to hide her incredulity.

"It's not as far-fetched as demonic possession," the constable scoffed.

"Possession?" Decker wondered where the constable had gotten such a notion. They certainly hadn't mentioned it.

"Yes . . . No . . . I mean . . ." The constable looked flustered, as if he had let slip something he shouldn't have. "Forget I just said that."

"But you *did* say it." Mina stepped closer to him. "Did the woman who survived say that was what happened? Did she say someone was possessed?"

"I'm not telling you what a witness said in an official interview." The constable's annoyance was evident.

"Then she did mention possession."

"Even if she did, the notion is ridiculous. There's no such thing. It's nothing but superstitious claptrap."

"You shouldn't let personal belief cloud your judgment, officer," Mina said. "It's not very professional and will only get in the way of finding out the truth of how these young people died. Besides, we have no proof the possession was demonic. There's more than one kind, you know."

"More than one . . . What are you talking about?" The constable was flustered. He took a moment to regain his composure and then pointed a forceful finger back toward the village. "All right. The pair of you, get out of here before I arrest you both for trespassing."

"Or you could let us conduct our investigation and look

inside that building." Mina met the constable's gaze with a hard stare. "We *are here* on behalf of the London Metropolitan Police after all, as we've already established."

"We haven't established anything. As far as I'm concerned, you're a pair of loafers up to no good. I'm giving you both one more chance to walk away before I'm forced to detain you."

"Come on," Decker said, touching Mina's arm. The last time he had gone head-to-head with a village policeman, his team had ended up in an Irish jail cell. "It's not worth getting on the wrong side of the local boys. Trust me, I know."

"All right. We'll leave . . . for now." Mina didn't look happy. She cast a rueful glance toward the workhouse doors.

"Well, what are you waiting for? Go."

Decker walked past the constable and waited for Mina to join him before starting off down the driveway. After a few steps, he stopped and turned back. "What's your name, constable?"

"Trent. Alfred Trent. Not that it's any of your business."

"Thank you. That will be most helpful." Decker flashed the constable a smile and kept walking.

When they reached the archway, Decker noticed a bicycle leaning against the stonework. It belonged, no doubt, to the constable.

As they passed it, Mina stopped and grabbed Decker's arm. "How is knowing that man's name helpful?"

"Because the only way that we will get any cooperation from that man is to put him in his place. When we get back to the village, I intend to call your Mr. Finch, assuming I can find a telephone. I think he may have the necessary influence to make the constable more amenable."

"And how is he going to do that?" Mina asked. "We can't reveal the Order."

"No, but I have a feeling that if asked, a certain officer within the Met will validate the story we just told up there."

"Detective Inspector Sim."

"Yes."

"Good idea. Now I just have one more question."

"Yes?"

"How are we going to get back to the village? Call me crazy, but if we're still hanging around when the good constable comes back down that driveway, we'll probably find ourselves spending the night in a cell."

"You're probably right," Decker said. They had hitched a ride with the local blacksmith, who was heading out to a nearby farm to shoe a horse. The man would not be returning with his cart for at least another hour. That only left one alternative. "I guess we walk."

# TWENTY-FIVE

THE BARTHOLOMEW MEADOWS workhouse lay a good three miles outside of the village of Mavendale. Mina and Decker walked in silence for the first half-mile or so, heads down to avoid the buffeting wind that blew across the landscape. Adding to their misery, it began to rain not long after they set out for the village. A relentless drizzle that found its way through their coats to leave them damp and cold.

Mina was the first to speak as they navigated a narrow country lane with trees overhanging at intervals and a low hedgerow marking the boundary between the road and the frozen fields beyond.

"I think it's time I explained myself," she said in a small voice.

"I'm all ears." Decker had hoped she would work out whatever she was struggling with. Now it appeared that she had.

"You probably think I'm an awful person for running out

on you yesterday the way I did, and then trying to leave London in such a hurry today without waiting to see you."

"I don't think any such thing," Decker said. "I'm sure you have your reasons."

"None that I'm proud of. I was scared."

"That doesn't sound like the Mina I know."

"That's just it. I'm not the Mina you used to know. When I first saw you in the office with Thomas, I was so excited. It had been so long, living alone in the past. To see you there . . . I could hardly believe my eyes. But then I got to thinking. What if I changed so much that you didn't recognize me? Worse, maybe you wouldn't like me. I was so young the last time I saw you. Barely more than a teenager. Now look at me. We are practically the same age. In fact, I think I'm older."

"I don't see what difference it makes," Decker said. "Honestly, this whole situation is my fault. If I hadn't allowed you to get involved with the investigation in London . . . If I hadn't allowed Abraham Turner to kidnap you . . ."

"Stop." Mina shook her head. "You don't understand. You are not the one to blame. It's all me. Even the pair of us being stuck in the past like this is my fault."

"I don't believe that for a second." Decker had carried the guilt of what happened to Mina ever since his encounter with Abraham Turner. For Mina to think she was the responsible party was just crazy. "I failed you."

"You did nothing of the sort. I don't know how to explain this any more than I did yesterday back in London, but I am the linchpin around which this timeline turns. As I said yesterday, everything that happened was destined to be. If I hadn't come back in time, there would be no Order of St. George and Abraham Turner would never have been caught. I set in motion the events that led to the encounter with Jack the Ripper that almost killed me. The organization you work for wouldn't even exist if it wasn't for what I have done here over the past quarter-century."

"That still doesn't mean—"

"You still aren't grasping what I'm trying to tell you. We didn't get thrown further back in the past because of some glitch in the Bermuda Triangle, but because of me. I am directly connected to Abraham Turner, and by extension, the watch that he carried with that infernal relic inside of it. When we flew into the lightning storm, that connection pulled me the wrong way. Instead of going home, I ended up here because on some level I became inextricably linked to Abraham Turner's watch when I absorbed his energy. Think of it like a rubber band stretched tight. The further into the future I was, the more tension there was on the connection. When we tried to go forward in time again, the rubber band snapped back and took me along with it. Does that make sense?"

"I think so," Decker said. "You're saying that Turner's watch dragged you back here because its influence was stronger than your connection to the future."

"Exactly. At least that's my working theory. After Abraham Turner was subdued with my help in 1889, his watch was placed in a protective box that shielded the relic contained within and blocked its influence. That was the only way we could ensure Turner remained catatonic and secure in his bricked-up basement lair. We also wanted to guard against others of his kind coming for the watch. But prior to that, Turner was carrying the watch openly. Its influence was at full force. That's why I ended up pulled back to 1887. It was the last time, more or less, that my connection to the watch was strong enough to pull me to it."

"Still doesn't explain me, though. I'm not linked to

Abraham Turner's watch or the relic within it, yet I'm here, too."

"I know. After I didn't find you back in the 1800s, I assumed you had made it home. But it appears that because we were holding hands when the lightning struck, I dragged you back with me. At some point while we were falling through the void, we got separated and you ended up arriving here a quarter of a century later than me. You see, I really am responsible for stranding you even further in the past."

"You don't know that for sure. At best, it's a working theory."

"I can't prove any of it, but I know in my heart that everything I've told you is true. There are things you don't know. Things that I'm not willing to talk about, even with you. I struggled when I first arrived here. It was a dark time, and I almost lost myself in that blackness."

"But you didn't," Decker said. "And whenever you're ready to talk, I'll be here to listen."

"I appreciate that." Mina's voice trembled. "I just wish I wasn't the reason you are still separated from Nancy, and on your wedding day, of all things. If we can't find a way back to our own time—and believe me, I have spent many long years looking—then you will surely die before she is even born."

"You don't need to carry that burden." Decker wished he could take Mina's pain away, but he didn't know how. "It's not your responsibility."

"But it is. You have meant more to me than practically anyone else in my life. You guided me and looked out for me, even though I was a royal pain in the ass."

"You weren't that bad." Decker couldn't help smiling.

"Yes, I was, and you stuck by me, anyway. Then I repaid you by wrecking your life."

"That remains to be seen," Decker said. "I've been in unpleasant situations before, and I've always found a way out."

"Have you ever been in one this bad?"

"No, I haven't," Decker admitted. "But that doesn't mean I'm going to give up. Nancy is out there in the future waiting for me. If it's the last thing I do, I'm going to get back to Singer Cay and marry her."

"I hope you're right," Mina said.

"I am," Decker replied. "And you're going to be there, too, because we can't have a wedding without the bridesmaid."

# TWENTY-SIX

CONSTABLE ALFRED TRENT watched the pair of strangers depart and wondered if he should have arrested them instead of seeing them off. But he had no proof they had done anything wrong, even though his policeman's intuition told him they were up to no good at the old workhouse and might even know more about the shenanigans that had occurred here the previous evening than they were letting on. If they did, he would get to the bottom of it, and then they would be looking back at him through the bars of a jail cell faster than their feet could hit the ground.

For now, though, he was content enough to let them leave because he had a feeling they would not be going anywhere anytime soon. The landlord of the Black Dog, Burt Granger, had informed him of their arrival earlier that afternoon. Visitors were infrequent in Mavendale, much less those from across the pond. Bert might have made a good copper if he had not gone into the hospitality business. One of the two, the woman, had slipped Bert some extra banknotes to ensure his discretion. Immediately suspicious, the landlord had done the exact opposite of what he promised and hightailed it straight down to the police station.

This wasn't the first time Bert had shown up to inform the constable about a shady-looking guest. It was, however, the first time anything ever came of it. With the four deaths up at the old workhouse still on his mind, Constable Alfred Trent had decided it was worth an hour of his time to investigate. And a good thing, too. Cycling up to the workhouse on a hunch, he found the strangers snooping around. They claimed to be working for the Metropolitan Police, but Trent didn't believe a word of it. He might be a country bobby, but he wasn't completely green. The Met didn't subcontract to outsiders, he was sure.

Trent waited a few minutes in case the interlopers returned, then ducked into the building to ensure nothing had been disturbed. He didn't think they had gone inside, and a cursory inspection supported that conclusion. Everything was as he had left it earlier that morning when the local undertaker had removed the four bodies in what was surely one of the busiest days of his year, if not the decade.

Satisfied that nothing was amiss and the strangers were long gone, the constable made his way back down the driveway. The pair were walking back to the village via the old carriage road. He knew this because he had seen them turn left out of the gates and watched as they started down the narrow lane, their heads bobbing above the hedgerows until they were lost from sight. Now he mounted his bicycle and pedaled off in the opposite direction, taking the longer route back to Mavendale.

When he arrived back at the two-room building that served as the village police station, he was surprised to find another stranger waiting for him.

The man was gaunt, his skin pallid. He wore a black suit and white shirt. A pair of thin wire-rimmed spectacles sat halfway down his nose. An instinctive shudder ran up the constable's spine. The man reminded him of an undertaker. Worse, he sat in Trent's chair with his feet on the desk as if he owned the place.

"Is there something I can do for you?" Trent asked, stopping in the doorway with a scowl on his face. He would have grabbed the man by the scruff of the neck and removed him from the seat, but something made him stop. Call it gut instinct, but he had a feeling that grappling with this particular stranger might not end well.

"You must be Constable Alfred Trent," the man said in a voice that lacked a discernible accent.

"I am." There was only one constable in the village, and Trent was in uniform. Moreover, they were at the police station. The stranger's deductive skills appeared less than impressive. "And you would be?"

The man waved a dismissive hand. "My name is not important. My business here, however, is very important."

"I see." Trent was taken aback. "I don't suppose you would mind vacating my chair?"

"I would mind very much." The stranger shifted his legs but did not remove them from the desk. He nodded to another chair on the other side of the desk. The one visitors usually occupied. "Please, take a seat."

For unfathomable reasons, Trent complied, even as he choked down a flash of anger.

"That's better." The stranger smiled to reveal a set of white teeth behind thin lips that, coupled with his pale skin, made him look positively ghoulish. "You are aware, I'm sure, of the guests currently staying at the Black Dog public house.

A man and a woman. They arrived earlier today and rented two rooms for five nights."

"What of them?" Trent wondered how the stranger knew as much as he did. Had he paid a visit to the pub and spoken with Burt Granger? If so, what else had the landlord told him?

"Do you know why they are here?"

"Not as such. They claim to be investigating the deaths that occurred last night on behalf of the Met if you can believe that."

"I take it that you do not?"

"I find their claim suspicious. They're probably reporters looking for a front-page story. The young people who died at the workhouse moved in affluent circles. Or at least, their parents do."

"I see." The stranger sucked in a long and rasping breath. "I would appreciate it if you would allow them to conduct their investigation without further interference."

"I'm just doing my job." Trent wondered why he felt the need to defend himself. There was an empty jail cell in the next room, and he didn't trust this stranger any more than the pair he had just found skulking around outside Bartholomew Meadows. There was one difference, though. On a primitive level, this man scared him. "Besides, what's it to you?"

"All in good time." The stranger swung his legs from the desk, pushed the chair back, and stood up. "For now, all you need to know is that I represent a department within His Majesty's government that deals with threats to the realm. I'm not at liberty to divulge any more than that, but rest assured that your compliance will not go unnoticed."

"What kind of department?" Trent felt another shudder run through him. The stranger was not only rake thin, but he was tall. At least six feet and probably more. "Who exactly do you work for?"

The question hung in the air, unanswered.

The stranger rounded the desk. "If and when you need to know more, I shall tell you. Can I count on your cooperation?"

"What would happen if I said no?"

The stranger loomed over Trent. His eyes were black and cold, like those of a snake. "I'll ask again . . . Can I count on your cooperation?"

This time, Trent nodded.

"Excellent." The man moved to the door. His footfalls were soft and silent. "I may require more from you later, but just stay out of the way for now."

Trent didn't reply. Not that it mattered because the stranger wasn't waiting for one. He stepped out of the police station and shut the door behind him. Only then did the constable realize he had been holding his breath. He expelled it in a long stream and went to the window, but the stranger had vanished as if he had never been there. The only person on the road was old Mr. Danforth, heading to the village store to buy tobacco like he did every afternoon at this time.

Trent stepped around his desk and sat in the recently vacated seat. Now that he was alone in the station, his encounter with the pallid stranger felt almost like a waking dream. He shivered and rubbed his hands together, noticing for the first time how cold the room had become, and tried to ignore the nagging suspicion that he had been visited not by a flesh and blood man but the angel of death dressed up in a suit.

# TWENTY-SEVEN

WHEN DECKER and Mina arrived back at the Black Dog public house, the landlord was behind the bar serving a smattering of customers from the village. Decker approached him and asked if there was a telephone in the pub.

The landlord shook his head. "I can't imagine you'll find one of those around here." He thought a moment. "Except for the police station. I think the constable had one installed a few months ago. Can't imagine he uses it much. Who's he going to talk to?"

"The constable," Decker said, with a sinking feeling.

The landlord nodded. "Don't hold me to that, though. I remember him talking about it one night in the pub, saying he was going to get one, but I don't know for sure."

Decker thanked the landlord and started toward the stairs leading to the second-floor guestrooms.

"If the only telephone in this village is under the control of that constable, we aren't contacting Thomas anytime soon," Mina said. "Even if I trusted him not to listen in, I can't imagine he would let us use it."

"I agree." Decker grimaced. "It looks like Detective Inspector Sim is not going to be much use to us, at least in the short term."

"It's worse than that. If the constable takes it upon himself to contact the Metropolitan Police about us and we haven't secured their cooperation in covering for us, he's going to find out we were lying."

"One of us could take a train back to London and make the necessary arrangements," Decker said. "It's a hassle but might be worth it."

"That isn't going to happen today. We've already missed the last train with service back to London. It stops in Mavendale at three-thirty."

As they reached the stairs, Decker glanced at a clock hanging on the back wall of the bar. It was a little after four. "I guess we'll have to wait until tomorrow and hope the constable doesn't check up on us in the meantime."

"God, I'd give anything for a cell phone," Mina grumbled. "You can't imagine what it's been like living here these past twenty-five years."

"I can hazard a guess. But even if you did have a cell phone, you wouldn't be able to call anyone on it for almost a century."

"At least I'd be able to play games."

"Until the battery went dead."

"Can you please let me have the fantasy?" Mina punched Decker's arm playfully.

"Sure, why not?" Decker replied with a grin. As they started up the stairs, he glanced back toward the bar and noticed the landlord watching them as he dried a pint glass with a dirty cloth. The man dropped his eyes and turned away quickly. Decker leaned close to Mina and spoke in a low voice. "I'm not so sure about that landlord. He seems friendly enough, but . . ."

"Yeah. I know what you mean," Mina replied as they reached the top of the stairs. "They probably don't get many visitors in a small village like this. Especially strangers with American accents."

"Kinda reminds me of Clareconnell." The landlord of the pub Colum, Rory, Hunt, and himself had stayed at in the small Irish village had acted in a similar manner and had almost gotten them killed before reluctantly helping to thwart Grendel. "I hope he's not going to be a problem."

"All the more reason for me to head back to London in the morning and secure the backing of Detective Inspector Sim," Mina said. "If we can get the local constable on our side, it will make our work here much easier."

"And in the meantime?" Decker asked, as they reached the doors to their adjoining rooms.

"You tell me."

"Okay. I think we keep a low profile until the constable is tucked up in bed, along with the rest of the village, and then we sneak back up to that workhouse under cover of darkness and take a look around."

"My thoughts exactly," Mina said, hand resting on her doorknob. "Before that, I think we should freshen up and then head down to the bar to find some food. If we're lucky, we might even come across a local or two who are sufficiently lubricated to chat with us."

"Good idea," Decker said. He opened his own door. "Meet you downstairs in an hour?"

Mina nodded and stepped into her room, turning on the light as she did so. Even though it was not even five o'clock, darkness had fallen.

Decker lingered in the corridor for a moment, his eyes

fixed on the shadows back toward the stairs. Because for a brief moment, as they were talking, he sensed movement, as if someone had made their way up and was lingering there listening to them. But if that were the case, there was no one there now. All he saw was light from the bar below spilling up toward the gloomy landing. Deciding he must have been seeing things, Decker turned and entered his own room. When he closed the door, he waited for a few seconds with his ear close to it, listening for stealthy footsteps in the corridor beyond. Just to be sure . . . but none came.

# TWENTY-EIGHT

AN HOUR later Decker met Mina in the saloon bar of the Black Dog. They ate a hearty meal of shepherd's pie and lingered, drinks in hand, being friendly to anyone who came their way in the hopes of learning more about the strange and disturbing incident that had occurred at Bartholomew Meadows Workhouse.

Not that it did much good. Most of the villagers were wary of their presence and engaged in brief pleasantries before making their excuses and hurrying off. The few that were willing to talk either knew nothing of consequence or did not want to tell what they knew. By ten o'clock, as the pub emptied of all but the diehard stragglers intent upon squeezing every ounce of boozy entertainment from the evening, Decker had reached his limit.

"Come on," he said to Mina. "Why don't we take in the night air before bed and go for a stroll?"

"Good idea." Mina hopped down from her stool at the bar. "I shall pay a visit to the powder room and meet you out front."

Decker nodded and watched her set off toward a narrow corridor at the back of the pub that led to the restrooms. When she was gone, he climbed from his stool, finished the last of his drink, pulled on the coat purchased for him that morning from the department store in London, and stepped outside.

The frigid November air hit him like a slap in the face. It was freezing. The temperature had plummeted since their afternoon walk back to the village. Worse, there was a fine mist of drizzle in the air. He wondered if it ever stopped raining in England. He was still pondering this when Mina appeared around the side of the pub. She was carrying a lantern in her hand.

"Where did you get that?" He asked as she approached.

"Beer cellar. The trap door is out back near the toilets in a small courtyard. It was unlocked, so I went down there to see what I could find. Figured there must be a lamp lying around somewhere, and I was right."

"Smart." Decker couldn't help but be impressed. "Now we can see what we're doing."

"Not much point in exploring if we have to do it in the pitch black."

"Let's just hope the constable is otherwise engaged at this time of night," Decker said as they started along the village High Street toward the lanes leading up to the workhouse. "I can't imagine he'll be thrilled to catch us up there again."

"He doesn't strike me as a twenty-four-hour-a-day type of policeman." Mina held the lamp at her side, keeping it concealed as best she could in case they ran into someone else out for a late-night walk.

"Me either."

They kept on walking, their heads bent against the inclement weather, and soon found themselves outside of the village, surrounded by a landscape that stretched off into blackness in all directions. They moved quickly, retracing the route they had taken earlier in the opposite direction. After forty-five minutes, they came upon the workhouse.

The first thing Decker saw was the stone archway looming out of the night like a sentinel. After passing through its ancient stones, the building appeared, its crumbling walls stark against the night sky.

This time, when they mounted the steps leading to the old manor house around which the rest of the facility had been built, no one was there to stop them.

Now Mina lit the lantern. It cast a pool of soft yellow illumination that pushed back the darkness and allowed them to proceed.

They edged past the half open doors and found themselves in a large entrance lobby dominated by a sweeping staircase that rose to the second floor. Part of the railing on the landing was missing. This was, no doubt, where two victims of the previous night's tragedy had fallen to their deaths. The other two had died on the ground floor, somewhere near where Decker and Mina now stood. Not that there was anything left to hint at the tragedy that had occurred here. The floor had been cleaned of blood. The splintered railing and shattered pieces of chandelier swept away.

"Looks like they're not big on crime scenes around here," Decker said, studying their surroundings with a critical eye.

"This is 1911," Mina replied. "They don't have the strict scene of crime protocols and forensic techniques you're used to. There are no CSI units and crime scene photography is still in its infancy. I bet the constable didn't even record any of this before he had the bodies removed and the area cleaned."

"Judging by our conversation with the only survivor of

what happened here, he's already made up his mind about what occurred here without the benefit of evidence or a thorough investigation."

"That's because he's a village bobby," Mina said. "He's not trained to investigate homicides and they aren't going to send an inspector from London. Not unless one of the victim's families has sufficient influence to force the matter. Even then, it's unlikely a trained murder detective would get here in time to preserve any evidence."

"I guess." Decker couldn't fathom how a crime scene could be cleared away and scrubbed like it was nothing but a nuisance, even in 1911. He gave the lobby one more hopeful glance and then sighed. "This is a waste of time. We might as well go back to the village."

# TWENTY-NINE

THE MAN in the black suit stood concealed in the unlit doorway of a grocer's shop on Mavendale's High Street and watched Decker and Mina leave the Black Dog.

It was late. After ten o'clock. The pub had mostly emptied, and there was no one else on the street except himself and the two people making their way along the High Street. When they were far enough away, he slipped from his hiding place and followed, making sure that they would not notice him until they turned onto the narrow lane leading up to Bartholomew Meadows Workhouse.

He suspected this was their final destination. They had made a similar trip there earlier in the day but ended up being chased away by the village's constable. Now they were returning under cover of darkness to complete their investigation of the old poorhouse.

Not that they would find anything.

The local funeral director had removed the bodies almost as soon as they were discovered, and the constable wasted no time cleaning the crime scene as if it were never there. He was, the man in the black suit thought, a buffoon. A more competent officer would have preserved the area for future analysis, maybe even brought in a photographer to document the scene, but not Mavendale's sole constable. With no experience in solving crimes of a greater magnitude than public drunkenness or the occasional stolen bicycle, he hadn't bothered to look for any explanation beyond a bunch of entitled aristocratic youngsters getting drunk and partying with tragic consequences. It didn't matter, though. Even if the best detectives in London descended upon the scene, they would not have discovered the truth because they would never accept the supernatural.

This was not true of the pair the man in the black suit now shadowed. The organization they worked for did nothing but investigate such things. It was their mandate, given to them decades before by Queen Victoria herself. The man in the black suit knew this because he had run into them before and would undoubtedly do so again once his current assignment was done.

In the meantime, he would ensure that no one, not even the constable, interfered with his current undertaking. This was why he had paid a visit to the policeman and warned him off, which turned out to be a relatively easy task. The constable was impressionable and naïve. The man in the black suit had merely implied that he worked within the government and that the pair were to be left alone to go about their business. He had told the constable that it was a matter of national security. The man in the black suit chuckled to himself. He had even extracted a promise of help from the constable, should it be needed. A useful ace that he would only play should it become necessary.

He hoped it would not.

Nonetheless, the assignment had recently developed a

wrinkle. The man who was accompanying his target. Who he was and where he had come from puzzled the man in the black suit. He had appeared suddenly and quickly ingratiated himself with the Order of St. George. So much so that he had accompanied the girl on this outing into the country. The man in the black suit did not know whether that would prove to be a problem.

He had watched the young woman for months, ever since his own organization had become aware of her. She was not like the others. She did not kill to sustain her life force. She did not even carry a relic. In truth, he wasn't even sure she was one of them.

The research he and his companions had conducted indicated that she had arrived in London around a quarter of a century before and had not aged appreciably in all that time. Usually, this would have been proof positive, but there was another curious aspect. She worked for an organization that fought supernatural creatures. It did not employ them as operatives. Even stranger, they could find no record of her existence before the young woman arrived in London. There was something special about the girl. He was sure of it. If she proved to be what he suspected, she would be invaluable.

But first, the man in the black suit must confirm what he was dealing with. That meant waiting until she revealed herself to be more than human, something she had not done so far. But she would slip up eventually, and when she did . . .

They were approaching the workhouse now.

As the couple walked up the driveway toward the building, the man in the black suit stopped at the archway. He pressed himself flat against the stonework and watched them enter. He felt no need to proceed further. They would do whatever they needed within the building and then come back out. He had no interest in their investigation beyond the fact that it drew the young woman away from the city, something that had not previously happened for as long as he was watching her.

He looked up at the sky and saw the faint impressions of rain clouds scudding through the blackness. He liked the night. It wrapped around him like an old friend. He especially liked evenings like this when the weather was inclement. People paid less attention to their surroundings in such conditions. They lowered their heads and focused only on reaching their destination. When he looked down again and glanced back toward the workhouse, the girl and her male companion were making their way back toward the archway.

The man in the black suit stepped backward and melted between the trees that lined the narrow trail. They saw nothing amiss when they passed by him a few moments later. They had no clue that he was even there. He waited a while until they were far enough ahead that his stealthy pursuit would go unnoticed, then he slipped from his hiding place and followed them back to the village.

# THIRTY

DECKER AND MINA had barely arrived back at the village when they heard the scream. It came from a nearby stone cottage with lights in its upstairs windows.

"What the hell was that?" Decker glanced toward Mina.

"Sounds like someone's in trouble," Mina replied just before a second scream, more panicked than the first, tore through the night.

Decker took off at a run toward the front door. When he tried the handle, he found it to be unlocked. He pushed the door open, but before he could step inside, Mina grabbed his arm.

"Be careful," she said in a whisper.

"Always am," Decker said. He stepped across the threshold and into the cottage. All the lights were off on the lower floor, but he could make out a narrow staircase. He headed to this, taking the stairs two at a time with Mina at his back.

There was a landing on the second floor, with two doors

leading off. Since most houses of this size would not have had indoor plumbing in 1911, Decker surmised that both were probably bedrooms. There would be an outhouse behind the property and bedpans for those times when the cottage's occupants did not wish to make the freezing journey outside to answer the call of nature.

Decker paused on the landing, listening for any signs of noise, but the house was silent now. Silent as the grave, he thought with a shudder.

"You take one room, and I'll take the other," Mina said, stepping around Decker and approaching the further of the two doors.

"Wait," Decker hissed. I don't think that's a—"

Before he could complete the sentence, the door flung open, and a woman in a cream-colored cotton nightgown appeared, almost bowling Mina over in her haste to escape the room.

If she was surprised to find two strangers outside the bedroom door, she didn't show it; such was her terror. "You have to help me. My sister. She killed her husband."

"It's okay. We've got you. You're safe," Decker said. He caught the woman by the arms mid-flight as she lunged for the stairs and tried to calm her down. "Tell me what happened."

"Let me go. She'll kill us, too." The woman ripped herself free and fled down the stairs and out the open front door into the night before Decker could do anything.

"Decker?" Mina was standing in the doorway, her eyes wide.

Decker came up behind her and peered into the room.

A crumpled body lay on the floor in a widening pool of blood. The figure was face down, but Decker could tell it was a man by his build and the pajamas he wore. Standing over him, brandishing a wicked-looking carving knife, was a woman in her mid-thirties with long brown hair and blue eyes. She looked down at the figure on the floor, her lips moving as if she were speaking even though no sound came out.

At first, she didn't register Decker and Mina standing in the doorway staring at her, but then she lifted her eyes and focused on the pair.

"Why don't you put the knife down," Decker said in the calmest voice he could muster.

The woman glared at him but said nothing.

"Please, lay down the knife." Mina took a step forward. She held out her hand. "You can give it to me if you want. Then we can summon help for your husband."

"He doesn't deserve to be helped," the woman said through gritted teeth. Her voice was rough and full of gravel. It sounded more like a man than a woman.

Mina took an instinctive step backward. She glanced at Decker, then turned her attention back to the woman.

"Who are you?" Decker asked, moving past Mina into the room. "Why did you do this?"

"I am the avenger of sorrows. The bringer of death." The woman's gaze snapped from Decker to Mina. She ran her tongue over her lips. "I bet you would be fun to hide inside."

Mina shrank back.

"Hey, leave her alone," Decker said, positioning himself between the woman and Mina. "Are you going to put that knife down or not?"

The woman's eyes burned with smoldering rage. Her mouth curled into a snarl. For a brief moment, Decker swore he saw another face hiding behind the first, superimposed over it like a barely visible mask. A ghostly countenance unlike any he had ever seen. Then, before Decker could react, the woman turned the knife upon herself, plunged it into her own stomach, and up in a violent slicing motion.

"No." Mina dashed forward and caught the dying woman before she fell. The knife clattered to the floor as Mina sank to her knees, cradling the woman in her arms.

"Tell me who you are," Decker commanded with as much composure as he could drum up. He wanted to know what they were dealing with before the woman expired. "Speak."

"Violet," came the reply in a voice that sounded nothing like the one they had conversed with moments before. Whatever entity that had been controlling the woman was gone. Her eyes grew wide with fear. She clutched at her ruined stomach and chest, her hands coming away red with her own blood. "It hurts. What happened?"

"Don't worry about that," Mina said. "We're going to get help."

But even as Mina said the words, Decker realized it was too late. The woman's eyelids fluttered. A rattling groan escaped her lips, and she went limp.

Mina laid the deceased woman on the ground next to her husband and climbed to her feet. The front of her blouse was stained crimson. She looked at Decker with searching eyes as if she couldn't comprehend what had just happened. "If I didn't know better, I would have said that this woman was . . ."

"Possessed," Decker said, finishing for her. "We have to fetch the constable."

"I don't think that's a good idea. He wasn't exactly friendly the last time we ran into him. We should leave right now before . . ." Mina's voice trailed off. She stiffened.

"Mina?" Decker felt his gut tighten.

"Mina isn't here right now," came the reply in that same insidious voice that had spewed from the lips of the dead woman, Violet, moments before. Mina turned to look at Decker, her face twisted into a leering grin. "I was right. She is fun to hide inside. So much fun . . ."

# THIRTY-ONE

MINA, or rather the entity that had taken control of her, reached down and snatched the discarded knife from the floor, never taking its eyes from Decker.

Realizing what was about to happen, he backed up toward the door. "Whatever you are, leave Mina alone."

Mina cocked her head sideways in a strange motion. She licked her lips. "Why? It's so cozy and warm in—"

The entity within Mina was abruptly cut off. Her face relaxed into a more natural expression.

"Decker. I can feel it inside my head. There's so much anger. It . . ." Mina's words trailed away. She doubled over as if in pain. A cry escaped her lips. "Get out of me."

"Mina, fight it." Decker resisted the urge to rush to her. The knife was still in Mina's hand. The entity might be luring him into a trap by letting her speak.

"I'm trying," Mina gasped through clenched teeth. She sank to her knees. "You can't have me."

"I can have whoever I want," said the entity within her in the same chilling voice.

"I don't think so." She lifted her head and screamed, the sound raw and guttural.

There was a blast of freezing air. Decker raised his arms against a sudden onslaught of stinging wind that ripped through the room like a miniature tornado. A vase fell from the nightstand beside the bed and smashed on the floor. The gas lamps flickered and almost went out. Then, the devastating wind died away as quickly as it had come.

Mina stood a few feet from Decker, looking startled. She glanced down at the knife in her hand and quickly discarded it.

"Are you okay?" Decker asked, hurrying toward her. "Is it gone?"

"Yes." Mina nodded. "It's not inside of me anymore. I expelled it."

"How?" Decker was baffled. "None of the other victims could escape its clutches, at least, until it killed them."

Mina shrugged. "I guess it never encountered someone like me before. I'm not a normal woman."

"Well, for once, I'm glad for Abraham Turner's parting gift. It probably saved both our lives."

"If it weren't for him, I wouldn't even be here to get possessed," Mina said somberly. She glanced at the two bodies lying on the floor. "We'd better make ourselves scarce before the constable shows up. There's just one problem. I'm not sure if he has the ability to find them, but my prints are all over that murder weapon."

"This is 1911. Is fingerprinting even a thing yet?" Decker asked.

"It's not widely accepted, especially in the provinces, but they can do it. There have already been convictions based on fingerprints."

"Better make sure we don't leave any evidence behind,

then," Decker said, going to a chest of drawers near the door. He opened the top drawer and took out a woman's cotton handkerchief with frilly edges, which he used to wipe down the drawer knobs. He went to the knife and wiped down the handle, then returned the handkerchief to the drawer. "Problem solved."

"John Decker, did you just tamper with evidence?" Mina feigned shock.

"Since we had nothing to do with these deaths, I would hardly call it tampering with evidence," Decker replied. He turned toward the door. "Come on. Let's go."

Mina nodded and followed Decker out onto the landing. They hadn't even started down the stairs when the front door opened below. The constable appeared with Violet's distraught sister steps behind.

"You two," he roared when he saw Decker and Mina standing above. "What the hell do you think you're doing?"

"This isn't what it looks like," Decker said, backing away from the stairs.

"I'll be the judge of that." The constable hurried up two steps at a time. He pushed past Decker and Mina and approached the open bedroom door. When he looked in, a pall fell across his face. "Good God."

"We had nothing to do with that," Decker said. "We were out for a late evening walk and heard screams. We rushed in here to investigate and came across the scene."

"You expect me to believe that?" The constable backed up, unable to tear his eyes from the gruesome tableau in front of him. "I don't care what your buddy from London says. If you did this, you'll hang. The pair of you."

"It wasn't them." Violet's sister was rushing up the stairs, her face contorted in panic. "They came to my aid. I wouldn't be alive if they hadn't found me."

"Is this true?" The constable glared at Decker.

"It's like she said." Decker felt a rush of relief. Ending up arrested for a double murder would scuttle their investigation before it even began, especially with no quick way to contact Detective Inspector Sim back in London to vouch for them. Then Decker realized what the constable had said moments before. "What do you mean, our buddy from London?"

A flash of panic crossed the policeman's face as if he had spoken out of turn without realizing it. He quickly recovered his composure. "I'll ask the questions if you don't mind."

"Surely you could give me an answer."

"That's it. I need you to go. Right now. Both of you." The constable pointed to the stairs. "And don't leave the village. I might need to talk to you again about this unfortunate situation."

"You should thank us," Mina said in a stern voice. "We just saved this woman's life and did your job for you."

"Is that so?" The constable's face turned red.

"Hey, let's get back to the Black Dog before the constable decides to arrest us anyway." Decker steered Mina toward the stairs again and started down, aware of the constable's angry gaze upon them as they descended.

When they exited the building, Mina took a deep breath. "That man's a jackass."

"He absolutely is," Decker replied. "And he clearly has no idea what's happening around here."

"I'm not sure we're faring much better." Mina shivered against the cold as they started walking toward the pub. "What do you think he meant by that comment about our buddy from London?"

"I don't know," Decker said as they reached the pub and let themselves in via a side door that led directly to the accommodations. As they climbed the stairs, he felt a tingle of unease. "We should watch our backs. I have a feeling the spirit that tried to possess you isn't the only danger in this village. There might be more going on in Mavendale than we anticipated."

# THIRTY-TWO

THE MAN in the black suit watched the commotion at the cottage with keen interest. He held back, lingering out of sight at the corner of a rutted dirt trail that led to a farm some quarter-mile distant. He had briefly considered moving closer, maybe even sneaking into the cottage to get a closer look, but he knew that would not be wise. It would be impossible to conceal himself in such a confined space, and he did not want Mina or her unknown companion to spot him.

When the hysterical woman had bolted from the cottage and fled shrieking down the street toward the end terrace house, the constable shared with his wife Molly near the village's High Street, the man in the black suit knew that his caution had been rewarded. If he had tried to enter the dwelling, he would almost certainly have encountered this woman, which would have made things difficult. When she returned less than ten minutes later with the constable in tow, he smiled.

The policeman would not arrest or otherwise unduly

harass Mina or her companion, he was sure, even though he didn't yet know what had occurred in the cottage. His performance earlier in the police station had been flawless. The constable had believed every word he said. It didn't hurt that the man was afraid of him. He could see it in the constable's eyes. This was not an uncommon reaction. The man in the black suit used his physical appearance to his best advantage, knowing that passive intimidation often got him further than outright threats.

The man in the black suit stood with his hands pushed deep into his pockets, ignoring the biting wind that chafed at his face, and the drizzle of rain that slicked his hair. He waited and watched until Mina and the stranger left together and hurried back toward the pub where they were staying. They were deep in conversation, but he could not hear what they were saying. It didn't matter. The investigation that had brought them here was of no concern to him. All that mattered was the girl.

When he was sure they were far enough away, he slipped out of concealment and strolled toward the cottage. But instead of entering, he kept going until he reached the constable's house and stepped into the darkness between it and a smaller single-story bungalow next door. Here he waited. The policeman would return eventually, and when he did, the man in the black suit would reinforce his message from earlier in the day, just to make sure the constable knew who was in charge.

# THIRTY-THREE

"DO you want to talk about what just happened?" Decker said as they reached their rooms on the second floor of the Black Dog pub.

"It's late. What I really want to do is hit the sack." Mina opened her bedroom door but lingered before stepping inside. "The spirit that tried to possess me sapped a lot of energy. I need time to recuperate."

"I can understand that," Decker replied. "But answer me this: did you get any sense of who or what the entity was?"

"Actually, I did." Mina nodded. "I even have a name. Bradley Wilcox."

"So, it's a human spirit we're dealing with, then?"

"I believe so," Mina answered. "And not a particularly nice one, either. There was so much anger bottled up inside that spirit. Seething rage. I can't be sure, but I got the sense that he only possesses women in order to kill their husbands or significant others."

"Which means there might be a revenge aspect," Decker

said. "I can't believe I'm saying this, but our ghostly killer has an MO."

"John Decker, Ghost Cop," Mina said with a grin.

"I think I like that title better than monster hunter. Maybe I'll keep it." Now it was Decker's turn to smile. Moments later, he was all business again. "I don't suppose you have any clue what this Wilcox guy's agenda is?"

"If you mean, do I know why he's possessing women to kill their husbands? The answer is no. All I could sense was the rage, but not the motivation behind it."

"I think I'll do some digging tomorrow," Decker said. "See what I can turn up on Bradley Wilcox. Given his violent agenda, there must be some significant event that triggered it."

"I would say that's a fair bet." Mina rubbed her eyes. "While you do that, I'm going to catch the early train back to London."

"Detective Inspector Sim?" Now more than ever, they needed verification of their cover story if they were to continue investigating, especially since they'd gotten caught at the scene of two crimes. "That's one reason," Mina noted. "But I think we need some help on this now that we know what we are dealing with."

"What kind of help?" Decker asked.

"The specialist kind. A medium."

"Seriously?" Decker raised an eyebrow. "Aren't those people mostly frauds?"

"Some are. Spiritualism became very popular during the Victorian era. A lot of fakers jumped on the bandwagon, rigging phony séances and using special effects to bilk naïve or desperate clients. But they aren't all fraudsters. The Order of St. George has worked with several very good mediums. The woman I have in mind to help us is anything but a faker.

Assuming that she's willing, I shall bring her back with me tomorrow on the afternoon train."

"Okay." Decker was willing to entertain the idea that certain people had the ability to commune with the dead. After all that he had experienced, it would be foolish to think otherwise. But he still wasn't sure why they needed such a person, and he said so.

"There's one simple reason," Mina replied. "The next time we encounter that spirit, I'd like to communicate with it and not get possessed in the process. It wasn't a pleasant experience."

"Makes sense." Now it was Decker's turn to yawn. "Speaking of which, are you suffering any ill effects from the possession?"

"Other than a slight headache and the lingering impression of the Spirit's anger, no. But I will tell you this much. It wanted to use me as a murder weapon. If I had not been able to fight off the entity, it would have attempted to kill you before it did the same to me."

"Thank goodness it wasn't able to complete its task."

"Agreed. I'm rarely grateful for what I have become, but I have to admit, my own supernatural nature served me well in this instance. The spirit struggled to remain inside my body."

"I wonder why?" Decker mused.

"I don't want to sound clichéd, but maybe it was because I'm one of the undead," Mina answered. "Or at least, my essence, or soul, if you want to call it that, is hovering somewhere between the two states. Think about it. Abraham Turner had lived long past his natural lifespan by stealing the life force of others. He should have been reduced to nothing but ashes centuries before. Likewise, I died in that London hospital from the wounds he inflicted upon me. I only recovered after you used the solid gold knife on Turner. He finally met his end, and I lived on thanks to his life force, which then became my own."

"That sounds like as good an explanation as any," Decker admitted. "Either way, I'm glad the spirit of Bradley Wilcox couldn't remain in control once you started fighting back."

"You're not the only one," Mina replied. "And I sincerely hope he's learned his lesson because it was not a pleasant experience."

Decker studied Mina's face. There were dark rings under her eyes, and her skin appeared paler than usual. Her shoulders were slumped as if the very act of staying on her feet was a chore. Whatever supernatural energy had enabled her to expel Wilcox had left her not just mentally, but also physically drained. "Go get some sleep. We'll pick this up in the morning."

"You don't need to tell me twice." Mina retreated into the bedroom. Before she closed the door she turned back to Decker. "For the record, I truly wish you had gotten back to Nancy, but selfish as this sounds, it's comforting to have you here."

"There's nothing selfish about it," Decker replied. He bade her good night and returned to his own room. Alone now, the silence closed in around him. For a while, while they were facing down the entity in that small cottage on the edge of town, Nancy had been far from Decker's mind. Now she was closer than ever. He felt a familiar tug of longing and quickly pushed it down. It would do no good to wallow in self-pity. Better to find a way to return both himself and Mina to their own time. The only problem was that he had no clue how to do it. Not yet.

He walked to the window and pulled the curtain back. The street outside was empty and dark. If they were in the twenty-first century, there would have been all sorts of response vehicles clogging the road by now, their red and blue lights painting the buildings in garish tones. But here there was none of that. If you didn't know what had so recently occurred inside that cottage, you would be none the wiser. He was about to turn away when he caught a movement in the darkness at the edge of his vision. He looked toward the spot where he thought he saw it, but just like earlier, when he sensed a presence on the stairs, there was nothing there. Decker studied the street for a few moments more, hoping to discover what had drawn his attention, but to no avail. With an uneasy feeling, he let the curtain fall back in place and turned toward the bed.

# THIRTY-FOUR

MINA WAS ALREADY GONE when Decker awoke the next morning. He found a note from her slipped under his door promising to be back on the afternoon train. That left him free to research the name she had come up with the night before. Bradley Wilcox. But how to go about it?

Under normal circumstances, his first inclination would be to search the web, but since there would be no internet for over eighty years, he would have to come up with another method of researching the spirit that had possessed Mina.

He thought back to their interview with the lone survivor of the original incident up at Bartholomew Meadows. She and her friends had gone to the workhouse because of a local legend regarding a spiritualist who was supposed to have trapped an angry ghost inside the crystals of a chandelier in the lobby. When one of them damaged the light fixture with an old iron poker, the spirit, probably Wilcox, was released. It wasted no time in exacting long simmering revenge.

Since Wilcox's choice of haunt was the workhouse, it was reasonable to conclude that he must have had a connection to the place. If so, he might have been local to the village. Maybe someone in the area had heard of him. An obvious place to start his inquiries, Decker thought, was the landlord of the Black Dog. As the social hub of the community, the public house would be the first place where rumors and tall tales circulated. If anyone held the information Decker needed, it would be their host.

He wasted no time in heading downstairs to the saloon bar. It was only nine in the morning and the establishment was not yet open. When Decker entered the bar, it was empty. At first, he thought it was too early. He stepped back into the corridor to retreat upstairs and wait, but then he spied an open door that led to the back of the building. From beyond, he could hear the clink of glass.

Decker found the Black Dog's landlord in a small rear courtyard stacked with beer barrels and cartons of bottles piled against the far wall. He was sorting through the previous night's empties, arranging them by brand into more cartons.

At Decker's approach, he turned. "We're not open yet."

"I know that. I was hoping to have a few minutes of your time."

The landlord dropped a couple of bottles made of brown glass into a half-full carton and then turned, wiping his hands on a bar towel looped over his trouser belt. "Is there a problem with your accommodation?"

"No. Nothing of the sort," Decker replied. "The rooms are just fine."

"Glad to hear it. I can spare five minutes, but no longer. It's the brewery's delivery day. What do you want to know?"

"Not what. Who," Decker said. "Bradley Wilcox."

"Sorry. Don't know the fella." The landlord picked up another bottle from a rolling tub of empties and placed it with the other ones that he had sorted. "He owe you money or something?"

"Not quite." Decker rubbed his hands together to keep them warm. "I think he might be dead."

"Kind of makes it hard to collect on a debt, then, don't it?"

"It would if he owed me money." Decker felt like he was getting nowhere with this line of inquiry. "I wondered if there were any stories about him circulating in the village. Rumors or local legends. Any tall tales. Maybe even a ghost story or two?"

The landlord shrugged. "Wouldn't know. Like I said, I've never heard of him."

"Do you have any idea who would know?" Decker asked.

"There's Mavis Corby. She fancies herself something of a local historian. Can't rightly say if she would know any more than me. Worth a try, though."

"That's very helpful. Where can I find this Mavis Corby?"

"She lives in one of the old almshouse cottages on Brook Street. Number six, I think."

"Thank you. How would I find Brook Street?"

"Easy. Take a right out of the pub onto the High Street and take the second road on the left. That's Brook Street. The almshouses are right there. You can't miss them. There's a big old stone plaque on the wall with the Grayson Family Coat of Arms on it. It was them what had the places built, probably to pay their way past the pearly gates. They were a mean bunch. Rich too. Built Bartholomew Meadows back in the 1840s to take advantage of cheap labor."

"Really?" The landlord might not know who Bradley Wilcox was, but he was providing a gold mine of background information on the workhouse.

"U-huh. They were scoundrels long before that, though. As far back as the late seventeen-hundreds, there were rumors of them rounding up people from the village and forcing them to work in the family's textile mills and factories hereabouts."

"What happened to them?" Decker asked. "Are there any descendants left in the area?"

"Goodness, no. Last one died decades ago. He was the workhouse master. His name was James Grayson, but everyone called him Old Flogger because of his addiction to the whip. And he had no children, probably because the good Lord didn't want to inflict that sort of misery upon them. He got what was coming to him, mind you. Ended up gutted by his wife with a meat cleaver. He must've been some piece of work. Even his own missus wanted him dead."

"Did she say why she did it?" Decker asked.

"Never got the chance. Used that same cleaver to slit her own throat right after dispatching her husband."

"That must've been why the workhouse closed down," Decker surmised.

"That it was. There were no inmates left, anyway. Before killing her husband, Bethany Grayson unlocked all the wards. Set the lot of them free to exact revenge on their tormentors. I was only a young boy at the time, but I remember that night well. Everyone who's old enough in the village does. It was a slaughter."

"What happened to the inmates after that?" Decker asked.

"The poor Law commissioners sent a bunch of coppers from London to round them up. Some were sent to other workhouses or straight to prison. A few, those who admitted to a hand in the killings, went to the gallows. It was a travesty. They should have been given medals instead of prison cells."

Decker was about to press the landlord for further

information, but before he could, the sound of horse hooves clacking on cobblestones reached his ears.

The landlord glanced toward the alleyway next to the pub just as an open cart loaded with barrels and drawn by two horses pulled into the courtyard. "That'll be my beer delivery."

"In that case, I'll let you get back your work," Decker said, as the drayman sitting up front brought the cart to a halt. Then he stepped into the alley and started toward the High Street to go in search of Mavis Corby.

# THIRTY-FIVE

DECKER FOUND the almshouse cottages right where the landlord said they would be. When he knocked on the door of number six, Mavis Corby answered almost immediately.

She was a white-haired old woman with a deeply lined face who Decker guessed must be in her eighties. She walked with a stoop. Gnarled, arthritic fingers curled around the knub of a cane that she used to support herself. A woolen shawl was draped over her shoulders.

Decker introduced himself, using the cover story that he was in the village on behalf of the London Metropolitan Police, and told her that the landlord of the Black Dog had pointed him in her direction. He explained that he was looking into the recent deaths up at the workhouse. In particular he was interested in the history of Bartholomew Meadows to see if there was a connection between the murdered staff all those years before, and what happened there two nights ago.

But when he mentioned the name Bradley Wilcox, hoping he might have been a local man, Mavis only looked apologetic. "I'm sorry. I've never heard of anyone in the village by that name."

"Could he have been an inmate there or maybe a staff member?" Decker asked.

"It's possible. The workhouse took in people from all over. James Grayson, the man who ran it owned at least two other workhouses and regularly transferred inmates between them. He treated those under his care more like free labor than people who needed a hand up. He was not an agreeable gentleman."

"That's what I've been told," Decker said. He looked up at the two-story stone cottage, one of four row houses. The Grayson coat of arms was placed prominently above the front door in carved stone. "And yet you live in one of his houses."

"It doesn't belong to his family anymore." Mavis looked slightly offended. "They sold everything he owned after his death. He had no direct heirs. Just a distant second cousin who had no interest in continuing the family's horrendous business. The one thing that wasn't sold was Bartholomew Meadows. Grayson owned the buildings and the land. He leased the beds to the workhouse commission. The more destitute souls he took in, the more he got paid. Then he put them to work to make even more money and paid the inmates just enough to cover the cost of keeping and feeding them. What he gave with one hand, he took with the other. It was a vicious cycle they could never break free from. Some of those people had been at the workhouse for decades."

"Why wouldn't they just leave?" Decker asked.

"They couldn't. The poor law wouldn't let them. To be discharged from the workhouse, you needed sufficient means to support yourself. All it took for Grayson to keep a captive labor force was to make sure that never happened."

"Because poverty is a crime."

"Yes. I look forward to the day when places like Bartholomew Meadows are shuttered for good. Every last one of them. The government should be looking after its people, not criminalizing them. But what do I know? I'm just an old woman."

"I think you have a better handle on the situation than most of the politicians in this age," Decker said. When he saw the perplexed look that passed across her face, he quickly moved on. "You said the man who inherited the workhouse from Grayson refused to sell it. Do you know if he still owns it?"

"It's empty, isn't it?" The old woman glanced in the general direction of Bartholomew Meadows, even though it was not visible from their location on Brook Street.

"So he does own it."

"As far as I know. I'm sure that if he had sold, someone would have reopened the dratted place by now."

"Do you know why he kept only that building and let it sit empty?" Decker asked.

"That's a question you would have to ask him," Mavis replied. "Although I suspect it was because the land is soaked in blood. After the atrocities committed there by his relatives, he probably wanted to make sure that no one else would suffer in that abominable institution."

"I don't suppose you know his name or where I might find him?" Decker asked. "You must have bought the cottage from him."

"That I did." The old lady gave a laugh that sounded more like a cackle. "But my memory isn't so good these days. It's been near on thirty-five years since the night Old Flogger met his end. Besides, he wasn't a local. He lived up north somewhere. I think it was Liverpool, but like I said, I don't remember like I used to."

"That's all right," said Decker. "You've been most helpful. Thank you."

"On the contrary, I should be thanking you. I can't remember the last time I had a visitor come to the house. I don't get out much these days." Mavis glanced down at the cane. "It's no fun getting old, my boy."

"I'll keep that in mind," Decker said with a smile. "If you remember anything else, I'll be staying at the Black Dog for the next couple of nights."

Mavis nodded and told him that she would be sure to get in touch.

Decker thanked her and made his way back toward the pub. It was only eleven in the morning, which meant that Mina would not return for several hours, and he had already exhausted his only lines of inquiry.

He decided to take a stroll through the village and soon found himself heading in the direction of the cottage where they had encountered the entity that had briefly possessed Mina the previous night. The front door was locked, and the cottage looked empty. If the constable was conducting a murder investigation, he wasn't doing a good job of it.

Decker toyed with the idea of tracking down the sister, who had probably shared the house with Violet and her husband, but then thought better of it. She was, no doubt, grieving her loss. Also, he did not wish to further draw the constable's attention to his and Mina's investigation. At least until they had proof of the story they had told him when he caught them up at the workhouse. With any luck, Mina would return with that proof from Detective Inspector Sim later in the day.

Even then, he wasn't sure it was worth interviewing the sister. She was nothing but an innocent bystander and would surely think them crazy if they raised the notion that Violet had been possessed.

With nothing else to do but wait, Decker walked back along the High Street toward the pub, which would be open by now. He hadn't eaten breakfast and could ignore his rumbling stomach no more. And as he went, his thoughts turned to the entity that possessed Mina the previous night. It was still out there, looking for a new victim. The question was, where?

# THIRTY-SIX

MINA ARRIVED BACK EARLY in the afternoon. Accompanying her was a woman in her mid-thirties wearing a white dress under a heavy coat. She had bobbed brown hair and striking blue eyes. In her hand, she carried a large travel bag.

"John, I'd like you to meet Skye Lockwood," Mina said when Decker answered his guest room door. "She's the spirit medium that I told you about."

"Hello," Skye said, flashing a bright smile. "You must be the monster hunter."

Decker shot Mina a disapproving look. "Are we supposed to be keeping a low profile?"

"Relax," Mina replied with an impish grin. "I've been working with Skye for ten years. She knows all about the order and what we do. You can talk freely in front of her regarding our work here."

"Very well." Decker stepped aside to let the two women enter the room. "But let's not do so in the corridor where we might be overheard."

"Of course." Mina waited for Skye to step inside, then followed her and closed the door. Satisfied that their privacy was assured, she turned to Decker. "Did you find anything out about Bradley Wilcox while I was gone?"

"Not a thing. I spoke to the landlord and also the unofficial village historian. Both of them have been in the village since before the massacre at Bartholomew Meadows. The landlord was a young boy at the time, and his memories are vague, but Mavis Corby is older and was able to provide a lot of useful information about the workhouse and what happened after it closed. She even lives in a cottage once owned by the workhouse master. His ancestors built it as a kind of private social housing project called an almshouse."

"But neither of them could provide any information on Wilcox?" Mina looked disappointed.

"He wasn't a villager, at least according to Mavis. She said he might have been involved with the workhouse, either as an inmate or a staff member. People came and went frequently because the master, James Grayson, owned other workhouses and moved inmates around as he needed them. He had a good racket going by all accounts. Took money from the workhouse commission to house the poor, then put them to work and paid them just enough to cover rent that he charged for their beds."

"It's not uncommon," Skye said. "The workhouse system is notoriously corrupt and deliberately harsh. The government wants to make sure that people do all they can to avoid ending up there by not falling into poverty."

"They make it deliberately unpleasant as a form of deterrent," Decker said with disgust.

"Yes." Skye nodded. "In the eyes of many, poverty is synonymous with laziness."

"None of that helps us to find out who Bradley Wilcox was in life, or why his spirit is so angry," Mina said.

"He must be angry indeed to be capable of possessing the living." Skye looked worried.

"You know what happened here, then," Decker said.

"Mina enlightened me in on the train journey from London," Skye replied. "Possession is a tricky thing for most spirits. Such feats require a lot of negative energy. If Wilcox can achieve that, who knows what else he might be able to do? We should proceed with caution."

"Speaking of which, how *do* you want to handle this?" Decker asked her. "I've never worked with a medium before."

"Very few people have," Skye replied. "And even fewer have worked with one who truly possesses the gift. There are a lot of fakers in my business, Mr. Decker."

"I'm aware of that."

"But I assure you, I am not one of them. Although sometimes I wish the universe had not granted me this ability, born as it was out of tragedy." Skye paused as a dark cloud passed briefly across her face. Then she regained her composure. "But none of that is important. In order to find out what we are dealing with, I would like to see the location where the spirit was released."

"You want to visit the workhouse?"

"Given how recently the spirit escaped its imprisonment, there may still be residual energy. Not to mention the newly disembodied souls of those who died at Wilcox's hands. Since they are beyond the veil and have probably not yet moved on, they might be able to give us some insight with regard to his motives."

"You think the ghosts of those people who died at

Bartholomew Meadows are hanging around there?" Decker asked, surprised.

"In my experience, the recently departed often linger at the scene of their deaths because they are unwilling or afraid to move into the spirit realm, Mr. Decker. This is especially true when they die by violence due to the sudden nature of their transition. But our opportunity to converse with them fades with each passing hour. Almost all such souls leave this plane once the shock of their death has worn off."

"Almost all?" Decker asked. "What happens to those who stay?"

"They become the wraiths that haunt our nights, Mr. Decker." Skye's blue eyes opened wider as she said this.

"I see." A chill ran through Decker. He turned to Mina. "Did you get what we needed from Sim?"

Mina reached into her pocket and withdrew an envelope. "I did, with a little help from Thomas. The detective inspector took a little persuading, but in the end, he wrote a letter validating us as civilian specialists conducting an investigation on behalf of the Met. It should keep the constable at bay if we run into him again. It even requests that he assist us as necessary."

"He's going to love that." Decker could imagine the constable's reaction when he saw the letter. But it didn't matter. He was unlikely to go against the wishes of the Metropolitan Police.

"It will be dark in a couple of hours," Mina said, glancing toward the window. "We should take Skye to Bartholomew Meadows before sunset. The spirit of Bradley Wilcox has struck on each of the last two nights. I have a horrible suspicion that this evening will make three."

The same thought had been lingering at the back of Decker's mind, and the odds of stopping a third night of violence were slim unless they found out who Wilcox had been in life, and what was driving his deadly rage in death. The village was small, but still boasted a population big enough to make finding potential victims near impossible without more information to go on. There was no time to waste. "We should leave as soon as possible."

"I agree." Mina's gaze shifted to Skye. "I know we have only just arrived, but are you in a sufficient state of mind to commune with the spirits?"

"I will be." Skye nodded. She glanced down at her travel bag. "I would like fifteen minutes to freshen up and prepare, and then we shall see what the dead have to say for themselves."

# THIRTY-SEVEN

THE BARTHOLOMEW MEADOWS Workhouse looked drearier every time he saw it, thought Decker as they trudged up the driveway toward the monolithic stone building.

With their previous transportation unavailable because the blacksmith shop was closed already—the smithy nowhere to be found—and not wishing to spend the time required to walk the entire way on foot, Mina had procured the services of a local farmer to take them there in his hay cart. She had found this unusual taxi service by talking to the landlord of the Black Dog while Skye was preparing herself in a third room they had rented for her at the pub. The farmer was only too happy to earn some extra money and had promised to return for them an hour later once their business at the workhouse was concluded. If he wondered what they were up to, he didn't ask, for which Decker was grateful. Better to stay silent than be forced to lie.

As soon as the trio entered the building, Skye stiffened.

"I can feel the negative energy here," she said in a strained voice. "It's all around us, like an ocean of anger and despair."

"Are there any spirits here?" Decker asked, glancing around the gloomy lobby.

"I think so." Skye set down a leather bag of the type doctors used to make house calls. She had carried it with her from the pub and now opened it. Reaching inside, she withdrew a glass vial containing a white granular substance that Decker realized was salt. This she spread around them in a wide circle sprinkling the salt on the floor. Next, she removed five candles and set them at equal distances around the circle, then lit each one in turn.

"What is all this for?" Decker asked.

"The salt is a protection circle to keep us from harm if there are any spirits here with bad intentions," Skye said. "Disembodied entities don't like salt. Don't ask me why."

"And the candles?"

"I place them at the five points of the pentagram to aid in opening a channel to the other side."

"There is no pentagram," Decker said, looking around him.

"Not a visible one." Skye reached into her bag one more time and removed a small silver hand mirror.

"I can't imagine what you're going to use that for," Decker said.

"So that I may see the spirits," Skye replied. "When I perform an evocation—that's the act of summoning those who pass to the other side—I see them reflected in the mirror and can thus communicate."

"They don't speak through you like at a séance?" Decker asked.

"No. Mediums and spiritualists who claim to be channeling those they wish to commune with are more often than not engaging in cheap parlor tricks. I have no need for such chicanery."

"Decker, we can discuss how it all works later," Mina said. "Right now, I'd like to get this over with as quickly as possible. I don't think we're safe here."

"Sorry." Decker motioned to Skye. "Please, go ahead."

"Very well." Skye checked the salt circle to make sure there were no breaks. Then she issued a warning to Decker and Mina. "Once I begin, do not step out of the circle for any reason. Do not interrupt me, regardless of what you see or hear. The spirits will respond only to me. When we are finished, I must close the connection to the other side. Only then will it be safe to leave the circle. Do you both understand?"

Decker and Mina both said that they did.

"In that case, I shall begin." Skye took up a position in the center of the circle. She kept the mirror at her side and began to speak in a voice that was little more than a murmur.

Decker could not hear what she was saying and leaned close, but still could not discern any intelligible words. It sounded like she was talking in another tongue, but what that language might be, he did not know.

This continued for more than a minute before the medium fell silent. She closed her eyes and stood motionless for a long while, her head cocking to one side more than once, as if she were listening to something only she could hear. Then, after what felt like a lifetime but had probably only been a couple of minutes, Skye's eyes snapped open. She stared straight ahead, still as a statue.

"Is she okay?" Decker whispered to Mina.

Mina shrugged. "I think so. I've only seen her do this once before."

"I thought you said—"

"Silence." Skye's attention snapped to Decker. "I require absolute concentration if I am to be successful."

"Sorry." Decker took a step backward.

Skye's gaze drifted forward once more. Her lips worked as if she were deep in conversation, but no sound came out. Or maybe she was reciting more of the same strange incantation under her breath.

Decker shivered, overcome with a sudden chill.

It was cold in the old workhouse. Freezing even. But now the temperature had plummeted to sub-Arctic levels. He could see his breath as an icy white mist. Beside him, Mina had wrapped her arms around her torso and was hugging herself tightly.

Whatever Skye was doing, it was working. Yet she appeared impervious to the suddenly frigid atmosphere. No mist escaped her own lips. Unlike Decker, there were no goosebumps on her neck. Her teeth were not chattering.

Then he noticed the sunlight, or rather lack of it. When they had walked up the driveway to the old building, the sky was a deep shade of winter blue without a cloud in sight. The sun was slipping low on the horizon but would not set for at least another thirty minutes. Yet the lobby of the old workhouse was full of shadows that crept from a sudden gloom that pressed in around them on all sides. It was as if the daylight had been sucked from the room.

Decker felt Mina's hand reach for his.

Her breath came in short, nervous gasps.

Skye remained motionless in the center of the circle, unconcerned by the encroaching darkness or the sharp drop in temperature.

Abruptly, her lips stopped moving. Her pale blue eyes grew wide. She lifted the mirror and peered into its glassy surface, unblinking. Then she uttered five small words that chilled Decker more than the frigid air swirling around him.

"The dead wish to speak."

# THIRTY-EIGHT

THE MAN in the black suit watched Mina and her two companions leave the Black Dog Public House and climb into a local farmer's hay cart before departing the village. He briefly considered following them, but then thought better of it. He had observed Mina depart the village early that very morning only to return in the afternoon with a companion. He was mildly curious regarding the woman who had accompanied Mina back to the village and wanted to find out who she was, just to be safe. He thought it unlikely that she was a supernatural creature like the one he suspected Mina to be. More likely, she was employed by the Order of St. George, but he had learned through bitter experience never to settle for assumptions.

Which was why, after Mina and the others departed the village, he entered the saloon bar of the Black Dog, and made his way to the door leading upstairs. He moved quickly, with a fluid gait that drew little attention from the pub's patrons. He didn't know why or how, but he possessed the ability to become almost invisible when it suited him. He could walk through a room packed with people and command nary a glance. Maybe it was because he exuded a natural confidence, as if he was meant to be there, regardless of his surroundings. Or maybe it was just that he was an unremarkable man with such mundane features that he blended into the background like a shadow. Either way, the man in the black suit didn't care. His natural stealth served him well.

Looking around to make sure no one was paying him any heed, the man in the black suit slipped through the door leading to the upstairs accommodations and soon found himself on the second floor. He proceeded quickly to the rooms occupied by Mina and her companions. All three were locked, as he expected, but that was no obstacle.

It took him less than thirty seconds to gain entry to the first room, occupied by Mina. Once inside, he wasted no time in searching every inch but found nothing out of the ordinary. It was, he thought, exactly as would be expected for a young woman who was traveling outside of the city. If he was hoping to find a clue regarding Mina's true nature, he was disappointed.

Unperturbed, he moved on to the room next door. The one occupied by the man who had accompanied Mina into the country. Again, he struck out. This room was even more bare than the last, with only a single suitcase packed with new clothes that had not been worn. When he left the room, the man in the black suit was none the wiser regarding the identity of Mina's companion.

That left one room. The one occupied by the most recent arrival who had disembarked the afternoon train with Mina after her brief excursion back to the city. It took him less than ten seconds to pick the lock securing her door and gain entry.

This time his efforts did not go unrewarded. A search of the newcomer's travel bag uncovered a thick volume bound in leather that he recognized as a grimoire. Such books were used by practitioners of magic because of the spells they contained, but they also aided in the summoning of spirits, demons, and other deities from beyond the veil. The latter was, he suspected, why this person had been brought here. Mina and the man accompanying her wanted to commune with the dead.

He lifted it out and examined the heavy volume. There were incantations inside, just as he expected, written on yellowed parchment. He closed the book and placed it back as he had found it.

This confirmed his suspicions.

The woman was a spirit medium.

In all likelihood, Mina wanted to commune with the recently crossed spirits of the young people who had lost their lives at the workhouse a couple of nights before. Their energy would still linger a short while, at least until they accepted their demise.

Now he was glad that he had remained in the village.

Opening a portal to the spirit world was a dangerous endeavor akin to visiting a lunatic asylum, then unlocking and flinging wide the doors of every ward just to speak with the man who ran it. Sure, you might get what you wanted, but you could also find yourself at the mercy of whatever else lurked within. And when it came to the great beyond, there were always entities, human or otherwise, looking for a way out.

He hoped the spirit medium knew what she was doing and was sufficiently skilled to ensure that nothing demonic slipped past her. If not, Mina and her companions would soon regret trying to commune with the dead.

The man in the black suit cast one last look around the bedroom, making sure he had missed nothing of importance, and then retreated back into the corridor. He still could not prove Mina's true nature, which meant that he would have to stay here and observe her until he was sure one way or the other.

Making sure he was unobserved, the man in the black suit hurried back along the corridor, down the stairs, slipped back into the Black dog's saloon, and weaved through the gaggle of afternoon patrons to the bar where he ordered a measure of scotch, neat. The oldest vintage available. Drink in hand, he found a table in the corner and settled down, then waited for Mina and her companions to return.

# THIRTY-NINE

DECKER DIDN'T NEED to be told that the spirits of the dead had arrived. He could feel their presence all around him, even if he couldn't see them. The atmosphere inside the workhouse had become thick and cloying. It was so cold now that a puddle of rainwater from the building's leaky roof had frozen solid on the tiles near the front door.

He glanced toward Mina, wondering if it was always like this when Skye Lockwood communed with the dead. The look on her face told him it wasn't.

Skye herself appeared oblivious to all but the mirror. She held it in front of her face and stared deeply into its glassy surface. Now and then, she would adjust the mirror's angle, as if she were following something only visible in the reflected room.

"I have the spirits of Daisy Elizabeth Cartwright, Felicity Braithwaite-Moore, Alastair Chamberlin, and Reginald Poulton," Skye said in a somber voice. "They have agreed to communicate with us."

"I don't see them," Decker said, looking around.

"Hush," Mina whispered, nudging him. "We aren't supposed to interrupt."

Skye ignored the interruption. "Who did this to you?" She asked of the dead air in a loud voice. "Tell me."

If an answer came, Decker didn't hear it.

"Do you know why he possessed you?"

There was a moment of silence while Skye listened to an answer only she could hear. Her gaze drifted to Mina and Decker. "I am conversing with Miss Cartwright. She has confirmed the identity of the spirit that killed her as Bradley Wilcox, just as you suspected. He suffered great misfortune before his death and is enraged."

"What misfortune?" Decker asked.

Skye ignored the question and turned back to the mirror. "Please, tell me more," she said, addressing the spirit. "I wish to hear all that you are willing to impart."

Silence descended upon the room once again as Skye listened intently to the spirit. She nodded once in a while and made small sympathetic sounds.

Decker was growing frustrated. He wanted to know what Skye was being told. Wanted to hear the voices of the spirits directly instead of having them relayed to him secondhand. He also wanted to ask his own questions but realized that interrupting Skye would only make it harder for her to do what she did. For once, he was relegated to the status of a spectator. Actually, not even that, because he could neither see nor hear the disembodied entities with which Skye was holding a conversation.

After a couple of minutes, as if sensing Decker's frustration, Skye turned her attention from the mirror once more. "Miss Cartwright isn't sure why Wilcox is so angry, but she thinks it has something to do with his wife, who suffered at the hands of the workhouse master."

"Do you have a name for the wife?" Decker asked, unable to stop himself.

"Her name was Fannie."

"Ask the spirits if they know where Wilcox and his wife lived when they were alive."

Skye nodded and turned her attention back to the mirror. She repeated Decker's request, then cocked her head to the side as if listening for an answer.

Mina edged sideways, positioning herself behind Skye and looking over her shoulder. She drew a quick breath, her eyes widening. "Decker," she whispered in a barely audible voice. "Look at this."

Decker joined her, careful to make sure that he did not step outside of the salt circle or disturb it. When he looked into the mirror, he saw why Mina had gasped. Behind the reflection of Skye's face, was the lobby of the old workhouse. But it wasn't empty. The distinct forms of four people could be seen inside the hand mirror's smoky glass. They were translucent and hazy around the edges. It was hard to make out the features of their faces. But they were solid enough for Decker to realize that two of them were male, and the other two, female. These, he realized, must be the disincarnate souls of the young people who lost their lives here a few days before.

"This is incredible," Mina whispered, leaning close to Decker's ear. "She can actually see ghosts in that mirror."

"More than that. She can communicate with them." One of the spirits was standing closer than the others. One of the women. This, he surmised, must be Daisy Cartwright. Or at least, the part of her that had transcended death. She was staring straight into the mirror as if locking eyes with Skye. Her lips were moving as she spoke in a voice that only the medium could hear.

Decker was spellbound. He had faced all sorts of monsters, but this was his first ghost. He moved closer, trying to get a better angle from which to observe the reflected souls, but as he did so, something changed.

The mirror's surface clouded over as if a swirling black mist had passed in front of it.

Skye let out a strangled cry and almost dropped the mirror in alarm. "Oh no. No, no, no."

"What is it?" Decker asked, the hairs on the back of his neck standing up.

"There's something else here." Skye's voice was breathless. She sounded scared.

"What sort of something?" Mina asked, abandoning any pretext of remaining silent.

"A dark entity." Skye stared at the swirling darkness filling the mirror. "A creature that lives in the space between life and death. A cacodemon. I thought we would be safe so long as we kept the summoning short, but I was wrong. It must have been here already, drawn to this place by all the suffering and death. We must end this. Now."

"How do we do that?" Decker asked.

"I must recite the closing incantation. Sever the connection between us and the spirit plane."

"Whatever you need to do, you'd better do it quickly," Decker said, still looking at the mirror. Because the swirling void was taking shape. The tendrils of writhing, dark mist had coalesced into a bestial face, more horrific than any Decker had ever seen. Its mouth twisted into a snarl that exposed jagged yellow teeth with sharp points. Bumps that looked like small horns protruded from the creature's forehead. It stared at them through the glass with burning red eyes full of malevolence.

A stench of sulfur filled the air.

Mina gagged and turned away.

Skye held the mirror at arm's length and recited the incantation to close the portal. But it was too late. Thin wisps of smoke curled out of the mirror, seeping from around the edges where the glass met the frame. They formed tendrils that snaked toward Skye as she hurried to finish her incantation and twisted around her neck before drawing tight like a noose. And as Skye choked and clawed at the amorphous bines with her one free hand, the face in the mirror pushed out from the smoky glass, eager to escape into the real world.

# FORTY

NO SOONER HAD the demon started to push its way out than Decker leaped forward and snatched the mirror from Skye's hand just as her eyelids fluttered, and she sank to her knees, on the verge of unconsciousness.

"It's going to choke her to death," Decker said, surprised that the wispy tendrils of smoke were still wrapped around Skye's neck despite his attempts to pull the mirror away. "If we don't free her, she won't be able to finish the incantation and close the portal with the other side."

"I'll do it," Mina said, stepping up next to Decker.

"Do you know what you're doing?"

"Does it matter? If I don't, the demon will escape."

Decker nodded. Mina's logic was impeccable. "All right. Do it quickly."

Mina closed her eyes and took a deep breath, then she began to speak in a language that Decker had never heard. Her voice was soft but authoritative, and the reaction was instant.

The demonic face pushing through the mirror's surface

twisted into a mask of pure hate. The creature growled and hissed, glaring at Mina even as more tendrils found their way out of the mirror and reached toward her.

"I don't think so," Decker muttered, batting at the amorphous strands. He was surprised to find that they were unexpectedly solid. One wrapped itself around his left arm and twisted, restraining him. Another coiled toward his right hand and looped around his wrist. It wanted him to drop the mirror and shatter the glass.

More tendrils found Mina. She swatted them away as she continued the incantation that would close the connection to the spirit world. Her voice rose in pitch and grew louder, and then, with one final utterance, she fell silent.

For a moment, Decker thought Mina had failed, but then the tendrils attacking them lost their cohesion and fell apart on a sudden wind that whipped through the lobby. The face in the mirror let out a torturous wail before it was dragged back into the mirror and vanished as if it had never been there.

For a moment, Decker saw the spirits of the four recently departed souls staring back at him in the mirror's reflection before there was a sharp splintering sound, and the glass within the hand mirror shattered and fell from the frame.

Freed from the demon's grip, Skye staggered to her feet, gasping for air.

"This building contains more negative energy than I expected," she said in a raspy voice. "That demon was feeding on the pain and suffering of all those who died here. I sensed more of them, too. We aren't safe here right now."

"We closed the portal," Decker said.

"That doesn't mean the demons can't hurt us. The veil between our world and the spirit plane is weak right now. We punched a hole through it, and until it mends, we shouldn't be here." Skye looked more like herself now. She discarded the broken mirror and threw it off into the gloom, then went around the circle, blowing out the candles. "We won't find any more information, anyway. The spirits told us all they know."

"In that case, let's get the hell out of here," Mina said. She took a step toward the edge of the salt circle. "This place gives me the creeps."

"Wait." Skye held out a restraining arm. She reached into her bag and produced a small glass vial. Unscrewing it, she sprinkled the liquid inside beyond the salt circle in all directions. When she noticed Decker watching her, she said, "Holy water. Just to be safe."

"That really works?"

"More than you would think. Although it's not so much that the water itself is imbued with any sacred powers, but more the belief of the person who blessed it. In this case, it was a cardinal ordained into the Minor Order of Exorcist."

"You're kidding me. A real-life exorcist gave you that holy water?"

"Don't sound so surprised, Mr. Decker. I don't adhere to any particular religion, but that doesn't mean I'm oblivious to the powers of faith. In my line of work, one can never be too careful."

"I guess so." Decker nodded toward the salt circle. "We good to go now?"

"I believe we are." Skye kicked the salt with her foot, breaking the circle. She went around and picked up the candles, placing them back into her bag, along with the empty vial of holy water. That done, she took one last look around and then stepped beyond the circle toward the doors leading outside.

Mina and Decker hurried along after her.

They descended the steps to the driveway and started down it toward the stone archway. The farmer that brought them here would be back by now, and Decker was eager to get back to the village and discuss what Skye had learned from the spirits. The sun was low on the horizon, filling the sky with fire reds and yellows. Soon it would be dark. He glanced back over his shoulder at the old workhouse and suppressed a shudder. The building's windows were dark and impenetrable, but Decker couldn't help wondering how many unhappy ghosts stood beyond them, watching the trio with envy as they left Bartholomew Meadows behind.

# FORTY-ONE

WHEN THEY ARRIVED BACK at the Black Dog, they went directly upstairs to Decker's room to regroup.

"What else did the spirits tell you before that demon showed up?" Decker asked, turning to Skye as soon as the door was closed.

"Enough to convince me that Bartholomew Meadows was not a nice place to find oneself, especially if you were female and attractive." Skye walked close to the window and looked out, her back to Decker. "They were more than happy to talk until that demon showed up and interrupted us. Daisy was the most vocal, speaking more than the others. It was her that told me about Fannie."

"Right. The wife," Decker said. "Did they know what the workhouse master did to her?"

"No. Not exactly. But Fannie and Bradley were separated because the workhouse master had designs on her. That's why Wilcox is so enraged."

"Is her ghost up at the workhouse? Maybe we could talk to her."

"I never sensed her, although there are other souls there. Spirits lingering from that tragic night. And they wanted us to know who we are dealing with. James Grayson was a cruel man. He was married, but that didn't stop his roving eye. If a young woman down on her luck entered the workhouse and caught his attention . . . well, let's just say that some inmates paid for their room and board with more than money."

"That's despicable." A strange look passed across Mina's face.

"He wasn't the only one abusing the female inmates. The workhouse physician was a monster subjecting those under his care to humiliating ordeals that went far beyond what might have been required in the scope of his employment."

"Do you think the workhouse master and the physician were working together?" Mina asked.

"It's possible. But whatever happened to Fannie Wilcox occurred at the hands of the workhouse master, not his depraved doctor."

"What about the wife?" Mina looked troubled. "She must have lived at the workhouse along with her husband. How could she not notice what he was doing?"

"Maybe she did, and turned a blind eye," Decker said. "It wouldn't be the first time."

"Or maybe she was a willing participant," Skye added in a somber voice. "Either way, it doesn't matter. Fannie Wilcox was being abused by the workhouse master. Whatever that abuse was must have been enough to enrage Wilcox, and he's been seeking revenge ever since."

Decker rubbed his chin. "Except that all the people involved in whatever happened back then are dead. There's no one left to exact revenge upon."

"Maybe he's just so angry that he can't stop killing," Mina speculated.

"I don't think so." Decker shook his head. "We still don't have all the answers. We need to find out more about Wilcox and his wife, and exactly what happened up at that workhouse in the days and months leading up to the massacre."

"But how?" Mina shook her head. "You heard Skye. We can't go back up there and hold another séance. We were lucky to escape unharmed this time."

"I'm aware of that." Decker folded his arms. "We'll have to do it the old-fashioned way. The workhouse must have kept records. That's a good starting point. I wonder where they went when it closed down?"

"Is there a library in the village?" Skye asked, turning back toward Decker and Mina.

"I don't know." Decker shrugged.

"Might be worth finding out. If there is, maybe the records went there."

"There could be other things, too," Mina said, her eyes sparkling with anticipation. "Bartholomew Meadows sounds like a horrible place. There must've been rumors swirling even when it was open. Maybe some of that stuff made it into the local newspapers. They might have an archive."

"Maybe." Decker didn't want to get his hopes up. "All of this happened so long ago. Even if the village has a library now, I can't imagine it had one back then."

"It doesn't matter. Any records or newspaper archives that were maintained would probably have been transferred there when the library opened."

Decker glanced at his watch. A classic silver timepiece lent to him by Thomas Finch before they left London. It was past five o'clock. "Even if there is a library, it won't be open now. It will have to wait until the morning."

"Which means we must get through another evening with

that vengeful spirit on the loose," said Mina. "It's killed each night since it was released. What if it strikes again?"

"I don't know," Decker admitted. "Maybe it isn't even here anymore."

"It's here," Skye said. "I can sense the negative energy."

"Maybe we should warn the village." Mina glanced between Decker and Skye.

"And say what?" Decker asked. "That an angry ghost is seeking revenge for the death of his wife three decades ago? Do you honestly think anyone will believe that?"

"Even if they did, what could they do about it?" Skye sighed. "You can't fight what you cannot see."

Decker nodded in agreement. "And we don't even know why Wilcox is targeting those that he kills. I can understand why Daisy and her friends incurred his wrath. One of them set the spirit free by breaking the chandelier within which it was trapped. But how do Violet and her husband fit into this? They were nowhere near Bartholomew Meadows when the chandelier broke, setting Wilcox free. Is there a method to his revenge, or is he just on an indiscriminate killing spree?"

"We won't know the answer to that until we know more about the circumstances that led him to this," Mina said. "But we know one thing. Wilcox has a distinct way of exacting his revenge."

"He possesses women to commit his murders before killing the person within which he is residing and moving on."

"What you are describing appears to be a Dybbuk," said Skye.

Decker turned to look at her. "What's a Dybbuk?"

"It's a malevolent spirit from Jewish mythology. The dislocated soul of a deceased person who possesses the living. The Dybbuk is always a male spirit that enters female hosts. Its name roughly translates as clinging spirit. Unlike the more traditional concept of possession, the Dybbuk only inhabits his host for long enough to achieve its goal, and then moves on."

"Sounds like a real charmer," Decker said. "I don't suppose Jewish mythology tells us how to defeat this Dybbuk."

"Not so far as I know."

"Perfect." Decker grimaced.

"We already know how to defeat it," Mina said. "We trap it in crystal, just like that spiritualist did the first time around."

"Do you have any idea how we accomplish that feat?" Decker asked.

"No." Mina looked glum. "Not a clue."

# FORTY-TWO

LATER THAT NIGHT, Decker was in his room preparing for bed when there was a knock on the door. He slipped his shirt back on and answered, expecting it to be Mina. Instead, he found Skye standing in the corridor.

"Mr. Decker, can we speak for a few moments?" Skye glanced toward Mina's door.

"Sure. Come on in." Decker stepped aside for Skye to enter. After closing the door, he turned to her. "What's on your mind?"

"I'm not sure if this is relevant to our reason for being here, but when I returned to my room earlier this evening, I sensed that someone had been there while we were up at the workhouse."

"What you mean, sensed?"

"Exactly what I said. My gift is a strange one, Mr. Decker. I can commune with spirits, but I am also sensitive to the vibrations of the world around me. The atmosphere in my room had been disturbed. I felt the same sensation when we were in your own room earlier, but I wasn't sure which is why I said nothing. I suspect that if we were to visit Mina's bedroom, we would discover that she had received an unwelcome visitor also."

"When you say that we received an unwelcome visitor, are you talking about a spirit?" Decker asked. "Or maybe a demon like the one that we encountered at the workhouse this evening?"

"No. This visitor was flesh and blood. Apart from what I sensed, there was more tangible proof. I have an affliction whereby personal items must be placed exactly in the position I wish them to be. I cannot abide things to be askew or out of place. To that end, I placed my travel bag at the end of the bed, exactly aligned with the folds of the top blanket. My personal items inside the bag were packed in a specific way. The bag was moved and opened. The personal items disturbed. A very important book that I carry with me, a grimoire that contains incantations used to summon the dead, had been removed and then put back. The intruder was careful to put everything back as he found it. Almost. A casual observer would notice nothing out of place, but to me, the book might as well have been lying open on the bed."

"I see." Decker rubbed his chin thoughtfully. In the twenty-first century, Skye would have been diagnosed with OCD. In the first decades of the twentieth, Decker surmised it was not so well understood.

As if reading his mind, Skye spoke again. "I know you must think me strange, Mr. Decker. But I assure you, it is a well-documented affliction. Sigmund Freud published a paper, not two years ago that documented a case of obsessional neurosis. The patient, whom Freud named Rat Man to protect his identity, became convinced that something terrible was going to befall members of his family. He suffered from murderous thoughts and developed a pattern of irrational and compulsive behavior."

"That doesn't sound like the same thing at all," Decker said. "You aren't fantasizing about murder, I assume."

Skye dropped her eyes and flashed a coy smile. "Of course not. However, Rat Man also developed rituals and habits that adversely affected his life, such as leaving his front door open between midnight and one in the morning without fail. He tried to control the events of his life through ritual. I fear that my own compulsive habits border upon the same obsession."

"Have you ever sought treatment?" Decker asked.

"No." Skye shook her head. "The structure I demand in my life helps me offset the uncontrollable nature of my supernatural gift. I can't control seeing and hearing spirits, but I do get to dictate the order of the physical world around me. Call it a psychic pressure valve. In this case, my need for everything to be exactly in its place provided proof that I was not wrong in thinking someone had been in my room."

"I don't doubt that you are correct," Decker said. "Since we arrived in the village, I've gotten the impression that someone was lurking around, too. It's nothing concrete. Just glimpses of movement from the corner of my eye as if we were being followed, and a general sense of unease."

"We should be careful," Skye replied. "The psychic impression left by the intruder was one of malice."

"Are you sure that the interloper was human?" Decker asked. "We had a run-in with the spirit of Bradley Wilcox last night, as you know. He tried to possess Mina."

"It's not Wilcox. We aren't dealing with a disincarnate entity. If we were, my impressions would be stronger. I might even see them. Whoever visited our rooms is flesh and blood, just like us. It's possible that they are connected to this investigation, but I couldn't begin to tell you how."

"There is one person who showed an interest in us," Decker said. "The village constable. He caught us exploring the workhouse and ran us off. He also showed up right after we witnessed the second incident. Another murder-suicide."

"It could be him," Skye replied. "But I can't give you a concrete answer. I sense impressions, but nothing more. Think of it like the ripples in a pond after a stone has been thrown in. By the time you see them, the stone is already gone. I'm sorry, but I can't identify any particular person as being the culprit."

"I understand." Decker paced over to the window and glanced out, overcome with the sudden sense that someone might be watching them at that very moment. But the street outside was empty and dark. "For now, let's operate under the assumption that the constable is watching us, at least until we find evidence that points to the contrary."

Skye nodded. "I think that's a good idea."

"Me too. In fact, it makes sense. I suspect he was snooping, trying to figure out who we are and why we are here."

"Since we agree that our activities here have drawn unwanted interest, we should tell Mina."

"I agree," replied Decker, already making his way toward the door. "I hate to disturb her, but I don't think we have any choice. We all need to be on our guard."

# FORTY-THREE

IT TOOK LESS than ten minutes for Decker to brief Mina on their fears about being watched. He was concerned that someone had taken the trouble to break into their rooms and wasn't entirely convinced that the constable possessed either the cunning or the skills to do so. But he could think of no one else with a motive. Mina appeared similarly troubled but agreed that the constable was the most likely suspect.

Once the conversation was finished, Skye and Decker left to return to their own rooms, but not before Mina took Decker aside.

"Do you think Wilcox will strike again tonight?" She asked.

"Your guess is as good as mine," Decker replied. "For all we know, he's moved on to wherever spirits go now that he's not trapped on earth anymore."

"He's still around," Skye said with a grim look on her face. "I can sense him."

Decker and Mina both turned to look at her. "What do you think? Is he looking for another victim?"

Skye raised an eyebrow. "The only way to know that is to wait."

Back in his room, Decker prepared for bed. Beyond the pub, the village appeared quiet and sleepy. But looks could be deceptive. The restless spirit of Bradley Wilcox might be out there right now, inhabiting the body of some poor unfortunate woman as she murdered her husband. But even he was better than the entity that had tried to push through the mirror during the séance. If that creature ever got free, Bradley's killing spree would look like a picnic. Of that, Decker was sure. He closed his eyes and tried to clear his mind, but to no avail. When sleep came . . . if it came . . . he was sure his dreams would be full of demons.

# FORTY-FOUR

THE MAVENDALE PUBLIC library was a Tudor building occupying a spot on the east end of the village High Street. Decker and Mina arrived there a few minutes before it opened and waited for the librarian, a heavyset woman with a round face and rosy cheeks, to let them in.

It was a Wednesday, one of only three days each week during which the library was open, the other two being Monday and Friday. The library's interior was dimly lit, which Decker found ironic for a building dedicated to reading. A musty odor hung in the air that probably emanated from the hundreds, if not thousands, of volumes lining the shelves. A long reading table with benches on each side stood in the middle of the room. The librarian's desk occupied a back corner.

Decker gave the librarian a few minutes to settle in, then approached her and explained what he and Mina were looking for.

"Workhouse records?" The librarian looked perplexed. "I don't think I've ever had anyone ask for those before."

"You have the records here?" Mina asked.

"Yes. In the special collections room along with the old parish birth and death registers and even some texts from the monastery that were salvaged during the dissolution," the librarian replied, glancing sideways to a door marked private. "We only allow viewing by appointment for our more important documents and texts. Would you like to make an appointment?"

Decker glanced around the empty library. "Do we need to?"

"Absolutely. Everyone who wishes to use the private collections room must book it."

"But there's no one else here. I can't imagine someone else has reserved the room today."

The librarian pushed a pair of spectacles higher on the bridge of her nose and looked down at the ledger sitting on the desk in front of her. She flicked through its pages and then looked up at him again. "You are correct. The last booking was in June. A scholar from Oxford University doing genealogy research."

"June?" Decker tried not to laugh. It was November. "You don't think you could just let us in there?"

"Rules are rules." The librarian made a tutting sound with her tongue. "Would you like to make an appointment?"

Decker wondered if the librarian was being deliberately obtuse, or if she had just spent so long sitting alone surrounded by the voices of long dead authors, that she had gone a little insane. "Can we make an appointment for today?"

Librarian licked her lips and looked down at the ledger again. "How about eleven a.m.?"

"That's almost an hour from now." Decker glanced sideways at Mina, who was trying hard not to grin, then back to the librarian. "You don't think you could fit us in right away?"

"Goodness, no. We reserve the room in one hour increments, and it's already gone ten."

"Of course you do." Decker sighed. "Eleven will be fine."

"I don't suppose you have newspaper archives, too?" Mina asked.

"Only local," answered the librarian. "They go back as far as the 1860s. That's when the Mavendale Standard was first printed."

"Are they in the special collections room as well?" Decker asked.

"No. We keep an archive in the room next door." The librarian looked at Decker without a hint of amusement. "You will need a separate reservation for the newspapers. Shall I pencil you in for noon?"

"Do we have much choice?"

The librarian raised a disapproving eyebrow at Decker's sarcasm. "Well, you could come back on Friday instead."

"Today will be fine. Noon it is." Mina kicked Decker's ankle.

The librarian scribbled in her journal again. "All done. I shall see you in a little under an hour. Please do not be tardy. I can't guarantee to hold your reservation if you are not here on time."

*Because people are lining up outside the door to get in there*, thought Decker. But he held his tongue and merely flashed the librarian the sincerest smile he could muster.

As they walked away from the desk, Decker leaned close to Mina and whispered in her ear. "Are all British people this obsessed with pointless rules, or is it just this particular librarian?"

Mina grinned. "Not all of them, but a good percentage. You'll get used to it."

# FORTY-FIVE

AN HOUR LATER, Decker and Mina returned to the librarian, who unlocked the special collections room. In the meantime, they had browsed the shelves looking through the library's local history section for any relevant material but found nothing of interest.

The special collections room was a cramped, windowless space lined with wooden shelves that held an assortment of oversized bound tomes. The librarian located the relevant volumes and deposited them on a wooden table of similar construction to the one in the main library, but smaller. That done, she retreated and left Decker and Mina alone. But not before issuing a terse warning to handle the records with care.

There were three thick volumes in all, each one covering about a decade. They decided that the first, dating from the 1850s was too early. A brief inspection of the second volume, which covered the 1860s and the first years of the 1870s, yielded nothing. When they came to the last volume, containing records of inmates admitted and released between the early 1870s and the date when the workhouse closed, they finally found what they were looking for.

"Look at this," Decker said, pointing to an entry from June 1875. The writing was hard to read and faded, the paper on which it was written having aged badly with heavy foxing. "It's difficult to make out, but this appears to be an intake record for Bradley and Fanny Wilcox."

Mina leaned close and examined the page. She pointed to another entry further down. "This appears to be a transfer for Bradley Wilcox. He was sent to another workhouse in Essex."

"The unofficial village historian that I paid a visit to yesterday morning, Mavis, told me that the workhouse master ran at least two more institutions. She said he would move people between them as he saw fit."

"But this transfer is only for Bradley, not his wife." Mina thought for a moment. "Do you think James Grayson sent Bradley Wilcox away so that he could gain unfettered access to Fannie?"

"Why would he need to?" Decker asked. "Grayson was in charge of the workhouse. He could do whatever he wanted, and Bradley Wilcox couldn't stop him. Didn't they keep the men and the women in separate wards, even if they were married?"

"Yes." Mina nodded. "I believe they did. But it still would've been easier to control Fannie with her husband out of the way. Maybe Grayson even blackmailed her, telling her she wouldn't see Bradley again if she didn't go along with his desires."

"It makes sense, but it's also pure speculation."

"I think we can assume that Grayson had ulterior motives. We know he was using the workhouse as his personal playground, not to mention a source of cheap labor. We also know that he coveted Fannie. If she had caught Grayson's eye and ended up forced into some sort of relationship with him, that would be more than enough to stoke Bradley Wilcox's anger and set him on a path to revenge."

"But how?" Decker asked, studying the remaining pages of the workhouse ledger. "Bradley Wilcox was in another poorhouse far from here. There are no entries concerning him being sent back to Bartholomew Meadows."

"You're forgetting one thing," Mina said. "Wilcox must have already been dead when the slaughter occurred at Bartholomew Meadows. After all, he possessed Bethany Grayson and forced her to kill her husband before taking her own life."

"Agreed. Which raises the question of how and when he died?" Decker flicked back through the pages of the workhouse ledger. "And I have a feeling we won't find the answer to that in these pages."

"Which leaves the newspaper archives." Mina closed the ledger and placed it back on top of the other two volumes. "There's bound to be mention of the massacre at the workhouse in there, but I wonder if there were any other incidents prior to that?"

"If only we had the internet," Decker said ruefully. "All of this would be so much easier."

"You can't imagine the number of times I've thought that over the past couple of decades." Mina returned the old volumes to the shelf. "I always imagined that it must've been so romantic to live in the Victorian era. Having been stranded in the past for a quarter-century, my eyes have been opened to the truth. If we ever get back to the twenty-first century, I'll never take my life for granted again."

"We'll get back there," Decker replied. "I don't know how yet, but I'm not willing to spend the rest of my life separated from Nancy."

A cloud passed across Mina's face. "I hope you're right. I really do. But I've been looking for a way home for so long that I'm not sure one exists."

Decker didn't know what to say. Mina had spent half her life stranded here, while he had only arrived a few days ago. He wanted to believe that she was wrong and that they would make it back to their own time, but he wondered if she was right. There might not be a way home. Because if there was, wouldn't she have found it by now?

"Hey." Mina must have noticed Decker's despondence. "I didn't mean to throw cold water on your optimism."

"No. You're right." Decker forced himself to focus. "It won't be easy to get back home. I need to accept that."

"That doesn't mean you need to stop looking."

"I have no intention of giving up. We escaped Singer Cay, didn't we?"

"And don't forget Celine. It was her getting thrown forward in time to your wedding that started all of this."

"You're right." Decker wondered why he hadn't thought of that before. Maybe there was a way home. It was a long shot, but just maybe . . . But Decker didn't want to raise Mina's hopes when all he had was a sliver of an idea. And besides, there were more pressing matters in the here and now. He glanced at his watch, noting that it was almost time for their appointment in the archive room next door. "Come on. Let's go paw through some moldy old newspapers."

# FORTY-SIX

WHEN DECKER and Mina reentered the main room of the public library, the librarian jumped to her feet and hurried toward them with a set of keys in hand, ready to unlock the archive room. But before she could complete her task, the main door opened, and Skye rushed in.

"I'm so glad I found you," she said in a breathless voice. "There's someone back at the pub that wants to talk with you."

"There is?" Decker asked, surprised. "Who?"

"Her name is Mavis. She was asking the pub landlord about you when I returned from a walk in the village. Sounded rather desperate to find you, so I intervened. She told me you visited her yesterday, inquiring about Bartholomew Meadows. Apparently, she has new information that you will find helpful."

"Did she say what that information was?" Decker asked.

"No. But she agreed to wait while I fetch you. Was most insistent, in fact."

"I had better talk to her, then," Decker said. He turned to

the librarian. "The newspapers in the archive room will have to wait, I'm afraid. Would it be possible to come back later this afternoon?"

"I'm sorry. The library closes at one on Wednesdays."

"Could you make an exception and stay open a little longer?"

"You're not the only one with a busy life, you know. Besides, I don't get paid outside of regular hours." The librarian looked peeved. "You'll have to come back on Friday. We open at ten a.m. Do you want to make an appointment?"

"Doesn't look like I have much choice," Decker replied.

"Wait," Mina said. "Why don't you go back to the pub with Skye, and I'll stay here and look through the archives."

"Good idea," Decker said. "We'll meet up back at the pub later and compare notes."

Mina nodded and waited for the librarian to unlock the door to the archive room, while Decker turned and followed Skye out of the library and back along the high street to the Black Dog.

When he got there, he found Mavis Corby sitting at a table in a corner of the bar with half a pint of bitter ale in front of her. When she saw Decker enter the pub, she waved.

"My associate tells me you remembered something important," Decker said, approaching the table with Skye at his side.

"Not so much remembered." Mavis waited for them to sit down before continuing. "It was more like a realization. I was reading the local newspaper. There was an article about that dreadful business up at the workhouse a few nights ago. It's been front-page news for the last two days. I suppose the newspaper's editor, Harry Theakston, is in his element with something more exciting than stray cats and the village fete to report on . . ."

Decker waited while Mavis took a sip of her drink before she continued talking.

"But anyway, that's neither here nor there. What is important is that I saw another story. One about Violet Hughes . . . poor woman. Did you know she killed her husband and then herself?"

"I did," Decker admitted, although he didn't mention that he was present at the time. "What was so important about those news articles that you rushed down here to see me?"

"Violet has a younger sister, Ada. She has just returned from London and was staying with them until she got on her feet. She left her husband. Anyway, according to the story in the paper, she claimed Violet wasn't herself, Mr. Decker. Said she was acting like she was under the influence of some evil force. Said her sister committed those heinous acts because of the workhouse curse."

"I'm sorry, the what?" Decker wondered why Mavis had not mentioned this to him before.

"The curse. Ever since the inmates escaped and slaughtered their jailers, there have been rumors of a curse placed upon Bartholomew Meadows. I always thought it was nothing but tall tales, to be honest. But then I saw that article, and it made me think. According to the curse, anyone associated with the workhouse will die a violent death."

"What does this have to do with the recent incidents?" Decker asked, sensing that a piece of the puzzle was about to fall into place.

"All of those people who died either had connections to that dreadful place or were associated with someone who did. I should have seen the pattern earlier, but it wasn't until I paid attention to the names of the victims that I realized. Alastair Chamberlain's grandfather served on the workhouse board. Lord Robert Braithwaite-Moore, the father of another victim, Felicity, tried to buy the old workhouse after it was closed down. He wanted to reopen it. Then there was Reginald Poulton. He wasn't a member of the aristocracy like his friends, but his great-uncle had worked at Bartholomew Meadows as a porter."

"I see," said Decker. "And what about the fourth person who died up the workhouse?"

"Daisy Cartwright," said Skye to Decker. "She's the young woman we conversed with last night."

Mavis shot them both a confused look.

"It's a long story," said Decker by way of explanation. "Was Daisy Cartwright associated with the workhouse, too?"

"If she was, the article I read didn't mention it. Perhaps she was just guilty by association."

"And what about Violet Hughes?"

"That one is easy. The whole village knows of her family's ties to Bartholomew Meadows. Her aunt was the matron who looked after the workhouse children. A horrible woman she was, by all accounts. Cruel as they come."

"There were children in that place?" Decker asked, horrified.

"Oh, yes. Some of them as young as five years old. And the matron was a scourge to them all. Violet was so ashamed to be related to her."

Decker exchanged a look with Skye, then focused his attention back on Mavis. "Just so I understand what you're telling me, pretty much all of our victims were connected to the workhouse or were in a relationship with someone who was."

Mavis nodded. "I really should have seen it before. It only occurred to me after I read that article in the newspaper."

"Thank you, Mavis. This has been a great help," Decker said. He motioned to the landlord and told him to provide

Mavis with whatever she wanted, on him. Then he turned his attention back to the old woman. "I have just one more question. Who else do you know in the village who still has a familial connection to the workhouse?"

"Well, only one that I can think of," Mavis replied. "Alfred Trent. The village constable. His grandfather was Robert Trent, one of the most feared men in the whole institution, at least among the female inmates."

"And Robert Trent was?" Decker asked.

"Why he was the workhouse physician, Mr. Decker," Mavis said. "And Grayson's partner in crime."

# FORTY-SEVEN

WHEN MINA RETURNED to the Black Dog an hour later, Decker was eager to tell her what he and Skye had discovered thanks to Mavis Corby. But Mina had news of her own.

They had gathered in Decker's accommodations upstairs, away from prying ears, and he could tell that she was eager to relay her findings, so he let her go first.

"I know why the spirit of Bradley Wilcox is so angry," Mina said breathlessly. "Our assumptions were right. James Grayson sent him to another workhouse to get him out of the way because he had designs on Wilcox's wife, Fannie."

"This was in the newspaper?" Decker asked.

"Yes." Mina nodded. "It took me a while to find because the archives are not well cataloged, but I came across a newspaper from about a week before the massacre up at Bartholomew Meadows. It appears that Wilcox freed himself from a workhouse eighty miles away in Essex, outside of a small town called Maldon. He was a determined man. He made his way back to Bartholomew

Meadows and waited in concealment for Grayson to take a walk on the grounds, as was apparently his habit each evening. Here he confronted the master and demanded that his wife be released."

"I'm sure that didn't work out well for him," Decker said.

"It did not," Mina replied. "He chose his spot to challenge Grayson poorly. Realizing that he needed leverage, Wilcox tried to take the workhouse master hostage in exchange for his wife. But he underestimated Grayson's strength and struggled to subdue him."

"Given that Wilcox had spent a considerable amount of time in the workhouse by then, and how far he traveled to reach Bartholomew Meadows," Skye said, "I would imagine he was probably malnourished and weaker than he otherwise would have been."

"Exactly. Otherwise, his plan might have worked," Mina replied. "According to the newspaper article, he was in possession of a hunting knife but dropped it during the struggle, which allowed Grayson to cry out and raise the alarm, drawing several of the workhouse porters and other staff to his aid."

"They must have been close to the building for anyone to hear him," Decker said. "Wilcox should have picked a better spot."

"He probably had no choice. Grayson walked the same route around the grounds each evening, following a path that circled the building."

"What happened next?" Decker asked.

"Grayson broke free and instructed the porters to restrain Wilcox. But before they could do so, he scooped up the knife and used it to hold them at bay, still demanding the release of his wife. A standoff ensued, that was only resolved when a member of the workhouse staff was able to circle behind

Wilcox and get the jump on him. There was a brief struggle, and Wilcox ended up on the receiving end of his own knife."

"That's terrible," Skye said, her eyes wide.

"It gets worse. As Wilcox lay dying on the grass outside of the workhouse, Grayson had Fannie brought out to witness what had befallen her husband. But not out of any compassion on the workhouse master's part. He wanted to make an example of Wilcox and show her what happened to those who broke the rules. She was not allowed to go to him and was taken back to the workhouse and locked in the women's ward even as Wilcox was drawing his last breaths."

"Do you think he did that to keep order in the workhouse or as a veiled threat for Fannie to go along with his desires?" Decker asked, reading between the lines.

"It's impossible to know, but my guess is that Fannie was not a willing participant in Grayson's advances, and he hoped that this would make her more pliable. She would truly be at his mercy with her husband dead."

"No wonder the inmates revolted and slaughtered the workhouse staff," Skye said. "With a master like that, you can only imagine how brutal the staff were."

"Exactly. But that revolt would not have been possible without Wilcox. He uttered a curse as he lay dying, saying that the master and all those who were complicit in his cruelty would not live to see the end of the month. He also condemned their families, saying that no one would be spared."

"I guess we know where the villagers got the notion of a curse on Bartholomew Meadows," Decker said, exchanging a glance with Skye. "Especially since the newspaper reported Wilcox's words almost a week before Grayson's wife released the inmates to kill everyone."

"Where did you hear about a curse?" Mina asked.

"Mavis Corby. Every one of our current victims has a connection to the workhouse."

"Wilcox is continuing to enact his revenge. It wasn't enough that he possessed Grayson's wife, freed the inmates, and killed the workhouse master. He wants to make the descendants of the workhouse staff suffer, too."

"There is still one thing that doesn't make sense," Skye said. "Why is he possessing women and then forcing them to kill themselves once he's done with them?"

"I can answer that," Mina said.

"A couple of days after her husband's death, Fannie found a way to join him. Distraught and inconsolable, she took her own life during a shift in the workhouse kitchen. She plunged a knife into her chest. It took her several hours to die in the workhouse infirmary, but during that time she swore her husband was present and had even spoken to her, lamenting her actions, for she would surely now go to hell."

"That must've been the last straw for Wilcox," Decker said. "Of all that Grayson had done, this must've been the worst. Putting Fannie in a situation where she felt her only way out was through death and eternal damnation."

"Even in the afterlife, they were denied the chance to be with each other," Skye said.

"And that anger has been fermenting inside of him ever since, even while he was trapped." Decker almost felt sorry for Wilcox. But not enough to excuse him for the misery he had caused. "Now he's lashing out at anyone he perceives as being even remotely responsible."

"Which means anyone descended from the workhouse staff is in grave danger," Mina said.

"We must warn the constable," Skye said. "I took a walk around the village today while you were both at the library, and everything was quiet. Wilcox did not strike last night. But

I can still sense him here. I can feel his anger. He won't wait long."

"Why the constable?" Mina asked.

"Because he might be one of the last people in the village with a direct connection to the workhouse," Decker said, remembering that he hadn't yet filled Mina in on what Mavis had told him.

"What kind of connection?"

"The worst kind." Decker paced back and forth. "Mavendale's village constable is the grandson of Robert Trent, the workhouse physician."

"How are we going to convince him?" Skye asked. "It doesn't sound like he's made any connection between the old workhouse staff and the deaths in the village, much less come to the conclusion that an avenging spirit is responsible."

"We'll have to be persuasive," Decker answered.

"Good luck." There was a somber tone to Skye's voice. "I've tried convincing skeptics that the spirit world is all too real, and most of the time it hasn't gone well. If the constable doesn't want to believe, nothing we say will change his mind."

"We don't need to change his mind." Mina glanced toward the bedroom door. "We have a letter from Detective Inspector Sim of the London Metropolitan Police instructing the constable to cooperate with us. Believe us or not, he'll have to do what we say."

"I'm not so sure it will be that easy," Decker said. "I've met his type before."

"Maybe." Mina folded her arms. "But I've learned to be quite persuasive over the past twenty-five years. One way or another, he'll do as we say. The bigger problem will be dealing with the spirit of Bradley Wilcox when and if he shows up."

"That's why we need a plan before going to speak with the constable," Decker replied.

"I don't suppose you have one of those rattling around in that mind of yours?" Mina asked, hopefully.

"The start of one, at least." Decker looked at Skye. "The last time Wilcox was defeated, they used a spiritualist to trap him in a crystal."

"I can't imagine he'll fall for that again," Skye said. "And I'm not sure I have the psychic strength to accomplish such a feat even if he does."

"Maybe not. But I know someone who might." Decker looked at Mina. "Fancy catching a ghost?"

Mina groaned. "Do I have a choice?"

# FORTY-EIGHT

THE MAN in the black suit stood in the corridor outside of Decker's room and listened with his head bent close to the door. The three people on the other side were careful to keep their voices low, and he struggled to hear everything they said despite his best efforts. But thankfully, his senses were finely tuned, including his hearing. He had listened in on conversations in much more challenging environments in the past. He heard enough of this one to realize that the local constable would play a larger role in the unfolding tragedies that had led Mina to this village than he had expected.

This was a most fortuitous turn of events. He was finding it difficult to observe Mina while staying in the shadows, but now he could use the constable in a greater capacity. With Mina and her companions worried he would become the next victim of whatever supernatural creature stalked this village, they would stick close to him. That meant the constable could watch Mina at the same time. If she displayed any unusual tendencies, anything that would lend credence to the man in the black suit's suspicion of her own supernatural nature, the constable would be able to report it right back to him.

The man in the black suit smiled. As always, fortune was on his side. Mina had been careful to hide her true nature. Maybe she was naturally cautious, or perhaps she was worried that someone like him would come along and realize what she was. But everyone slipped up eventually. Even someone as disciplined as her. Events in Mavendale were shaping up nicely to force such an error. And with the constable in close proximity, the chances of that error being observed had just increased exponentially.

The conversation inside the room was ending. The man in the black suit stepped away from the door and hurried back down the corridor to the stairs. He descended to the saloon bar and breezed through it. It wouldn't be long before Mina and her companions paid the constable a visit. He would do so first, just to smooth their way.

# FORTY-NINE

CONSTABLE ALFRED TRENT stood at the window and watched the stranger in the black suit stroll down the High Street as if he owned the place. The constable shuddered and turned back to his desk. Until three nights ago, his job had been one monotonous workday after another, with little more than an occasional drunk or squabble between husband and wife to deal with. And he liked it that way. It was easy. Simple.

The last seventy-two hours had been anything but easy or simple. First, those self-entitled rich brats had trespassed up to the old workhouse and got themselves killed. All but one, that was. And the story she told was, frankly, ridiculous.

Then Violet Hughes lost her mind and killed her husband before taking her own life just one night later.

If this didn't count as the worst week of Alfred's professional life, he wasn't sure what would. And it was made all the more frustrating by the strangers who had rented rooms at the Black Dog. He had already caught them poking around the workhouse and been forced to warn them off. He didn't appreciate people meddling in his investigations. Hell, for all he knew, they were somehow responsible for this sudden glut of strange deaths, although he could not see how.

Then there was the undertaker, as he now thought of the man in the black suit. After three visits, the constable was no less creeped out than he had been the first time he laid eyes upon the man. The last one had come only minutes before when the undertaker showed up at the police station unannounced to once again reiterate that he should refrain from interfering in the business of the strangers staying at the Black Dog. But this time, he went further. He wanted Alfred to assist them. They were, the undertaker assured him, about to pay a visit to the constable. Without going into detail, the undertaker instructed Alfred to go along with whatever they told him to do . . . No matter how strange or unbelievable it appeared. In addition, Alfred was to pay attention to the young woman named Mina. He was to report any unusual occurrences. This was all in the name of national security, of course, and the constable would be rewarded for his efforts.

Alfred glanced back toward the window. It only now occurred to him that he really didn't know who the undertaker worked for. The man had shown him no credentials of any kind and had not even mentioned which specific branch of the government or police he answered to. The constable found this troubling and decided to press the issue when they next crossed paths. In the meantime, he would do as the undertaker requested, at least until it reached a line he was not willing to cross. He did this partly because he didn't want to run afoul of an organization that could spell trouble for him if he didn't, but mostly because the man in the black suit scared him.

Alfred stood and went to a small room at the back of the

police station that served as a kitchen. He put a kettle on the stove and waited for the water to boil, then made a pot of tea. It would take a few minutes to percolate. When he returned to the main room, he found more visitors waiting for him.

It was the pair who had shown up at the scene of both recent incidents, and another woman he didn't recognize. In her hand she clutched a bag like those that doctors carried. It looked heavy.

"Is there something I can do for you?" The constable asked, with the undertaker's instructions fresh in the back of his mind.

"Actually, it's more what we can do for you," Mina said.

Her male companion—the constable remembered his name was John Decker—spoke next. "We fear that you and your family may be in danger."

"Danger, huh?" The constable didn't bother keeping the incredulity from his voice. He went to his desk and sat down, then motioned for his guests to do the same. "You'd better take a seat. There are only two chairs, so you'll have to fight over them."

"I don't think that will be necessary," Decker said, allowing his female companions to sit down while he hovered behind them with his arms folded.

The woman with the bag set it on the floor next to her chair with obvious relief.

The constable observed his visitors with narrowed eyes, milking a moment of silence before he spoke again. "I think you'd better tell me all about this danger."

"That is why we came here," the man named Decker said. "But first, we have something for you. To prove our credentials."

The young woman, Mina, produced a folded letter and pushed it across the desk toward him. The constable picked it up and read it quickly, noting the London Metropolitan Police letterhead and the signature at the bottom. Detective Inspector Harry Sim. The document looked genuine. At least on the face of it, these people were telling the truth. They really did work for the Met. Which raised the question of who exactly the man in the black suit worked for? The Undertaker had claimed to represent a department within His Majesty's government. If so, it must outrank the Metropolitan Police. Unless the ghastly man was lying. If so, he would find himself locked up in short order. But until then, the constable would continue as promised, and this letter only made that task easier.

Alfred folded the letter and placed it back on the table. "All right. Let's hear it, then. Tell me about this danger."

And so they did. And when they were done, the constable wondered if the Metropolitan Police had lost their minds in hiring these people. More to the point, he wondered if he was in the presence of three downright lunatics.

# FIFTY

"LET me see if I'm hearing you right," the constable said from across his desk. "The ghost of a man who died at the workhouse over three decades ago wants revenge on me because my grandfather just happened to work there."

"Yes," Decker said with a nod.

"And that same ghost is going to possess my wife in order to murder me."

"Correct," Mina said.

"And then it will make Molly kill herself."

"That about sums it up," Skye replied.

"You sound crazy. All three of you."

"Crazy or not, it's the truth." Decker rested his hands on the back of Mina's chair and leaned forward. "While we can't offer proof of our claim, your own interview with the survivor of the incident at the workhouse, Beatrice Warburton, should corroborate our claim. She told you that her friends were possessed, after all."

"She said as much," the constable admitted grudgingly. "But she was also hysterical and in shock."

225

"And what about Violet Hughes?" Mina asked. "She lived in the village. It's a small place. You must have known her well."

"That I did."

"Did she strike you as the type of woman who would commit a heinous act like murder?"

"No." The constable rubbed the back of his neck as if relieving a knot of tension. "Honestly, she was about as gentle as they come. I've known her since we were children. In all that time, she never harmed a fly, let alone took up a weapon against anyone in anger. I'm struggling to believe that an angry spirit is responsible for what's going on around here, but I have to admit, I don't have any other good explanation."

"Does that mean you believe us?" Decker asked.

"I'm not sure what to believe." The constable was still rubbing his neck absently. "I've never put much stock in such things. To be honest, I'm not even much for religion, although I attend the local service because it's expected of me."

"Good enough." Decker was relieved. He had expected more resistance from the constable. "Where is your wife at this moment?"

"The village shop. She works there a couple of days a week just to help out. She's a good friend of the owner, Gladys Thorpe. Honestly, I think the woman is a gossip, but Molly won't hear of it."

"Can you ask your wife to come home?" Mina leaned forward and placed her elbows on the desk. "The village was quiet last night, but I can't guarantee it will remain so this evening."

"And you're sure that Molly and I are the most likely targets of this angry spirit?"

"Quite sure." Decker hoped he was right. Mavis had identified the constable as the only villager left with a direct link to the workhouse, but that didn't mean she was correct. "Your grandfather was the workhouse physician. By all accounts, he was a reviled man who worked closely with James Grayson."

"They were pretty much partners in crime," Mina said. "Excuse the expression."

"I'm well aware of what my grandfather did up at that place. I was only an infant when he died, so I don't remember him, but I've heard the stories. My dad was ashamed of his own father's actions and refused to talk about him, but others in the village were not so tight-lipped. Even the other children at school teased me. I hated my grandfather before I was even old enough to understand his crimes. I became a policeman, in part because of what that man did. Believed the scales could be balanced by good deeds to offset the misery my grandfather caused to so many."

"A noble attitude," Mina said.

"And a naïve one, if what you say is true." There was a note of sorrow in the constable's voice. "My family are going to pay the price for his sins regardless of any good we have done since."

"That's what we're here to stop," Decker said. He glanced toward the window. The shadows were getting along. It would be dark within the hour. "We don't have much time. We should fetch your wife and bring her here."

"The shop doesn't close until four-thirty. She'll go straight home after that. We can meet her there."

"I don't think we can wait that long," Decker said. "And I would rather we bring her to the police station. It's a more secure environment than your house."

"If you think so," the constable said with a shrug.

"I do. Each minute we delay increases the chance that Bradley Wilcox will strike before we are ready for him."

"Which brings me to my next question," the constable said. "How do you plan to protect us if this spirit does try to possess my wife?"

"Let us worry about that," said Skye.

"That's a big ask." The constable didn't look happy. "It's Molly and me who will end up on the receiving end of this if you fail."

"I'm aware of the stakes." Before they had left for the police station, Decker had outlined his plan to Mina and Skye. It was risky. If anything went wrong, the consequences would be catastrophic, but no more so than if they did nothing. At least for the constable and his wife.

"Could you at least tell me what you intend to do?"

"No. It's too risky. Wilcox will possess your wife, I'm sure of it. When he does, he might have access to her knowledge."

"Or he might not," the constable countered.

"True, but if he learns what we are going to do, we won't be able to save her. We can't take that risk," Decker said. "You need to trust us."

The constable was silent for a few moments, then he nodded. "All right. I'll put my trust in you. But if anything happens to Molly, I'm going to hold you responsible, not some ephemeral ghost. Do you understand me?"

"You've made your position clear," said Decker. "Now, if you don't mind, please fetch your wife and bring her to us immediately."

"What are you going to do while I'm gone?" The constable asked, standing up.

Skye glanced down at the doctor's bag sitting on the floor next to her chair. "We're going to set a spirit trap."

# FIFTY-ONE

WHILE THE CONSTABLE went to fetch his wife, Decker watched Skye get to work, preparing for what might turn out to be a harrowing night. He wasn't sure that their hastily conceived and untested plan would work. He wished there was some other way to stop Bradley Wilcox.

"Hey, it's going to be okay," Mina said, coming up beside him and placing a hand on his shoulder.

"Is it that obvious?" Decker asked.

"Just a bit." Mina forced a smile even though Decker could see she was nervous. "We've been through so much together, and both of us are still here. Whatever happens tonight, we'll handle it."

"Can I get a little help here?" Skye asked. She was pulling items from her bag. First came the five candles that they had used up at the workhouse. She also removed a tub of salt. Next came the vial of holy water, which was now refilled.

"Where did you get that?" Decker asked. "Didn't we use it all up at Bartholomew Meadows yesterday?"

229

"I stopped in at the local church during my walk in the village this morning," Skye replied. "The vicar there was more than happy to bless some font water for me, although he said that if I wanted true holy water, I was in the wrong house of worship. But he pointed out that a blessing is a blessing and that, in theory there shouldn't be too much difference between the two. Just to be safe, I took my remaining salt along and had him pray over that, too."

"Wasn't it already blessed?" Mina asked. "I thought that was kind of the point."

"It was, but I thought a second round of blessings couldn't hurt." Skye reached into her bag and brought out one last item. A heavy polished piece of quartz crystal about eight inches long and shaped like an egg, which she placed on the Constable's desk.

"You had that lying around, just in case?" Decker asked, leaning down to study the crystal. It was clear and flawless, almost like a piece of cut glass.

"In my line of work, you never know when a crystal will come in handy. I find it channels my energy like a magnifying glass."

"And it's handy if you want to trap an evil spirit," Mina said.

"That too." Skye grinned. "Although this will be the first time I have had to do that."

"Join the club," Decker said. "I don't like this ghost stuff. Give me a flesh and blood monster any day."

"And that's why I call him Mister Monster Hunter." Mina's eyes sparkled as she said that.

"Do I want to know?" Skye asked, raising an eyebrow.

"Probably not." Decker picked up the crystal. "You realize this will need to be put in a safe place once we trap Bradley Wilcox in it?"

"I know." Skye looked at the crystal wistfully. "Shame. I've had this since I was a teenager. What will you do with it?"

"The Order of St. George has a secure vault back in London," Mina said. "The crystal and its unwilling inhabitant will be kept safe and out of harm's way. Wilcox won't bother anyone ever again."

"I'm sure the Order will provide you with a new crystal in exchange," Decker said, placing the gleaming egg back on the desk.

"Not that easy, I'm afraid." Skye touched the crystal as if it were the most precious thing in the world to her. "Only certain crystals will work. I will need to find a replacement with similar harmonics if our energies are to align."

"I wasn't aware of that," Decker said.

"Why would you be, Mr. Decker?" Skye asked.

"You know, you can call me John."

Skye hesitated, then smiled. "Very well, John."

"See. That's better. Everyone in this century is so stiff and formal."

A brief look of confusion passed across Skye's face.

Mina shot Decker a warning glance.

"Let me guess," Skye said. "Some unrelated strangeness the Order is mixed up in?"

"Exactly," Mina replied. "You should probably ignore it."

"Always do." Skye stepped back from the desk and surveyed the assortment of items spread upon it. "Everything we need is here."

"Except the constable and his wife," Mina said.

"And Wilcox," Decker added. "Although a part of me hopes he won't show up."

"I wouldn't count on that." Skye glanced toward the door.

"He's close. I can sense him. His anger is like a dark cloud. Are you sure you want to do this?"

"I think we're past the point of no return," Decker said. "If we don't, Wilcox will surely kill the constable and his wife."

"And if we keep going, he may kill all of us," Skye said. "You know, just so we're aware of what could happen if we fail."

"I'd rather not dwell on that if it's all the same with you." Decker was getting restless. The constable should have returned with Molly by now. He went to the window and peered out. There was no sign of them, but he couldn't help but notice the dark clouds that were gathering over the village even as the sun slipped below the horizon. "Looks like a storm is brewing."

"I don't know why," Mina said. "But somehow, that just seems fitting for a night like this."

"And dangerous." Skye paced across the room and joined Decker at the window. She glanced up at the loaded, ashen sky. "The last thing we need is a thunderstorm right now. Spirits draw their power from the surrounding energy. It will make Wilcox even stronger and harder to defeat."

"Nothing we can do about that unless you think he'll agree to wait for more favorable weather."

"What do you think?" Skye didn't sound happy.

"I think we're in it up to our necks." Decker was about to turn away from the window when he caught sight of a solitary figure hurrying toward them along the High Street. It was the constable.

"Where's his wife?" Skye asked, a hint of panic in her voice.

"That's an excellent question," Decker said as the constable drew closer. "I have a bad feeling about this."

"Me too," Skye replied as the door opened, and Alfred Trent walked in with a worried look on his face.

"She wasn't at the shop," he said, voice trembling. "The door was standing wide open, the till was unlocked, but Molly wasn't there. She's gone."

# FIFTY-TWO

MINA TOOK a step toward the constable. "What do you mean, your wife is gone?"

"Exactly what I said. The shop was empty. She wasn't there. The open sign was still in the window, but the door was wide open as if she had just gotten up and walked out. Molly would never leave the shop unattended with the door like that."

"Maybe she went home for some reason?" Decker said. A tingle of dread crawled up his spine. "You can't live far from the shop."

"Less than a minute. It was the next place I went, but she wasn't there either." The constable paced back and forth. "This isn't right. Something has happened to her. I know it."

"Is there anywhere else she would have gone?" Decker asked. "Any friends she might have visited or errands she may have run?"

"No. Sometimes she helps the older villagers with their shopping. Carries it back to their homes for them. But she always closes up first, and she's never gone for more than a few minutes. The village isn't large."

"I hate to state the obvious," Skye said. "But it looks like Wilcox may already have found the constable's wife."

"If he did, then where is she?" The same thought had occurred to Decker, but it left him wondering what the vengeful spirit's intentions might be. Every other time Wilcox had possessed someone, it had quickly ended in bloodshed. If the constable was the next target, his wife should have been close at hand. Instead, she appeared to be missing. It didn't fit the pattern, and that concerned Decker.

"Maybe Wilcox knows what we're planning to do," Mina said. "He could be avoiding us."

"I don't buy that." Decker shook his head. "He wouldn't need to possess the constable's wife in order to hide from us."

"We don't know that he possessed my wife," the constable said, a glimmer of hope playing across his face. "Not for sure."

"True. There may be a more mundane explanation," Decker replied. "But you said it yourself. Your wife would never leave the shop unattended and the door open for no good reason. Until we know otherwise, we must assume that Wilcox is in control of her."

"Which brings us back to the question of what he's up to," Skye said. "If we assume that Wilcox is unaware of our trap, then there must be another motivation for his change in behavior."

"I agree." Decker turned back to the window and studied the streetscape beyond. It was almost dark now. The village was swathed in a strange and gloomy twilight. He watched a man in a flat cap hurry toward the Black Dog Pub, shoulders hunched against the weather, even as the rain started falling. The weather was declining rapidly. A flicker of lightning flashed across the sky, followed a few seconds later by an ominous rumble of thunder. Decker turned away from the window and observed his companions. "We should search the village. Check everywhere we can think of. The constable's wife must be out there somewhere."

"It will go quicker if we split up," Mina said, reaching for her coat. "I'll go with the constable and take the east side of the village."

"Skye and I will head in the other direction toward the pub." Decker was already on his way to the door. He stopped and turned back to the constable. "Can you think of any friends or acquaintances that your wife might have gone to?"

"There's Betty Thomson at number thirty-six Folkestone Street," the constable replied. "That's the road behind the pub. She plays bridge there on Friday nights with a couple of the other village women. I can't see any reason that she would go there now, though, especially when she is supposed to be working the shop."

"We'll check there anyway," Decker said. "Anywhere else?"

"No. Molly has a couple of friends on the other side of the village, but I can check there myself."

"Fair enough." Decker waited for Skye to join him and opened the door. "Let's meet back here in thirty minutes."

"I doubt it will take that long," the constable said. "The village is small and there aren't many places Molly would go."

"In that case return here as soon as you're done." Decker stepped out into the rain. It was coming down heavy now. Huge drops that soaked him within moments despite the heavy coat that he pulled around his frame.

With Skye at his side, Decker started toward the Black Dog, wishing he had possessed the forethought to purchase a cap. The constable and Mina headed in the other direction. When Decker glanced back, they were nothing but gray silhouettes shrinking into the rain-drenched night.

"Do you really think we'll find her in the pub?" Skye asked. "Or at a friend's house?"

"Not for a second," Decker said. "But we have to eliminate the most obvious places before we decide what to do next. At this point, we're not even sure if the constable's wife has fallen under the influence of Wilcox or is just helping someone home with their heavy groceries."

"I hope you're right," Skye replied as they neared the pub. "But my sixth sense is telling me that something is dreadfully wrong."

"Yeah. Mine too." Decker pulled the pub door open and stepped inside, shaking the rain from his coat. The saloon was empty except for a couple of diehard regulars that he had seen once or twice in passing.

The landlord was behind the bar wiping glasses with a cloth. He glanced up as they approached. "You look like a pair of drowned rats. Whatever were you doing out in that weather?"

"Looking for the constable's wife, Molly," Decker replied. "Have you seen her?"

"Not today." The landlord set down the glass he was holding before turning his attention back to Decker and Skye. "Have you tried the corner shop? She works there on Wednesdays until five."

"Yes. She's not there."

"Can't help you, then."

Decker asked the landlord to keep a watchful eye and turned to leave. There was one more place to visit. He didn't think for one moment that Molly would be at her friend's house, but they must leave no stone unturned, as the saying went.

He made his way back toward the door, and as he went, he noticed a gaunt man in a black suit sitting in the furthest corner of the barroom. He was tucked back into the shadows, melting into them almost like a chameleon. Were it not for his sallow complexion, the man might not have drawn Decker's attention.

There was something about the man that set Decker's nerves jangling. He hesitated, taking a small misstep. He almost changed direction and headed toward the odd gentleman in the black suit, as much to satisfy his own uneasy curiosity as to ask about the constable's wife. But the man folded his arms and looked down into a pint of dark beer sitting on the table in front of him in an apparent effort to avoid contact. Decker almost continued anyway, but then thought better of it. There were more pressing concerns than investigating a stranger sitting in the bar, no matter how unorthodox his manner might be.

"What are you waiting for?" Skye asked, reaching for the pub door and pulling it open.

"Nothing." Decker shook off his disquietude and stepped through the door, back out into the pouring rain.

# FIFTY-THREE

IT TOOK LESS than ten minutes to confirm that Molly Trent was not at her friend's house on Folkestone Street. They hurried back through the village toward the police station, looking forward to getting out of the storm. Along the way, they came to the corner shop. An open sign still hung in the window, but the door was closed, no doubt by the constable after he ascertained that his wife was not there.

Decker was curious. He reached out and tried the handle, finding it unlocked, and hurried inside. Skye hesitated a moment on the pavement, then followed him in.

"What are you doing?" She asked. "We already know that Molly Trent isn't here."

"I figured it couldn't hurt to take a second look," Decker replied. "I don't wish to disparage the constable, but he doesn't strike me as the most observant fellow. He may very well have missed some small detail that would alert us to his wife's location."

"You mean like the odor hanging in the air?" Skye said. "It's faint, but definitely there."

"Yes, just like that," Decker said. He hadn't noticed until now, but once Skye mentioned it, he became aware of a mild smell of rot permeating the shop. It reminded him of the stench up at Bartholomew Meadows when they encountered the demon, only much less obvious. "Unless there are some rotten eggs around, I think we just found proof that Molly was possessed."

"Curious." Skye looked perplexed. "I wouldn't have expected a spirit like that of Wilcox to give off such a malodor. Sulfur is usually associated with a truly malevolent entity. One consumed by pure evil."

"You don't think Wilcox is evil?" Decker moved further into the shop. "He has killed six people in the last week, and that's not counting those who died either directly or otherwise at his hands during the workhouse when the inmates were set free."

"True. But his motivation was revenge. He wasn't an inherently evil man." Skye wandered down one of the aisles, her gaze roving one way and then the other. After a moment, she looped back and returned to the front shop. "The smell is stronger near the counter."

"Where Molly would have been."

"Presumably." Skye came to a halt near the door and closed her eyes. She breathed deeply, as if centering herself.

Decker watched in silence, unsure what was happening but sensing that he should not interfere.

When Skye opened her eyes again, she looked concerned. "Wilcox was definitely here. I can sense the lingering remnants of his energy laying heavy in the air like a fog of evil. Wilcox might have been motivated by revenge when this began, but now he's driven by pure hatred."

"Which begs the question, why hasn't he gone after the

constable yet? There's no other reason he would take Molly Trent."

"Maybe he wanted to separate us first," Skye said. "If I can sense him, then he can sense me."

"I wish you hadn't said that." Decker felt his chest tighten. Mina was with Alfred Trent at that very moment. If Molly and the evil entity that hid within her were out there right now hunting the constable, then both of them were in a world of danger. "I think it's time we got back to the police station."

"I agree." Skye was already halfway through the door. But then she stopped and backpedaled, slipping past Decker back into the shop. "Hold on."

"What are you doing?"

"Stocking up on supplies." She hurried toward the back of the shop and grabbed several items from a shelf. When she returned, her arms were loaded with as many packages of table salt as she could carry. "If we are going to battle with a spirit consumed by evil, we need the ammunition to fight back."

"Will that work?" Decker asked. "It's not blessed."

"Salt that has been sanctified will work better, but any garden-variety sodium chloride will do, especially if I cut it with the blessed stuff I already have." Skye scooped up a brown paper bag from the counter and deposited the packages of salt inside, then headed back to the door and stepped past Decker back outside and into the raging storm. "I'll settle up with the shop owner later."

They hurried along the road toward the police station.

A flash of lightning so bright that it lit up the High Street as if it were daylight streaked across the sky, followed immediately by a boom of thunder that shook the ground under their feet.

They reached the police station and tumbled inside, drenched and freezing.

Decker was disappointed to find that they were alone. The constable and Mina had not returned yet.

Skye went to the desk and set about preparing the salt she had acquired, mixing it with what she already had.

Decker stood in the open doorway and peered out, scanning the street for any sign of the others. "Maybe I should go back out and look for them."

"We're safer here," Skye said. "If Wilcox comes looking for us, we stand a better chance of defeating him on friendly ground."

"It's not us he's looking for," Decker reminded her.

"You can't know that. At this point, he might just be hunting for anyone he perceives as having wronged him, and Mina repelled his attempts to possess her. Pushed him out. That could make her a target."

"Which is why I need to find them before it's too late," Decker said.

"If you feel that's the best course of action, I can't stop you," Skye said, turning to Decker. "But keep in mind, you will play into the spirit's hands by further separating us."

"Then come with me." Decker was growing tired of this debate. Every moment spent discussing their next move increased the likelihood that something awful would befall Mina and the constable.

"That's a terrible idea." Skye shook her head. "If we encounter Wilcox out there in the storm, I can't perform a ritual to trap him. We won't be able to draw a salt circle or light the candles. We will be at a distinct disadvantage."

"Better than the alternative." Decker could feel the frustration rising inside him like a dark wave. Inaction was the enemy of success. He was about to tell her to do whatever she wanted and head out into the storm alone, but then he caught a movement from the corner of his eye. He turned toward it and saw two figures stumbling toward him through the maelstrom.

It was Mina and the constable.

They hurried up the steps and into the police station, dripping water on the floor as they peeled off their sodden coats.

Then Mina turned to Decker and spoke in a grave tone. "We know where Molly Trent has gone. And you're not going to like it one bit."

# FIFTY-FOUR

"BARTHOLOMEW MEADOWS," Mina said as if the very words themselves were loaded with evil. "Molly went to the workhouse."

"How do you know that?" Decker asked.

The constable stepped forward. "We ran into Sarah Hemming. One of the ladies in Molly's Friday night bridge club. She was on the way back from visiting her mother and saw my wife walking out on the old carriage road. She called out to her and asked where she was going. At first, Molly acted like she didn't hear, but then she stopped and told Sarah to give me a message."

"She said the constable had until seven this evening to meet her up at the workhouse, or he would regret it," Mina said. "Sarah was on her way here to find the constable and deliver the message when we crossed paths with her."

"Seven o'clock?" Decker glanced at the clock near the door. It was almost six already. "That doesn't give us much time."

"We can't go along with that ultimatum. It's crazy." Skye's

brow knotted with concern. "You saw what happened yesterday when we went up there. We almost unleashed an inhuman entity with the power to wipe out the entire village. It's too dangerous. Wilcox will be too strong. Especially with that storm raging outside. And let's not forget, the demon is still up there, too."

"That might be why Wilcox went back there." Decker hated to admit it, but Wilcox had outplayed them. "We're going to need a new plan of action."

"If only we could wait for the weather to clear," Mina said. "Without the storm's energy to draw on, Wilcox might be weaker."

"Even then, it wouldn't be a fair fight," Skye said. "He'd still have the advantage. That place is steeped in negative energy. Better to avoid it altogether. Wilcox won't harm Molly. Not until he gets what he wants. I suggest we stay right here and force him to come to us. When he does, we'll be ready for him."

"You want to call his bluff?" Decker didn't like that idea.

"It might be our best option."

"Or he might get angry when I don't show up and just kill my wife," the constable said. "I have no intention of sitting around here hoping Wilcox will play the game we want him to. The rest of you can do what you want, but I'm going to Bartholomew Meadows."

"You can't go up there alone. It will be a death sentence." Skye took a step toward the constable. "For both you and your wife. It's not just Wilcox. There are dangerous entities up at Bartholomew Meadows. Inhuman ones."

"Demons," added Mina.

"I don't believe in demons," the constable replied. "And if I sit around here cowering in fear, Molly might not survive the night."

"The constable is right," Decker said. "We must go to the workhouse. All of us. One way or the other, this has to end."

"Did you not hear what I said?" Skye shot back, her voice rising in pitch. "There's at least one cacodemon up there. And it's angry. We denied it entrance into this world. Do you have any idea what it will do if we return there?"

"What's a cacodemon?" The constable asked.

"One of the worst kinds of supernatural entity. Think of it like a regular demon, only bigger, angrier, and meaner. Everything that haunts your nightmares."

"And my wife is up there with that thing?" A look of anguish crossed the constable's face. He made for the door. "That settles it. I'm going to get her back."

Decker stepped in his path. "Not on your own. We stick together." His gaze shifted to Skye. "Look, I know you're scared, but we don't have a choice."

"I don't think you understand what we're up against." Skye folded her arms in defiance. "This isn't some troubled spirit that doesn't know it has passed over. It's evil incarnate, and it wants out. Maybe if I had more time to prepare—"

Mina shook her head. "We're going to the workhouse right now. If you refuse to come with us, then at least tell us how to fight this thing."

There was a moment of silence. Skye glanced toward the paraphernalia spread across the desk. The holy water, salt, candles, and the egg-shaped crystal. For a moment, she wavered, then threw her arms up and went to the desk, collecting everything and putting it back in her bag. "Damn it. You'll never survive up there without me."

"You'll come with us then." Decker breathed a sigh of relief.

"Against my better judgment." Skye reached for her coat. "But here's the thing, if we're going to do this and stand a chance of surviving, everyone will have to do exactly as I say."

"Just tell us what you need us to do," Decker said. "We're ready."

"It's a cacodemon. Trust me, you're not ready." Skye grabbed the bag and started toward the door. "There's no time to waste. I'll go over everything you need to know on the way up there."

"Thank you," the constable said, looking relieved. "I appreciate this."

"Don't thank me yet," Skye said, before opening the door and stepping out into the storm. "For all I know, we'll all end up as ghosts ourselves by the end of the night."

# FIFTY-FIVE

THIRTY MINUTES LATER, they arrived at the stone archway leading to Bartholomew Meadows in a horse-drawn cart the constable had borrowed from the village greengrocer, because it was the closest transportation on hand. It was open topped and did nothing to protect them from the raging storm. Lightning flashed across the sky like angry spears of crackling energy thrown by the gods, illuminating the landscape below in brief flashes of stark white brightness. Peals of thunder rumbled with such frequency that it was almost impossible to hear Skye's instructions. She was forced to shout at the top of her voice, battling the screaming wind and booming sky.

At the gates, they jumped out of the cart and waited while the constable tied the horse to a post lest it get spooked and run.

Skye waited for him to complete the task then turned to them. "Does everyone understand what they need to do when we get in there?"

One by one, each of them affirmed they did.

Satisfied with their answers, Skye turned and led the way up the driveway on foot toward the workhouse. They walked in a tight group, hunched against the storm. No one spoke. At the doors leading into the lobby, Skye paused again. She placed the bag on the ground and opened it, pulling items out and distributing them. She gave Mina and the constable packages of salt. To Decker, she handed the five candles. Lastly came the crystal, which she kept for herself.

"When we get inside, there won't be much time," Skye said. "Do your job quickly, and whatever happens, don't let yourselves get distracted."

"Is it going to work?" The constable asked.

"I don't know." Skye cradled the crystal in one hand and pushed the door wide with the other. She kneeled and rummaged in the bag one last time, lifting out a ragged leather-bound book.

"Is that your grimoire?" Decker asked.

"Yes. The incantation to trap a spirit is in here."

"You don't have it memorized?"

"I know some of the more common incantations, like the one we used to open a channel to the spirit world the last time we were here," Skye said. "But this is different. Instead of opening the doorway, we are trying to draw a spirit into the crystal and slam one shut. It's not like I do that every day."

"Point taken."

"Good. Now let's get this done." Skye stepped inside with the grimoire in one hand and the crystal in the other.

The constable carried a lantern that he had brought with him. Before they followed Skye across the threshold, he lit it.

"She's not here," he said, holding the lantern high and turning in a circle, watching the flickering orange light push the shadows away.

"Trust me, she's close by," Skye said.

"Is the spirit still inside of her?"

"Yes. And his energy is getting stronger. Your wife will show herself soon enough." Skye made straight for the center of the room and set the crystal down. "We have little time left."

Decker nodded and placed the candles at the five points of the pentagram, just like they had done before and lit them with matches from a box Skye had given him on the way up to the workhouse.

The constable placed the lantern on the ground next to the crystal. He stepped back, still clutching the box of salt. He and Mina headed in opposite directions, sprinkling it as they went. But instead of drawing a protective circle around them with salt, they spread it across the front doorway and around the edges of the room. Instead of forming a protective barrier around themselves, the salt would prevent Wilcox from leaving. In effect, they were sealing themselves in alongside him. Because once Wilcox realized what they were going to do, he would try to take flight, and they couldn't allow that.

Their trap set, everyone congregated in the middle of the room and waited to see what would happen next. It didn't take long to find out.

# FIFTY-SIX

"I SEE the constable did as he was told. And he brought some friends with him."

The sudden voice startled Decker. He looked up to see a middle-aged woman in a torn and sodden yellow dress standing on the second-floor balcony above them near the broken railing.

"Molly!" Constable Trent took a step forward.

"That's not your wife," Skye warned him.

"I assure you it is. Or at least, it's her body." Molly spoke in a rasping voice that sounded strange coming from a middle-aged woman. It was too low. Deep. Decker recognized it as the same voice he had heard coming from the lips of Violet Hughes right before she killed herself. Or rather, before Wilcox killed her. "But don't worry. Her consciousness is rattling around somewhere. I can hear it nagging at me, screaming to be set free."

"Let her go." The constable was trembling with rage. "If you hurt her . . ."

"What will you do?" Molly stepped away from the

251

railing and walked toward the stairs. She descended slowly, her eyes never straying from the constable. When she reached the bottom, her gaze flicked briefly to the oval crystal sitting in the middle of the room, surrounded by candles. A wicked smile stretched across her face. "Ah. I see. You want to trap me just like that unpleasant spiritualist the villagers sent up here did all those years ago."

"That's right," Skye said, stepping forward with the grimoire in her hands. She opened it and turned to a page marked by a slip of paper, then began reciting the incantation written upon it in a commanding tone.

Molly came to a halt. A strange look passed across her face, as if she were in mild discomfort, but it vanished as quickly as it had appeared. "Is that all you've got?"

Skye ignored her and kept going.

Decker wished there was something he could do to help, but everyone except Skye had been reduced to bystanders.

Molly started forward again, heading straight for the constable. She raised her hand, and Decker saw the knife, previously hidden in the folds of her dress.

Skye had seen the knife as well. She recited the words faster. The incantation tripped from her mouth as it built to a crescendo. She balanced the book in one hand, then reached down and picked up the crystal, holding it in the other. She held it forward, aiming the narrow curved top of the stone toward Molly as if it were some kind of psychic gun.

The constable's wife hesitated. She took a faltering step. The knife dropped lower.

Decker saw his chance. He sprinted forward, intent on disarming the woman.

Molly anticipated his assault. She sidestepped and brought the knife down in a wide slashing arc that caught his arm. He felt a stinging pain and warm blood welling from the wound as he sailed harmlessly past her.

Decker flailed wildly, trying to stop his forward momentum and stay on his feet. He turned back in time to see Molly lunging toward her husband.

Mina let out a savage cry and leaped forward, pushing the constable aside in the nick of time.

Skye finished the incantation and slammed the book shut, holding the crystal at arms-length. If she expected something to happen, she was disappointed.

Molly gave a low chuckle and turned to the spirit medium. "Foolish woman. That won't work on me twice. I'm stronger now."

The building's front doors flew back on their hinges with a mighty crash. A sudden gust of rain-soaked wind whipped through the lobby, extinguishing the candles. The lantern tipped sideways onto its side. The flame inside flickered and waned.

Decker made a mad grab for it, aware that if the lantern went out, they would be plunged into total darkness. He scooped it up just in time to save the flame, which steadied itself and flared bright again. When he looked up, he expected to see Molly advancing on the constable once more, but Wilcox had other ideas. He turned toward Skye, a vicious snarl contorting his host body's face.

"I've had enough of these petty games," he said, moving toward her like a big cat stalking its prey, the knife still clutched in Molly's hand.

Skye scooted back to evade the sudden attack, but Molly was too quick. She darted forward with such speed that Skye had little time to react. All she could do was throw her arms up to fend off the knife that she expected to come arching toward her at any moment.

But it didn't.

Molly had other ideas. She swatted the crystal from Skye's hand and sent it tumbling to the ground. It hit with a thud and rolled away, coming to rest at the foot of the stairs.

Decker was crestfallen to see a large crack weaving through the previously perfect oval of quartz. He didn't know if that would affect its power, but he suspected the crystal was now useless.

"Decker," Mina screamed.

He turned to see that Molly had Skye in her grasp. She had gripped the spirit medium by the throat and lifted her from the floor in a display of inhuman strength.

Mina rushed forward but stopped short when she saw the knife in Molly's free hand.

Skye kicked and gasped for breath, batting at her assailant with her free hand. Her bulging eyes locked on to Decker's and an unspoken understanding passed between them.

She lifted the grimoire and tossed it clumsily in Decker's direction even as Molly tried to bat it away.

The book sailed past her and landed on the floor a few feet from Decker.

He made a diving grab for it as Molly turned, Skye still in her grasp, and tried to intercept him.

This time, Mina was ready. She barreled into Molly, sending her staggering sideways just as Decker lunged at the book and snatched it up.

Molly brought the knife around.

Mina jumped sideways, barely avoiding a slashing sweep that threatened to rip her open.

The constable stood rooted to the spot, locked in indecision.

"Page sixty-six," Skye gasped, pawing at Molly's hand

around her throat in a futile attempt to break free. "The portal incantation. Use it."

Decker flicked through the pages until he found the right one. But then he hesitated, his eyes lingering on the warning written above it in scrolling handwriting. "This says it will rip open a gateway between the spirit world and our own," he said, remembering the demon that had appeared when they used Skye's hand mirror to talk with the dead. If this truly breached the veil, who knew what might come through?

"Just do it," Skye sputtered, even as her eyes rolled up into her head and she lost consciousness.

"There's no time," Mina screamed. "Do what she wants. Read the incantation."

Decker hesitated a moment longer, but he knew there was no choice. Skye wouldn't survive much longer in the grip of the vengeful spirit possessing Molly. With a heavy heart, he looked down at the page and started to read.

# FIFTY-SEVEN

THE REACTION WAS INSTANT. The room around them crackled as if it were alive with electricity. Fingers of electrical energy arched overhead. From somewhere behind Decker, there was a blast of fetid air. He turned in time to see a shimmering crack appear in the middle of the room as if the very air itself was being torn apart.

He took a step back in alarm and almost dropped the book, but somehow managed to keep it firm in his grasp and continued reading.

The crack widened, spilling blinding white light into the lobby.

"It's working," Mina shouted over the howling supernatural wind that erupted from the quickly opening portal. "Keep going."

"What is that?" The constable stumbled backward. For a moment, he looked like he might turn and bolt from the room in a panic, but then he regained his wits.

"No." Molly spun around, releasing Skye, and throwing

her across the floor, where she landed in an unmoving heap. "You can't do this."

"Just watch him!" Mina screamed at the infuriated woman, even as Molly lunged forward to pry the book from Decker's hands in an attempt to stop him.

Decker stepped sideways and barely avoided the constable's wife and the spirit that possessed her.

He kept reading. Faster now.

Molly swiveled and lunged again. This time, she anticipated Decker's attempts to evade her and gripped the book, almost wrenching it from Decker's hands.

He struggled to hold on to it, felt himself losing the battle.

The incantation was almost complete. As his fingers slipped from the leather-bound volume and Molly tossed it away with a triumphant howl, he shouted the final words from memory.

A loud crack like a sonic boom echoed through the building. The portal's edges folded back to reveal a shimmering and translucent nothingness with undulating flickers of brighter whiteness that played across it like waves on a pond. And from this strange realm, figures appeared. They were nothing more than ghostly silhouettes at first, but then they became more solid even as the portal itself faded away and dissipated into the ether on gossamer threads.

Decker could hardly believe his eyes. There were at least twenty ghostly entities. They wore clothing that looked old-fashioned. A nurse's uniform. Overalls. Button-down shirts and coarse workman's trousers held up by suspenders. These were the people that died on that fateful night so many decades ago, killed by the newly freed inhabitants of Bartholomew Meadows.

"Decker," Mina breathed. "Are you seeing this?"

"Yes," he replied, unable to look away. And then Decker

realized something. Molly was not attacking him anymore. Instead, she stood with her arms at her sides and stared at the cadre of phantoms that had appeared from the void. Or rather, at one particular phantom.

She stood in the center of the group wearing a long, flowing white dress. Her cascading hair was the color of freshly mowed hay. She looked at Molly, or rather the spirit inside of her, as if she were seeing an old friend for the first time in decades. Or maybe not an old friend. Maybe a husband.

"Bradley," the apparition said in a voice that somehow sounded close and far away both at the same time.

"Fannie. Is it really you?" The spirit inside of Molly sounded awestruck.

"It's me." the apparition nodded, then looked around the lobby. "Bradley. You have to stop this. The killing. It's not right."

"I did it for you," the spirit inside of Molly sounded desperate. "To avenge what they did to you in this place."

"There's nothing to avenge. Not anymore. Everyone responsible for my suffering is long dead."

"But their children still live, and their children's children. It's not right that they should enjoy life while you suffer in hell."

"Foolish man. I'm not in hell. I've been waiting for you all this time." The woman's face softened into a radiant smile. "Come with me, Bradley. Leave these people alone and come with me."

"I can't. I don't know how." Molly took a step forward, reached a hand toward Fannie Wilcox.

"It's easy. Just let that poor woman go. Release her."

Molly nodded.

Decker backed away from the cluster of apparitions. He

glanced toward Skye. She was still unconscious. He resisted the urge to go to her, for fear of enraging the spirit within Molly once more.

But when he looked back at the constable's wife, she was walking toward the apparitions with her hands extended. Fannie met her halfway and their fingers touched. There was a momentary flash of light, and then Molly stumbled backward in a daze, leaving the ethereal form of Bradley Wilcox standing with his wife.

Decker held his breath even as the constable raced to embrace Molly.

Then, one by one, the spirits faded. They turned away and walked into thin air, returning to wherever they had come from. Soon, only two apparitions remained. Bradley Wilcox and his wife, Fannie. They lingered a moment, staring at each other like a pair of long-lost lovers, and then they turned hand-in-hand and faded from view.

"Is that it?" The constable asked, mouth agape. "Are we safe now?"

"Safer than we were ten minutes ago." Decker rushed to Skye's side. As he reached her, she groaned and pushed herself up.

Her hands went straight to her throat and rubbed it. When she spoke, her voice was hoarse. "I knew I'd regret coming here. Damned evil spirit almost throttled me."

"It didn't turn out to be so evil in the end," Decker said.

"Easy for you to say when you weren't having the life crushed out of you." Skye glanced around. "What happened, anyway? Did you open the portal?"

"Yes, and the spirits came through just like you thought they would. Including Fannie Wilcox. She convinced her husband to join her on the other side."

"Huh. That wasn't my plan. I figured if we opened a

gateway to the hereafter, the spirits of all those people who died because of Wilcox would come and drag him down to hell."

"I like it better this way," Decker said. He climbed to his feet and extended a hand toward Skye, and helped her up. "I guess all that's left to do is clean up our mess and get out of here."

"Sounds good to me," Skye said, but then a cloud passed across her face. "John. Where's Mina?"

Decker looked around, scanning the lobby. When he didn't see her, an alarm bell went off in his head. "I don't know. She was here moments ago." He looked at the constable. "Did you see where she went?"

"No. I was too busy tending to my wife."

"I have a bad feeling about this," Skye said. "Did you see anything come through the veil when you opened that doorway to the other side? Anything other than human spirits, I mean."

Decker shook his head. "Nothing. Why?"

"Because we aren't alone. I can sense it. An inhuman entity took the opportunity to slip into this world." Skye looked scared. "It's the cacodemon. It was waiting, biding its time."

"So, where is it?" Decker asked, looking around frantically. "I don't see anything."

"That's because it found somewhere to hide," Skye said. She reached out and gripped Decker's arm. "There's only one reason Mina would be missing. The demon took her."

# FIFTY-EIGHT

"MINA," Decker said in a small voice. He gripped the lantern and held it high, examining the lobby for any sign of where Mina might have gone. When he came up empty, Decker grimaced. "This place is enormous. We'll never find her."

"She was near the stairs," the constable said. "I think she might have gone up."

"Why didn't you stop her?" Decker turned on the policeman.

"Why would I?" The constable shrugged. "Besides, I wasn't really paying that much attention to her, what with everything else going on. And anyway, it's not like I would've known that there was a demon inside of her."

"John," Skye said. "We can talk about this later. Let's find her first."

"You're right." Decker started toward the stairs. The constable stayed where he was, attending to his wife, but Skye hurried to catch up with him. Decker stopped and shook his head. "No. Stay here."

"But—"

Decker cut her off. "You almost died. You aren't in any state to face off with a demon. I'll go alone."

"You can't. It's not safe."

"Agreed. But it won't be any safer with you by my side, and it might even be a hindrance. I'll have one more person to look out for. This isn't up for discussion. Stay here and catch your breath. I'll find Mina and bring her back." With that, Decker turned and started up the stairs. For a moment, he thought Skye would follow anyway, but then she slumped and sat down on the first step, apparently still suffering the effects of her near strangulation.

The second level of the old manor house was in worse condition than the lobby. A landing ran in both directions, the railing rotten in places. To his left, Decker could see a break where the railing had collapsed several nights before during the deadly incident that had originally brought him and Mina to this place. The floorboards under his feet creaked and moaned. They felt soft in some spots. Plaster hung from the ceiling above him, peeling back from the joists.

Decker proceeded with caution. He went to the right first, holding the lantern ahead of him to light the way to make sure he didn't put his foot through a rotten floorboard. There were two rooms off the landing, both of which appear to be bedrooms, although neither contained any furniture. There was no sign of Mina, either.

Doubling back, he headed in the other direction, past the shattered railing. There were more rooms on this side of the stairs. Decker remembered from his research that the workhouse master had kept a suite on the second floor. The first door that he tried turned out to be a small box room that contained a mop and pail and some antique tools, all covered in a thick layer of dust. But the second door opened into a much larger space that still held remnants of the furniture that must've belonged to James Grayson and his wife, Bethany. An upright piano stood against one wall. There was a couch, too, its fabric torn and faded. One leg had collapsed, causing the piece of furniture to sit askew. A rug covered in mildew sat underneath it, the pattern indistinguishable thanks to the dust that covered everything and flaking plaster that had fallen from the ceiling. This must have been a lounge or drawing room area, Decker surmised. A door to his right stood open, leading into what looked like a dining room area. On the far wall, he could see a set of pocket doors, one of which was standing half open.

Decker poked his head into the dining room but found it empty. Another door led to a kitchen that was also empty.

Decker hurried back to the drawing room and approached the double doors. He pushed them wider, stepping through. This inner space appeared to be a private study. There was a desk and bookshelves that still contained large volumes with unreadable spines.

There was no sign of Mina.

That left one door on the other side of the study.

When Decker pushed it open, he found a bedroom beyond. A four-poster bed stood against one wall, the fabric of its curtains threadbare and rotted. A vanity with a tarnished and cracked mirror on top occupied the opposite wall. Heavy drapes covered the windows. Even during the day, very little light would have penetrated. Now, with the storm raging outside, the room was swathed in inky blackness.

Decker swung the lantern around to push the gloom away. At first, he thought this room was empty, just like all the others. But then he noticed the smell.

Sulfur.

It permeated the air, getting worse the further into the room Decker went.

The hairs on the back of his arms stood up. Decker couldn't explain how, but he knew he was not alone. The atmosphere in the darkened room was thick with malevolence.

Then he heard the voice behind his back. It sounded like Mina, but he could tell it was not really her. "I've been waiting for you."

Decker spun around. The lantern swung wildly, sending long shadows leaping across the floor. But at first, he still didn't see her. At least until he noticed a pair of eyes glowering at him from a corner that appeared to be draped in impenetrable darkness. Eyes that smoldered an unnatural yellow.

Decker stepped forward with the lantern arms-length until he could make out Mina's face in the shadows.

"Let her go," he said, edging as close as he dared to the demon that occupied his friend's body.

"I'd rather not." The voice sounded less like Mina now. The words almost slithered across her lips, chilling and inhuman. "It's so cozy in here. I like this body."

"Please, just release her," Decker pleaded, desperately trying to think of any way that he could force the demon out of her. He came up blank. "If you want a body, take mine instead."

"I appreciate the offer, but I'll stay where I am," the demon sniggered. "But I should probably thank you for setting me free. You really aren't very good at this monster hunting thing, are you? I guess it must run in the family."

"What do you mean?"

"You really want me to tell you?"

"Sure. Why not?" Decker knew he was being baited, but the longer he kept the demon engaged, the more chance there was for Mina. Which was why he lowered the lantern and met the demon's insidious gaze. "Tell me."

# FIFTY-NINE

"POOR LITTLE JOHNNY BOY," the demon said in a sibilant whisper that sent a chill running up Decker's spine. "I've spoken to your mother in hell. She sends her regards."

"You leave my mother out of this," Decker said. "She's not in hell."

"Oh, but I beg to differ." The demon inside Mina grinned. "She told me all about your father and what he did. The Loup Garou took her as punishment for his sins."

"That's not true." Decker took a step forward, closing the gap between himself and Mina. In response, she moved further into the shadows. Only her eyes, glowing an unnatural shade of yellow, were visible in the darkness. The smell of sulfur was overpowering now.

"Yes, it is, and you've always known it. Even when you were a young boy sitting in that morgue with your mother's lifeless body lying on a cold metal table, you knew it. Even as your father lead you away from that place, his heart heavy because he knew why she had died and what he had done, the thought was in your head. And then you grew up to kill that same Loup Garou. Poor Annie Doucet. Didn't deserve what happened to her. I bet it must have felt so good when you finally got your revenge on the creature that took your mother away."

Decker felt his chest tighten. He swallowed and tried to speak, found that the words would not come.

"What's wrong?" The demon cooed. "You didn't know that your mother was killed by the same unearthly creature that plagued Wolf Haven all those years later? The clues were there all along. You just had to find them. After all, it was your own father that created the creature. He lived with that knowledge for his entire life. That's why he cut it short and left you alone in the world. He couldn't take the guilt. Would you like to ask him about it? I can fetch him for you. He's in hell right alongside your mother."

"Stop it," Decker screamed. "Stop it now. You know nothing about my family."

"I know everything about your family."

"No. You're lying, I—"

"Decker?" The voice changed. It was no longer the demon talking. Mina stepped from the shadows; her face contorted with the effort. Tears streamed down her cheeks. "Don't listen to him. He's trying to—"

"That's enough of that." The demon was back. It cut Mina's plea short and stepped back into the corner, merging with the darkness. "She's a sneaky one, slipping out like that when I wasn't looking."

"Mina." Hope surged through Decker. "If you can still hear me, fight back. Push him out."

"I don't think so." The demon chuckled. "This is my body now. And what a fine body it is. I could live a thousand years in here just on the life force she has stored up right now. A real vampiric. Maybe I'll even live forever if I do what that pathetic girl would not and feed on the human cattle all around me. So much potential. Such a fascinating creature."

"Mina. Resist him. You can do it." Decker hoped he was getting through. If she could not fight the demon off, then he had no other way to defeat it. He didn't even want to think about the carnage such a creature would wreak upon the earth if it were set free for a thousand years or more. "I believe in you."

"How touching." The demon's eyes flashed. "Would you like to say bye-bye to your little friend before I send her into eternal darkness?"

"How about you let her go instead? Leave her body and go back to where you came from."

"You really are an optimist." The demon shifted in the darkness. "I'm tempted to let you live just because it amuses me. The thought of you spending a lifetime knowing I'm out there, living inside of this pretty girl . . . keeping her soul locked away in agony . . . I have to say . . . it's appealing."

Decker wished he still had the grimoire, or maybe the crystal. Anything with which to fight back. But the crystal was irrevocably broken, and the book was back in the lobby. Not that he thought there was an incantation powerful enough to defeat the creature he now faced. All he had were words. "I'll never stop hunting you. I won't stop until I get Mina back."

"I realize that. Which is why I can't let you live. I took a gander through her memories. They make fascinating viewing. You're dangerous. If you were anyone else . . . But not John Decker. You really will follow me to the ends of the earth."

"You'd better believe it."

"Oh, but I do." The demon stepped from the shadows, the darkness falling from him like a discarded cloak. "Now I think it's time we ended this pathetic charade. I'm growing weary of sparring with you. I have places to be. Scores to settle."

"Wait," Decker said. He held the lantern high so that he could see Mina more clearly. An idea had occurred to him. It was a long shot, but it was all he had. "You said I can say goodbye to Mina. At least let me do that before you kill me."

The demon contemplated this a moment, then Mina's lips curled back in a leering grin. "What the hell. If I'm going to send you into eternity, I might as well give you something to ponder until the end of time. You could have spared her, after all. If only you hadn't used that book and set me free."

"Just let me speak to her."

"Very well. I'll grant a dying man one last wish." The demon closed his eyes. When they opened again, the yellow flames that burned within them were gone.

"Decker." It was Mina's voice. "You need to run. Right now. He'll kill you."

"Or you could fight back," Decker said. "You did it before when Wilcox possessed you. You can do it now."

"No. I can't. Oh God, it hurts so much in here. It feels like I'm being torn apart limb from limb. I can't even think straight."

"Focus," Decker said, realizing his opportunity was brief. The demon had let Mina surface, but if he pushed her back down into whatever dark hole he was keeping her in, she might be lost forever. "Don't let him win. If you do, he'll make Abraham Turner look like an amateur."

"I can't . . ." Mina's face contorted in pain. "I'll . . ."

"I believe in you, and I'm not going anywhere. Either you fight back, or the demon will kill me. Your choice."

"Decker . . ." Mina grimaced. She gasped and shook her head before her face relaxed into an expressionless blank.

When she next spoke, the demon was back. "I think that's a good enough farewell." The creature fixed Decker with its flickering yellow eyes. "I have an idea. How about you run and make this a bit more interesting for me? I'll even give you a head start. I haven't hunted a human in so long. What do you say?"

# SIXTY

"I'M NOT GOING ANYWHERE," Decker said defiantly. "If you want to kill me, then get it over with."

"I admire your bravado," the demon hissed. "Pointless as it might be. Although I must admit to being a little disappointed. It would have been nice to make more of a game of it. You might even have escaped."

"I don't believe that, and neither do you." Decker circled around the demon. "You both know I'm no match for a creature such as yourself."

"True. But hope is a powerful motivator. I wonder what you think might be gained by sacrificing yourself?" The demon folded his arms. "Perhaps you're trying to buy time for your companions to escape? The constable and his wife. That inept spiritualist. If so, it's a pointless effort. I'll find them as soon as we're done here. Silence them."

"On the contrary, I'm waiting for Mina," Decker said.

The demon laughed. "Still hoping that she'll—"

There was a moment of silence. A strange expression passed across the demon's face. The yellow glow behind the demon's eyes faded to be replaced by the iridescent blue of Mina's own eyes before it grew bright again.

"No." The demon cocked his head to one side. "I'm not letting you—"

The yellow glow faded again. "Decker. It's me."

"Fight him, Mina. You've got this." Decker took a step forward toward her.

"I'm trying. It's . . ." Mina's voice faded to be replaced by the demon. "I won't allow this. You can't have her back."

As if fighting an internal tug-of-war, Mina reappeared. "Get out of me."

Decker reached for her. "That's it. Keep going."

"Stay away." Mina took a step backward into the darkness at the edge of the room. "I can't keep you safe if—"

"What she means is I might kill you and use your soul as leverage to free myself of her," the demon said in an undulating voice.

"Dammit, Mina." Decker lifted the lantern high and advanced, pushing the gloom back. "Don't let him win."

"She's already lost." The mocking tone of the demon's voice made Decker's heart fall.

But then Mina lifted her head and let out an angry shriek. "This isn't your body to have."

She stumbled forward, clawing at the air as if she were fighting an invisible adversary. Her face twisted into a pained expression, her teeth bared, eyes wide. The yellow glow behind them faded in and out as she fought for her life.

"No." The demon screeched and clawed at its own face . . . At Mina's face.

Decker resisted the urge to intervene, unsure how he could fight an enemy that he could not see or touch.

Mina turned to him, her eyes pleading.

She shook her head as if trying to clear her mind.

Small whimpering sounds mixed with animalistic grunts escaped her lips. Apparently, neither she nor the demon was in control long enough to form a coherent sentence.

And then, before Decker's eyes, Mina's face appeared to blur and morph into two separate countenances. One was the gentle young woman that Decker knew. The other was a frightening visage that he recognized as the creature from the mirror. They flowed over each other, fading in and out like a bad TV picture.

Mina fell to her knees. She arched her back and held her head as if it might split open.

Then, with a scream of anguish, the demon reared itself up, exiting Mina's body like a snake shedding its skin, and stood facing Decker.

With a whimper, Mina dragged herself across the floor away from the devilish creature. She could barely hold her head up and soon slumped to the ground.

The demon looked around as if it were confused to be outside of her body.

It stood over six feet tall, with scaly, rough, mottled brown leathery skin that was pockmarked in places. Its fingers ended in curved talons that it flexed as if it were about to gut him.

But at the same time, it didn't look entirely solid. The creature was not flesh and bone, but rather, it was opaque. He could make out the vague shape of a window behind it.

But that didn't make it any less dangerous.

Decker stepped back instinctively, unsure what the newly expelled demon would do. He glanced toward Mina, who lay unmoving on the dusty floorboards several feet away. He was relieved to see that she was still breathing.

"Hey." A voice spoke from behind him.

Decker turned to see the constable standing in the

doorway. In his hand was the vial of holy water they had procured in the church earlier.

"Skye told me to bring you this." He tossed the small bottle into the room.

Decker snatched it in midair with a one-handed catch and twisted the stopper out. Without waiting, he flung the contents toward the startled demon.

The effect was instant. The water, which would have been harmless under other circumstances, might as well have been pure acid.

The creature recoiled and let out a shriek as the liquid passed through its non-corporeal form. It writhed and twisted. Welts appeared on its skin and burned through as if the water were consuming it. Then, even as it turned and staggered back to Mina, looking for a haven within which to hide, the demon's body broke apart and dissipated into strands of wispy mist that soon faded.

"Is it gone?" The constable took a step into the room and looked around. His eyes were alight with fear.

"I think so." Decker approached Mina and kneeled beside her.

She groaned and pushed herself up on one elbow. Her skin was clammy and drenched in sweat despite the freezing air inside the room. "Did I do it?"

"You did it."

"I'd really like to get out of here now," the constable said from behind Decker. "I left my wife downstairs with that medium woman, and I'd really like to get her away from here before anything else happens."

"Suits me," Mina said, clambering to her feet. She rubbed her neck and winced. "I have the worst headache. Feels like someone put a spike through my brain."

"Can you walk?" Decker asked.

"What do you think?" Mina hurried past him toward the door. "If that demon had snapped off both my legs I'd still find a way to walk out of here." She paused and looked back at Decker, a hint of humor flashing in her eyes despite all she had gone through. "No wonder people don't like the workhouse if this is how you get treated."

# SIXTY-ONE

"HOW LONG WERE YOU STANDING THERE?" Decker asked. They were walking back to the downstairs and the lobby below. At the top of the staircase, he cast a quick glance back to make sure the demon hadn't reappeared.

"Long enough," the constable replied. "Is that creature really gone?"

"I don't know," Decker admitted as they descended the stairs to where Skye and Molly were waiting.

"What if it comes back?"

"Your guess is as good as mine." Decker was relieved to see that the color had returned to Skye's face. The constable's wife looked bedraggled and cold but otherwise in good health. "If you want my advice, you should probably lock this place down tight and stop anyone from ever trespassing in here again."

"You won't get any argument from me on that score." The constable rushed to his wife and put an arm around her.

Skye approached Decker and Mina. "Considering that

you're both here, I assume the demon has been sent back to where it came from?"

"I don't know about that, but it's certainly gone off somewhere to lick its wounds."

"Which means we shouldn't linger here any longer than necessary." Skye looked around nervously. "Creatures like that don't take long to recover. If it didn't end up back in hell, it will come after us again soon enough, and next time we might not be so lucky."

That was all Decker needed to hear. He helped Skye scoop up the candles and the broken crystal. Then they left the workhouse behind, careful not to break the perimeter of salt they had sprinkled around the lobby of Bartholomew Meadows earlier. It would be one more barrier for the demon to traverse if it really was still in there. Decker hoped it wasn't.

The weather was still lousy as they rode back toward the village, sore and tired, but at least the storm had mostly passed. A light drizzle dampened the air, but Decker didn't mind. Anything was better than the oppressive atmosphere inside the workhouse.

At one point, the constable glanced toward him and spoke in a low voice.

"All the stuff that creature said about your friend, Mina?" He asked. "Is it true?"

"Like what?" Decker replied. He had hoped the constable hadn't overheard his conversation with the demon. It appeared he was wrong. He wondered how long the constable had been standing in the doorway, listening.

"Why did the demon think she would live a thousand years?" The constable glanced toward Decker. "And how did she fight it off? What is she?"

"I'm not sure," Decker answered, and it was the truth. "I'm not even sure that she knows herself. All I can tell you is that something happened that changed her. That's how she was able to fend off the demon. She has more resilience than any of us."

"And a much longer lifespan, apparently."

"That remains to be seen." Decker didn't want to be having this conversation. "I know that what you saw up at Bartholomew Meadows tonight was far from ordinary, even fantastical. But I'm going to request that you keep everything you saw and heard to yourself."

"Your request sounds more like a command."

"That's because it is," Decker said. "I can't divulge who we work for, but I can promise that you will be doing your patriotic duty by keeping silent."

"Shouldn't be too hard," the constable said. "Who would ever believe me?"

"Just keep that in mind."

The village was ahead of them now. Decker could see the twinkling lights burning in the windows of cottages and the pale glow of gas lamps that illuminated the High Street. It was a welcome sight.

At the police station, they climbed from the cart and parted ways. The constable took his wife home while Decker, Mina, and Skye retreated to the warmth of the Black Dog pub.

Entering the building, they found a smattering of locals sitting at the bar, nursing pints of beer, but the place was mostly empty.

"I don't know about you, but I could use a stiff drink," Skye said as they made their way through the bar toward the door leading upstairs to their accommodation.

"Me too," said Mina, even though she looked like she was

about to collapse. "But I think I'm going to take a hot bath and climb into bed instead. I'm not sure I have the energy to keep my eyes open much longer, and I still have a killer headache. I don't know what the demon was doing inside there, but I wish he hadn't done it."

"Fair enough." Decker opened the door and waited for the two women to pass through before following them up to the second floor. When they reached Mina's room, he stopped and looked at her. "Are you going to be okay?"

"Sure." Mina forced a smile. "I'll see you in the morning. We'll catch the early train to London."

"Sure." Decker waited for Skye to enter her own bedroom, then turned back to Mina. "Maybe on the journey, you can tell me a little more about what you've been doing all this time. You've been so tightlipped."

"I know." Mina nodded. "I spent a quarter of a century on my own here. I've wanted to share my experiences with you, but it's been so weird having you around again. I'd given up hope."

"I'm here now," Decker said.

Mina laid a hand on his arm. "And I wouldn't have it any other way. Tomorrow, okay?"

"Tomorrow." Decker bade her good night and moved off toward his own room. Once inside, he stood there for a long while contemplating what it must have been like for Mina to be trapped in the past for so long with no hope of rescue. But it was different now. He'd found her, and even better than that, he might even know a way to get them both home. But all that could wait. There was nothing he could do at that moment.

Decker quickly changed into dry clothes, freshened up, and stepped back out into the corridor. Then he went downstairs to warm himself by the flames roaring in the saloon bar's fireplace and have that stiff drink. When he got there, he found Skye had beaten him to it. Even better, she had a double measure of scotch sitting on the bar with his name on it.

# SIXTY-TWO

CONSTABLE ALFRED TRENT waited until his wife was asleep, then stood up from the chair in the corner of the bedroom where he had been sitting since bringing Molly home and putting her to bed several hours before. She was exhausted but otherwise physically fine. He still didn't understand exactly what had happened up at the workhouse, but he was relieved the ordeal was over and Molly was safe at home.

As for John Decker and his two companions, the constable would not relax until they were gone from the village. They had brought nothing but trouble since their arrival, and he didn't care who they worked for. He wanted his life to go back to the way it was before. No unexplained deaths. No creepy strangers in black suits skulking around. No portals to the spirit realm. But in order for that to happen, he still had one thing left to do.

After double checking that his wife was asleep, Alfred went downstairs. As he put his coat on, the grandfather clock in the hallway chimed ten somber peals, reminding him how late it was. Alfred paused a while, listening to make sure his wife had not stirred, then opened the front door and slipped out into the cold and dark night. The storm had passed hours ago, and the sky was clear now. He could see stars twinkling like a million tiny lanterns across the firmament. The almost full moon hung low above the rooftops. It lit his way as he hurried toward the High Street and the Black Dog.

When he entered the bar, he spied the man in the black suit immediately. He was sitting in the pub's snug, a small room made up of stained-glass panels and dark oak on the left side of the bar that afforded those within more privacy. The drinks cost a little more if you want to sit in the snug, but the constable didn't care about that. He went to the bar, ordered himself a large rum and black to stave off the deep chill that had wormed its way into his bones, and approached the man he had gone there to see.

"Do you have the information that I require?" the man in the black suit asked as the constable settled into a chair opposite him.

The constable nodded. "That girl ain't right. There's something strange about her, that's for sure."

"Please, elaborate." The man sipped his own drink. Neat scotch that he consumed without expression.

The constable suppressed a shudder and divulged everything he had overheard. He told him about what had occurred up at the workhouse and the confrontation between John Decker and the demon that had possessed Mina. When he got to the part about her living a thousand years, he almost didn't repeat it, not because Decker had asked for discretion, but because it sounded insane. But then he decided it was no less crazy than anything else that occurred that day and blurted it out.

When he was finished, a silence fell between them that

was only broken when Alfred shifted nervously in his seat. "If that's all you need, I'll be off back to my wife."

The man in the black suit remained silent for a moment longer before nodding slowly. He fixed the constable with piercing gray eyes. "If it becomes necessary, I know where to find you."

"Right-ho." The constable picked up his rum with shaking hands and drained it in one go. He couldn't wait to escape the snug. Being in this man's presence made his skin crawl. And worse, he wasn't sure whether that last remark was an innocent observation or a threat. To Alfred, it sounded more like the latter. He placed the tumbler back on the table, a little too hard, and jumped up.

He mumbled a hurried farewell and retreated back through the bar, heart pounding in his chest. It was only when the constable was outside in the frigid night air that he felt safe again.

# SIXTY-THREE

THE MAN in the black suit sat and watched Constable Alfred Trent leave the pub. Then he sat there some more, contemplating the dregs of his drink, before finishing it and standing.

It was almost eleven. Closing time. Only a couple of hard-core stragglers remained perched at the old oak bar on two stools. Neither paid any attention to him as he smoothed out his suit jacket and crossed the room toward the door leading upstairs. The publican, busy with a mop, cleaning assorted beer spills and drips from the floor behind the bar, paid no heed either as he opened the door and slipped through.

Less than a minute later, he was standing outside room six. He glanced around to make sure the corridor was empty, listened a moment for any sign of movement from the other rooms. When he was satisfied that no one else would disturb him, the man in the black suit gave the door of room number six a pair of short, quiet raps with his knuckles.

After a few seconds, the door opened to reveal a young

woman dressed in a cotton nightgown covered by a flannel robe, which she quickly tied closed.

"I think you might have the wrong room," the young woman said.

"Oh, I don't think so." The girl who stood before him was young and pretty, but the man in the black suit would not be fooled by her exterior appearance. He knew what she was. And he knew who she was. "Mina, will you please let me inside?"

"I don't think so." A look of alarm passed across Mina's face. She tried to slam the door, but the man in the black suit made sure that the toe of his shoe was next to the frame, stopping it from clicking shut.

"Trust me, my dear, this will go much easier if you just do as I say." The man in the black suit glanced toward the room occupied by Mina's companion. The man named John Decker, who had arrived in the village with her. "Unless you want something very unfortunate to befall your friends."

"Threats don't scare me." Mina tried to kick away the foot, stopping the door from closing. She almost succeeded. "I don't know who you are, but if you don't leave right now, it is you who will find misfortune."

"Very well." The man in the black suit sighed. He would have to do this the hard way. Not that he had expected her to comply with his requests. He feigned a retreat, mostly to stop her from crying out and alerting her friends. As he did so, one hand slipped into his jacket pocket and closed around a small glass vial. He pried the top off quickly and withdrew it, his other hand shooting out and catching the door, pushing it wider before Mina had a chance to react.

He brought up the vial and flung its contents in Mina's face. A billowing cloud of gold dust.

She coughed and sputtered. Staggered backward.

The man in the black suit followed, stepping across the threshold into the bedroom and closing the door behind him. The gold dust had not done what he expected it to. Gold was toxic to others of her kind, but not to Mina. It irritated her, certainly. He could see a slight rash blossoming on her cheeks. But it did little to incapacitate her. Perhaps that was because of her unique situation as a hybrid. Part human, part vampire.

No matter. He had planned for this eventuality.

The man in the black suit reached into his pocket again and removed a second vial, this one containing a clear liquid, along with a cloth which he casually doused. Unlike gold, this chemical would work on humans.

But Mina had other ideas. Having cleared the gold dust from her face, she lunged forward, eyes narrowed with rage.

The man in the black suit stepped deftly aside at the last moment and brought his arm up, catching her under the chin with a jarring blow. Mina staggered backward, stunned. Her legs hit the end of the bed, and she toppled back onto the mattress. That was all the man in the black suit needed. A moment later, he was upon her and pressing the cloth over her mouth and nose, even as she struggled and kicked and fought back against him. At least, until the chemicals on the cloth kicked in . . .

# SIXTY-FOUR

AT A LITTLE PAST eleven in the evening, John Decker climbed into bed. He was exhausted. The events of the past few weeks had left him drained. Now that Bradley Wilcox had passed over to the other side and the demon up at Bartholomew Meadows had been exorcised, he hoped there would be some breathing room to turn his attention to the bigger issue. Getting himself and Mina back to the twenty-first century. An idea had been forming at the back of his mind over the last few days. He wasn't ready to share it with Mina yet, because he didn't want to get her hopes up, but he thought there was a chance it might work.

Decker yawned and slid down under the covers. The room was dark, lit only by a narrow shaft of moonlight that pushed through a crack in the curtains. In the darkness beyond, the village lay still and quiet. Tomorrow, he would take the train back to London. Mina had promised to be more open with him, and Decker looked forward to that. Ever since he found her again, she had been guarded. Secretive.

He closed his eyes, letting his exhaustion gain the upper

hand, and for a second, he forgot where he was and reached for his cell phone to text Nancy before he fell asleep, as he often did when he was away on a mission. But his cell phone was not on the nightstand, of course, because he had lost it on Singer Cay after they traveled back in time to the 1940s. And even if he could have somehow sent a text in an age that had only just discovered radiotelegraphy, a gulf of decades separated him from his bride. Which was why, as sleep overcame him, Decker mouthed her a silent good night and hoped that somewhere in the distant future, Nancy would hear it.

# SIXTY-FIVE

DECKER AWOKE the next morning as the first rays of sun pushed through the curtains, sending a splash of pale light across the floor. He rose and dressed, then packed his meager belongings into a travel bag and made his way downstairs to meet the others. Today, they would take a train back to London. What he did after that, Decker wasn't sure. Whatever happened, he was going to be stuck in the past for a while, even if the half-formed plan lingering at the edges of his mind came to fruition. The Order of St. George might have plucked him off the streets, but he was still not sure if they would accept him into their fold permanently.

Decker entered the empty saloon bar and found Skye already there. The morning train would depart for London in less than an hour, and she appeared eager to put Mavendale behind her. He couldn't blame her. Being a spirit medium, Skye was more susceptible to the supernatural forces swirling around Bartholomew Meadows and the village. He wondered what it was like to sense spirits, actually feel their presence. He decided it must be unsettling at best, and did not envy her that particular skill.

"Good morning," she said as Decker dropped his bag next to hers.

Decker glanced around. "Has Mina come down yet?"

Skye shook her head. "Haven't seen her since last night."

"Me either." The last time he had seen Mina was upon their return to the Black Dog the evening before. She had declined a drink at the bar and went straight to her room. After her ordeal at the workhouse, he didn't blame her. Mina had looked worn out. It must have taken a lot of mental energy to battle the demon that had tried to possess her. A demon Decker hoped was gone forever.

"You think we should go wake her?" Skye asked. "I'm sure she doesn't want to miss the early train."

"I'll go see where she is." Decker started back toward the stairs. When he reached the second floor, he headed straight for Mina's room and knocked twice.

There was no movement from the other side of the door.

Surprised, Decker knocked again. "Mina, it's me."

Silence was his only answer.

A sense of foreboding overcame Decker. He didn't know why, but he knew something wasn't right. He tried the doorknob and found that it turned. Mina would not have left her door unlocked like that.

Decker pushed the door open and stepped into the room. The first thing he saw was her travel bag sitting on the floor under the window. There was a hairbrush on the dresser. But Mina was not there.

He stepped back out of the room and went along the corridor to the bathroom that was shared by all the guest rooms, expecting to find Mina there. But the bathroom was empty, as was the separate lavatory.

Decker returned to Mina's room and checked it one more time before heading back downstairs. When he reentered the saloon, Skye looked up from her perch on a stool at the bar.

"You didn't find her?" She asked, her voice heavy with concern.

"Her bag is there, but Mina isn't in her room."

"Maybe she went for an early morning walk."

"When she knew we were leaving for the train?"

"Can you think of another explanation?" Skye slipped down from the stool and went to the bay window at the front of the bar. She peered out.

"No." Decker joined Skye at the window. "Which is why I'm worried."

"Then let's find her," Skye said, turning away from the window and starting toward the back of the pub, beyond which came the clink of bottles.

Decker followed her through the door next to the bar, along a short corridor, and out into the small courtyard that sat behind the pub. He had been here once before. More beer barrels had appeared since then, stacked one atop the other along the far wall. The landlord was busy at work dealing with the previous evening's empties.

He didn't acknowledge Skye and Decker until the medium tapped him on the shoulder. "I wonder if we could bother you for a moment of your time."

The landlord turned, wiping his hands on a dirty rag that hung from his belt. "Pub won't be open for another two hours."

"That's not why we're here," Skye said.

"We're checking out and heading back to London today," Decker added.

"I see." The landlord folded his arms. "You're paid up

through tomorrow. No refunds if that's what you're looking for."

"Actually, we're looking for our friend, Mina."

"Have you seen her?" Skye asked.

"The young woman you checked in with?" The landlord looked at Decker.

"Yes." Decker nodded. "We haven't seen her since last night. If we don't find her soon, we will miss the early train."

"I wouldn't bother wasting your time if I were you," the landlord said. "She's gone already. Left late last night with another gentleman."

"What?" The knot of tension in Decker's gut flared to full-blown panic. "Are you sure?"

"U-huh. It was almost midnight. I'd just finished tidying the bar and closing up when I heard a noise outside the pub. An engine running. I went to the window and looked out. There was an automobile sitting in the side alley. A fancy one with chrome hubcaps and big running boards. Caught my attention because there shouldn't have been anyone out there at that time of night. At first I didn't see who it belonged to, but then two figures came from behind the pub. They must've come out the back door and through this courtyard. One of them was your friend."

"And the other person?"

"Tall, gangly gentleman in a black suit. He's been hanging around the last few days. Had an arm around your friend's waist, holding her up. Looked like he was helping her along because she was having trouble walking. Another man got out of the automobile and came around. Together they bundled her into the back seat and then they drove off."

"And you didn't think to intervene?" Skye asked with alarm.

"Look, I run a pub. You know how many people have to be helped out of here at the end of the night?"

"Mina wasn't drinking," Decker said. "She went to her room when we returned last night and didn't go out again. She certainly wouldn't leave with a stranger."

"I beg to differ," the landlord replied. "It was definitely her, and she looked three sheets to the wind. Not very ladylike, if you ask me."

"No one's asking you." Decker felt like grabbing the landlord, shaking some sense into him. But he didn't. Instead, he took a deep breath. "Describe this man."

"As I said, he was tall and thin. Kind of creepy looking in that black suit. Almost like an undertaker. Had deathly white skin, like he'd never been outside. He was in here last night until closing. Drank at least two whiskeys."

"You remember anything else?" Decker wished he hadn't left Mina alone the previous evening, but he had believed the threat to be over. He was wrong. "Think hard. Any little detail."

The landlord shook his head. "That's it. Honestly, I wouldn't even have noticed the gentleman yesterday evening if it wasn't for the whisky he purchased. Single malt Glenbain. Most expensive scotch I carry. I'm not even sure why I ever stocked it. Six years and I've only sold three drams. Two of them last night."

"Was he a guest here at the pub?"

"No. Must have been staying somewhere else, although I don't know where that would be. One thing I do know. He wasn't a local."

"What about the car?" Decker asked. "Do you know what model it was?"

"Sorry. It was dark, and it's not like I know much about automobiles. Give me a good horse any day."

Decker realized there was nothing more the landlord could tell them. He thanked the man and returned to the empty bar.

When they were out of the landlord's earshot, Skye turned to him. "You think Mina went willingly with that man?"

"Not a chance." Decker didn't believe for one moment that Mina was drunk or that she would leave of her own free will with a stranger. "It sounds like she was drugged and abducted."

"For what purpose?" Skye's voice was high-pitched. She looked at Decker with questioning eyes.

"Your guess is as good as mine." Decker pondered the description of the man who had taken Mina. It had stirred a memory. A pale, thin stranger in a black suit sitting in a dark corner of the pub the previous day when he was searching for the constable's wife. Decker had gotten a strange vibe as he passed the table. Something had set his nerves on edge. Now Decker wished he had followed through with that intuition. If he had, maybe Mina would still be with them.

"What are we going to do now?" Skye looked around the bar as if she expected her friend to appear at any moment.

"We find her," Decker said. "Return to London, beg the Order of St. George for help if we have to, and get Mina back."

# SIXTY-SIX

**TWO WEEKS LATER.**

THOMAS FINCH OBSERVED Decker from across his desk situated in a lavishly appointed office below the streets of the capital within the abandoned and forgotten London Bridge tube station that now served as the clandestine headquarters for the Order of St. George.

"We have used every resource at our disposal," Finch said in a grave tone, "and found no trace of Mina's current whereabouts or the identities of those who took her."

"There must be something," Decker said, not bothering to hide his frustration.

"If there is, we haven't discovered it." Finch leaned forward and rested his elbows on the desk. He looked worn out, with dark bags under his eyes and hair that appeared grayer than it had only a few weeks prior. "Your own inquiries have turned up no more than ours. It saddens me to say this, but whoever took Mina covered their tracks with impeccable skill. Even after finding the accommodation in

Mavendale used by the man in the black suit, we are no closer to knowing who he is or why he took her."

"He gave a false name," Decker said. He had returned to Mavendale only a few days before to see for himself the upstairs room in a small cottage occupied by Mina's abductor. The man in the black suit, who gave his name as Samuel Fehir, had rented the room from an elderly villager after seeing an advertisement in the local newspaper. The woman, a widow with limited income, was looking for a long-term lodger to help pay the bills but had agreed to let the man stay there because he paid three months of rent in advance for what he claimed would be a one-week stay at most. A sum of money that bothered Decker because it proved that the man in the black suit and whatever organization he might represent were well-funded. It also meant that Mina's abduction was not random, but premeditated and planned. "Do you think she was taken because of what she is?"

"It's probable," Finch replied. "But until we ascertain more about the person or persons who snatched her, we can't say for certain. What I can say is that only a few trusted people knew of her abilities. And other than the two of us, nobody is aware that she is from the future. I can't imagine how her abductor could have discovered her true nature."

"Somebody did," Decker said. "There's no other reason to stalk her."

"I agree." Finch rubbed his chin. "Would you recognize this man again if you saw him?"

"Absolutely." Decker would never forget that sallow countenance. It was burned into his memory. He hated to think of Mina in that man's clutches and what he might be doing to her.

"Good. Then let's hope he shows his face again."

"You think he will?"

"Who knows?" Finch leaned back and rubbed his temples. He met Decker's gaze. "I won't stop looking even if I have to direct every single ounce of the Order's resources to the search. You realize that. I won't rest a moment until she is safely back with us."

"I'm pleased to hear it," Decker said. He sensed a determination behind the words that was fueled by more than friendship. He wondered just how well Thomas Finch and Mina had once known each other. But now was not the time to ask.

"And what of you, Mister Decker?" Finch asked. "It's been two weeks, and at some point, you have to lay your search for Mina aside for a moment and focus on your own future. I know you don't want to hear this, but we may not find her anytime soon. Maybe things are different in your own time, but in the here and now, there are many circumstances under which a person can vanish and never be seen again. It is not an uncommon occurrence, even when the disappearance is not meticulously planned."

"I'm trying not to dwell on that possibility," Decker replied. "And to answer your question, I don't know what to do going forward other than to continue my search for Mina."

"Which will be hard without the Order's resources."

"Undoubtedly."

"Then might I suggest that you join us."

"You mean work for the Order of St. George?"

Finch nodded. "At least until such time as you find a way back to where you came from, if that is even possible."

"It might be," Decker said. "But not in the short term, and certainly not without Mina. I have no intention of abandoning her here."

"Good. In that case, you are now an official Order of St. George operative. I took the liberty of securing you permanent accommodation on the assumption that you would say yes. It's close by and yours for as long as you need it. Eunice has the address and keys. Just head up to the solicitor's office and she'll take care of everything."

"And Mina?" Decker asked.

"The search will continue round the clock," Finch replied. "We will find whoever took her, Mister Decker. We will get her back. I promise you that. And what's more, we will do it together."

*The next books in the John Decker Series*
**A Ghost of Christmas Past**
*and* **Deadly Crossing**

*New Decker Universe Novella Series - The CUSP Files*
*Book 1 -* **Deadly Truth**

# ABOUT THE AUTHOR

Anthony M. Strong is a British-born writer living and working in the United States. He is the author of the popular John Decker series of supernatural adventure thrillers.

Anthony has worked as a graphic designer, newspaper writer, artist, and actor. When he was a young boy, he dreamed of becoming an Egyptologist and spent hours reading about pyramids and tombs. Until he discovered dinosaurs and decided to be a paleontologist instead. Neither career panned out, but he was left with a fascination for monsters and archaeology that serve him well in the John Decker books.

Anthony has traveled extensively across Europe and the United States, and weaves his love of travel into his novels, setting them both close to home and in far-off places.

Anthony currently resides most of the year on Florida's Space Coast where he can watch rockets launch from his balcony, and part of the year on an island in Maine, with his wife Sonya, and two furry bosses, Izzie and Hayden.

Connect with Anthony, find out about new releases, and get free books at www.anthonymstrong.com